JUNKYARD DOGMA

JUNKYARD DOGMA

THE ELVEN PROPHECY™ BOOK FOUR

THEOPHILUS MONROE

MICHAEL ANDERLE

LMBPN

DISRUPTIVE IMAGINATION

Copyright © 2021 LMBPN Publishing
Cover copyright © LMBPN Publishing
A Michael Anderle Production

LMBPN Publishing
PMB 196, 2540 South Maryland Pkwy
Las Vegas, NV 89109

Version 1.00, July 2021
ebook ISBN: 978-1-64971-888-4
Print ISBN: 978-1-64971-889-1

THE JUNKYARD DOGMA TEAM

Thanks to our Beta Team

John Ashmore, Rachel Beckford, Kelly O'Donnell

Thanks to our JIT Readers

Veronica Stephan-Miller
Dave Hicks
Zacc Pelter
Dorothy Lloyd
Peter Manis

If We've missed anyone, please let us know!

Editor
The Skyhunter Editing Team

CHAPTER ONE

I didn't want to talk about it. Maybe, if we just got in the car and drove, the situation would change.

Layla pulled Agnus onto her lap after she'd buckled up in the backseat of my Mitsubishi Eclipse. It was Aerin's turn to ride shotgun. Who would have thought having two wives would be as infuriating, at times, as I imagine it would be like to have two children?

Not like I was the mature one in the relationship.

Based on the rings that bound our souls together, we were all three equally mated. At least that was the significance of our "bonding" according to drow custom. Layla was the one I loved.

"So what happened, Casp?" Layla asked as I pulled out of the parking lot at St. Ensley's. Never heard of St. Ensley, patron saint of practical jokes? It was the old church that the cult formerly known as the Order of the Elven Gate purchased for their gatherings. Now, with the cult divided between those who sided with the elves and the few who backed me as the "chosen one," they'd named their quasi-church after the trickster fairy and king of the fae, who'd given his life helping us escape Brightborn and his legions.

After that night, we hadn't heard a thing about Brightborn and the elven legion's whereabouts. We didn't have a clue what they were up to. Not until our little "cult" gathering at St. Ensley's was interrupted by a visit from the President, and of course, a cadre of Secret Service agents.

I grunted as I pulled my Eclipse onto the Interstate, switching the transmission into Sportronic mode, which allowed me to manually shift gears with two little paddles on the back of the steering wheel instead of the clutch. A gimmick, perhaps. I didn't use it much. But I wanted to accelerate faster than the usual automatic shifting allowed. Get as far from the city and where the President was, as I could, as fast as I could.

"You didn't answer me," Layla said. "What did the President have to say?"

I snorted. "I don't want to talk about it. Not yet."

"That bad?" Aerin asked, raising one eyebrow.

I sighed. "Yeah, it was bad. Just give me a minute to gather my thoughts." I touched my pocket and felt the faint outline of the card the President had given me. The one with a direct line to his phone. When I was ready to make my choice, to decide which side I'd take, I was supposed to give him a call.

"I don't understand what he could possibly have to say that you couldn't repeat," Layla interjected.

I shook my head and turned on the radio, dialing to the satellite channel that played nineties alternative twenty-four hours a day.

Agnus was used to my steady stream of music from my youth. He knew the words to most of the songs.

"I love thee, like Walter," Agnus sang, botching the lyrics of *All Over You* by Live.

I chuckled, turning down the volume a notch. "It's 'our love is like water,' you got the words wrong."

"No it isn't!" Agnus protested. "That makes no sense. After

that, he sings, 'pinned down and abused for being strange.' You can't pin down and abuse water, Caspar."

I shook my head. "And you think it makes sense concerning some random dude named Walter?"

"You never know," Agnus said. "Maybe Walter likes being pinned down and abused."

"My vote is with Agnus," Aerin said. "Most of the men I've courted were like that."

I bit my lip. "That's because the drow culture is matriarchal. It doesn't matter. I'm telling you, that's not the lyric."

"Does it really matter, Casp?" Layla asked.

"Yes!" I shouted, tapping another preset on my radio. Classic Rock. My usual backup station was saved to the second preset, reserved for when the nineties alternative station decided to play Ace of Base.

I smiled. Creedence Clearwater Revival. One of my favorites.

Agnus immediately piped up and started singing, "There's a bathroom on the right!"

I shook my head and turned down the music again. "There's a bad moon on the rise."

"I think I'm siding with Agnus again," Aerin said. "I'm pretty sure he said that there's a bathroom on the right."

"I agree," Layla added. "Why would the moon be bad? I mean, it's the moon, right? It's not really good or bad. Sort of morally neutral."

I gripped my steering wheel tightly. "He's not singing about trying to find the damn restroom! Why would anyone write a song about that? It's not exactly an inspiring experience."

"Could be," Layla said. "If you've really got to go."

"The name of the song is *Bad Moon Rising*," I shouted. "I know I'm right about this!"

Aerin looked at me, cocking her head. "Are you okay?"

"I'm fucking fine! Why wouldn't I be fine?"

"Caspar…" Something about the tone of Layla's voice calmed me. She was the love of my life. Probably the only one who could console me at the moment. "Just turn off the music. Let's talk about it."

I took a deep breath and released it before turning off the radio. "The President considers them refugees."

"He's giving my dad's legion asylum?" Layla asked. "After they killed all those soldiers?"

"The elves are invading this planet and this country," Aerin said. "They didn't come here looking for asylum."

I shook my head. "That's not how he sees it. They came from a world devastated by war. Destroyed to the point that it is no longer inhabitable. The President believes the only reason they attacked was that we greeted them with hostility."

"What a pussy!" Layla blurted.

I raised my eyebrow. I'd expect something like that from Jag, but I don't think I'd ever heard Layla refer to someone with the p-word. "That's not the worst of it," I said, shifting gears and accelerating past someone driving below the speed limit in the fast lane. "He said if I try to fight them, if I attack them at all, they'll arrest me."

"On what grounds?" Layla asked, raising her voice.

"Because I murdered Fred."

"Murder?" Layla asked. "My dad basically forced you to do it!"

I nodded. "I tried to explain that. He just said that every one of the King's legionnaires witnessed it."

"But they aren't citizens!" Aerin protested. "Not even of this *world*, much less the United States of America."

I shook my head. "It doesn't matter. You don't have to be a citizen to be called to testify in court."

"Then why did the President come talk to you?" Layla asked. "That sounds like something the FBI, or maybe the police would be involved in."

"Because he hopes it won't come to that. He wants me to support this so-called alliance. To speak up on behalf of the elves.

Apparently, after my performance at the trials went viral, there are some in Washington who don't support the President's position."

"An alliance?" Layla asked. "Granting them asylum is one thing, but..."

"I'm guessing that your father made an offer he couldn't refuse," I said, cocking my head, realizing I'd inadvertently quoted Marlon Brando from *The Godfather.*

"What kind of offer?" Layla asked.

"Military aid," Aerin said. "Think about it. What else could the elves offer the US government that would merit an alliance? If the military could wield their power to control the weather, think of what they could do. No need for missiles. No loss of human life. If they can just send massive storms and earthquakes on their enemies."

"And it wouldn't cost billions of dollars," I said. "For now, it seems that Brightborn isn't trying to convince the government to cede him power, at least."

Aerin scratched the back of her head. "Power like that could be more devastating than nuclear weapons. If the elves are controlling it, but doing it in the name of the US government..."

"It would start a world war," Layla finished, shaking her head as I glanced at her in the rearview mirror.

"They've got me by the balls," I said. "If I don't speak up to try and convince Congress to support the alliance, to authorize the use of power..."

"They'll charge you with murder," Layla said. "Even if you don't convince Congress like he wants, what are the chances they'd support you once you're a convicted killer?"

"How much time did he give you to decide?" Aerin asked.

"One week," I said.

"There's one option," Layla said. "From what I've studied of this society, there's one thing that might complicate this matter for the President."

"What's that?" I asked.

"Politics," Layla said. "What if you were so popular, if you had so much support, that your arrest would be political suicide?"

I shook my head. "The President wouldn't arrest me himself. He doesn't have that power. He'd have some US attorney indict me. The FBI would arrest me. He'd play it cool politically. Separate himself from the issue as much as possible. Probably urge people to allow the justice system to do its job."

"But he could pardon you," Layla said, "if arresting you is so offensive. People would see through what's happening. The facts are out there."

I shook my head. "I don't know. It's like I'm damned either way. I can't do what the President wants. That's as good as surrendering to Brightborn. I don't know, say we decide to challenge him and turn popular opinion against the elves? How do we even start to do that?"

"If we use any magic at the ranch, the elves will know," Aerin said.

"If you use *your* magic, true," Layla said. "But we already know that the fairies can't detect my magic. I'm only starting to scratch the potential of what this angelic power I've been given might allow me to do. I don't know what I could do that would help, but maybe there's something."

"Then we'd be playing into your father's hands. He's already trying to sell the elven legion on the idea that you are the true chosen one."

"Still, if I come out against my father. Maybe that would sow some discord amongst the legion."

"Caspar, even if they do arrest you," Aerin added. "It isn't like there's a prison that could hold you. Not with your power."

I shook my head. "I don't know if I could do that. The book of Romans says we're supposed to obey earthly authorities."

"Even if they're unjust?" Aerin asked.

I nodded. "Jesus even rebuked Peter for drawing his sword on the centurion when they came to arrest him in the Garden of Gethsemane."

Layla snorted. "I'm not a Bible scholar, Caspar. But didn't God send an angel, once, to break Paul out of prison in the New Testament?"

I bit my lip. "Let's just hope it doesn't come to that. In the end, I *did* kill Fred..."

The car was silent for a few moments, so I turned up the volume on my radio and switched it back to my nineties alternative station.

R.E.M.'s *Losing My Religion* was on. I chuckled to myself at the irony of the song, given everything I'd been through lately. What timing.

Agnus piped up and started singing again. *"Let's pee in the corner! Let's pee in the spotlight..."*

I wasn't going to win the argument. Instead, I gripped my steering wheel and joined in. *"Losing my religion!"*

CHAPTER TWO

The floorboards of the old farmhouse creaked and flexed louder than I was comfortable with as I stepped through the door. I don't know how long it had been since someone had lived there before we arrived. It still smelled a little musty, but since we'd been leaving the doors and windows open as much as possible, the odor had improved to the point that it was tolerable.

Of course, the pile of dirty laundry didn't help. I half-suspected Agnus had peed in it to protest the lack of electricity at our off-grid ranch since his luxury self-cleaning litter box was no longer in operation.

For at least a decade, the locals—I'm using that term loosely since there aren't any other houses within three square miles—had been using the old ranch as a dumping ground. I'd never seen so many inoperable kitchen appliances in my life. That's really saying something since I grew up in Missouri, and a good number of my home state's residents typically use their defunct appliances as lawn ornaments.

Waste not, want not. Why buy a flower pot when you have an old toilet bowl just sitting around?

It was thrifty. Having been a Boy Scout in my youth, I could appreciate that. Thrifty, brave, clean, and reverent. The last four components of the Scout Law. Someone would have to be brave following me in the bathroom, rounding out the Scout Law. I'd often knelt before the porcelain deity in reverence in my drinking days. It just made sense to be thrifty about the toilet bowl once it had outlived its usual purpose.

Not the only way the Boy Scouts had prepared me for this new adventure. We'd purchased a bunch of tents, on Aerin's dime, of course. There was a whole army of warrior drow motel-hopping while they waited for us to set up shelters for them at the junkyard ranch.

We'd piled the tents up, still in their original boxes, just inside the farmhouse door. I grabbed three of them and headed out the door.

"Going to go set those up?" Layla asked.

I nodded. "Something to do. Not to mention, I could use the fresh air."

"Mind if I join you?"

I shrugged. "Sure, why not? It's usually easier to set these things up in twos anyway."

Layla grabbed two more tents and followed me out the door. We'd already cleared the weeds from a small area behind the farmhouse.

"This is just temporary," Layla said. "Aerin said she's buying some old shipping containers that could be repurposed into little houses."

I bit my lip. "Yeah, she'll buy those. She'll use all her princess money to get us a generator, too. Maybe several of them. Hell, if we're lucky, maybe she can pull some strings and get those handsome twins on HGTV to renovate our whole fucking house. It'll be a regular redneck oasis in no time."

Layla and I dropped our tents on the ground. "Are you okay, Caspar? I've never seen you so...sarcastic about, well, everything."

"Me? Sarcastic?" I raised my left eyebrow as I unpackaged one of the tents. "Never!"

Layla chuckled. "I see what you did there."

I sighed. "I guess it's just I feel so fucking helpless about all this shit. I can't use any of my powers here because, well, if I do, the fairies will know and find us, which means your father will know where we are. And now, well, I guess I have to worry about the goddamn government finding us here, too. With their resources, it's probably just a matter of time."

"So this is all about you not being able to use your powers?" Layla asked.

I shook my head. "It's more than that. Never thought I'd have to rely on a sugar momma to provide for me. Besides, what's the point? The way I see it, you're right. This is temporary because pretty soon, one of two things is going to happen. I'll either have to give up and do what the President wants or I'll end up in prison, wearing orange and taking it up the butt from some guy named Cliff."

"Cliff?" Layla asked. "Why does it have to be Cliff?"

I scratched my head. "I don't know. That was the first name that came to mind. It sounds like the name of someone who might be in prison, and I can't imagine anyone named Cliff being on the receiving end of such extracurricular prisonhouse activities."

Layla unrolled the tent and started putting together the poles. "Neither of those things is going to happen, Caspar."

"You really think we can just defy the government without consequences? Think about it, Layla. The way it looks, it's my fault that *all* those soldiers died at the rivers when the elven legion came through. I didn't just kill Fred. I killed all of them. The fact that I'm not in federal custody already is a small miracle."

"You're a man of faith, Caspar," Layla said, looking at me with wide eyes. "After all that has already happened, everything you've seen and all you've done, you mean to say you don't believe in miracles anymore?"

I grabbed one of the tent poles that Layla assembled and started fishing it through the channel on one of the tent's corners. "What do you think, Layla? That all of this is just some big test of my faith?"

"Could be," Layla said. "In your Bible, do you know anyone who did anything worthwhile who didn't endure a time of testing? You said it just before the government showed up at St. Ensley's."

I shook my head. "I don't even remember what I said. I was just talking."

"If I heard you correctly," Layla said, "and if everyone else heard you clearly, you made the point that it was one man, a son of a carpenter, who sparked a movement that ultimately led to overcoming the mighty Roman Empire."

"Yeah," I said. "But they also arrested him and crucified him. And I hate to break it to you, but I'm not Jesus. I'm not going to rise again on the third day."

"But what about his disciples?" Layla asked. "Didn't they change the world?"

"They did," I said, nodding. "But almost all of them were also killed for their faith. The only one who wasn't ended up in exile. But at least he was on a nice island and had cool visions from God to get him through it. He didn't have to set up camp in some junkyard. As far as I know, John the Apostle never killed anyone."

"You didn't kill anyone, Caspar," Layla said. "You saved my life!"

"You were there, Layla!" I protested. "You saw what I did. How can you say—"

"My father is to blame for that," Layla interjected. "If Fred's blood or the blood of those soldiers is on anyone's hands, it's my father's. Not yours."

I shook my head. "Not sure a jury of my peers will see it that way."

"They certainly won't," Layla said, "if you don't believe it yourself!"

With the last pole in place and the first tent set up right, I grabbed one of the stakes, shoved it through one of the loops along the tent's base, and stomped it into the ground. "I just can't believe the President is so gullible. He really thinks that your father is going to help strengthen the military? After all we told him before? After Brag'mok told him how your dad basically exterminated all the giants?"

"I suppose we all are tested in our own ways," Layla said. "It seems that my father tempted him, successfully, with the allure of power."

"When your father betrays him, and he will, it will be too late. He'll already have given the elves a chance to get a foothold here, and plenty of time to practice their abilities with all of the Earth's magic at their disposal."

Layla nodded. "Too late for your government, perhaps. But I don't have any faith in any of this world's governments."

"There aren't any saviors on Capitol Hill," I said. "Never have been."

"I believe in you, Caspar. I always have. But despite telling you as much a hundred times, you don't seem to get the message. When all else fails, when your government fails, you'll still be there."

I snorted. "Yeah, probably locked up and taking it up the tail from Cliff."

"Shut up, Caspar," Layla said. "Stop being such a baby."

"I'm not being a baby!" I shouted, clenching my fists. "I'm being a realist!"

"That's what you call this? Being realistic? Because your faith has always been based on what's realistic, right? You talk about a man who rose from the dead. You've healed people! Remember

Grace, Cecil's daughter? What about Doris, that woman who was having a stroke in your church? What you did, there, totally realistic, right?"

I huffed. "I suppose not."

"Everything you ever thought was real has been blown out of the water, Caspar. A few months ago, you didn't even believe that elves were real, or fairies, or magic. Much less did you believe you could subdue powerful, magical elementals, or fly across the city like a superhero. How can you say what's realistic when you don't even know much about what's real at all?"

"Dammit, Layla…" I put my hands on my hips.

"Damn *what*, Caspar?" Layla asked.

"I'm here trying to have my own little pity party, and you're pissing all over it with belief and hope."

Layla smiled. "That's why I'm here."

"To piss on me? Sorry, Layla, I'm not into that sort of thing."

Layla shook her head. "See, there you go. You're trying to be funny again. That's the Caspar I know and love."

"How about we just finish these tents?" I asked.

Layla put her hand around my waist. "Or we could climb inside this one…"

I chuckled. "What exactly do you have in mind?"

"Well, usually, when you're pitching a tent for me, I'm pretty good at handling it."

"See, now you're the one with the jokes," I said, taking Layla by the hand and ducking into the tent. "One question, though."

"What's that?" Layla said, laying down beside me.

"Would it be too weird if I moaned the name 'Cliff' in the middle of it all?"

Layla poked me in the side. "You better not, you doof!"

CHAPTER THREE

Layla rested her head on my chest while we caught our breath. Funny how a little extracurricular fun with my hot elf wife could clear my mind.

I was still conflicted. I didn't have a clue what we should do next. We only had a week before the President's ultimatum expired. However, as I'd learned in AA, the only thing I could do was the next right thing. At the moment, that meant putting my pants back on.

I gave Layla a quick peck on the lips. "I guess we'd better get the rest of these tents put together."

Layla sighed. "I was thinking we could go again!"

I chuckled. I almost took her up on the offer. I wasn't sure if I had the stamina for it, but I was willing to give it a go until the sound of ruffling fabric and a few curse words stole my attention.

Slipping my shirt back over my head, I stepped out of the tent.

I started laughing.

One of the tents was over Aerin's head, and she was flailing around and grunting in frustration.

"Aerin?" I asked. "Need a little help with that?"

Layla, also laughing her ass off, went over to Aerin and helped her pull the tent off her head.

"How the hell are these dumb things supposed to stand up?" Aerin asked with a look of total exasperation.

"Well," I said, pointing at the pile of poles and stakes at her feet. "I think you need to use those to hold it up."

Aerin grunted. "I wondered what those things were for."

I smiled. "I suppose Princess Nightshade hasn't ever pitched a tent before?"

Aerin shook her head. "This is what men are for! No, I've never pitched a tent. Why on earth would I have ever wanted to do that? That's what houses are for! Stupid tents!"

"It's not as difficult as it looks," I explained, putting the poles together.

"About time you two decided to take your hands off each other and do something!"

I cocked my head. "Aerin, we weren't trying to…"

"Never mind," Aerin said. "I'm just annoyed."

"Obviously," Layla quipped. "We can handle this, you know."

Aerin nodded and stomped off back to the farmhouse.

"I think you should go talk to her," Layla said.

"Talk to her?" I asked, raising my eyebrows. "Why? She's just a little out of her element."

"I don't think it's just about the tents, Caspar," Layla said.

"Well, what do you think she's so bitchy about?" I asked. "She's been like this ever since we got here. Ever since…"

"Ever since the wedding?"

I nodded. "Yeah. Pretty much."

"Has it ever occurred to you, Caspar, that this isn't exactly what she wanted for her life, either?" Layla asked.

I scratched my head. "Didn't really think about it. Wasn't this whole marriage thing what she wanted ever since she showed up?"

Layla nodded. "But I don't think she wanted it like this. You and me together, her always on the outside looking in."

"Layla," I said. "You aren't suggesting we let her join in..."

Layla looked at me blankly. "Are you really that dense, Caspar? That's not what I'm saying at all."

I tossed the tent pole I was assembling on the ground. "I know. I get it. But wouldn't you be better to talk to her about that?"

Layla shook her head. "You're the one she thought she was destined to marry, Caspar. I'm the one who, well, got in the middle of it all."

I nodded. "All right. You got this?"

Layla smiled. "I can handle the tents."

I shook my head. "I don't know what I can say to her. It's not like I have any answers that will make this whole situation normal."

"It isn't about giving her the answers, Caspar," Layla said. "She just needs someone who will listen to her. I'm not saying either of us should sleep with her. But is it really so bad to be a friendly ear?"

"All right," I said. "I'll be right back."

Layla nodded and picked up the pole I'd just thrown down.

I jogged back to the farmhouse and stepped inside.

I heard her sobbing in her room. The farmhouse only had two bedrooms, and since I was only intimate with Layla, it made sense for her to have the other. I knocked on the door. She didn't respond, so I walked in. Aerin was sitting in a corner, her face in her hands.

"That little patch of the floor looks awfully comfortable," I said. "Mind if I join you?"

Aerin wiped her wrist across her upper lip, probably to gather her snot. Gross, I thought, but we've all been there. She scooted a little to her left, which I took as permission to sit beside her.

"I'm sorry about all this," I said, sitting down and leaning against the wall, my legs bent in front of me with my feet flat on the floor. "I know this isn't the kind of marriage you wanted."

Aerin shook her head. "It's not that. Not entirely."

I shrugged. "Then what is bothering you?"

"All right, so it is sort of related to the marriage. This just isn't what I ever dreamed about as a little drow girl, you know? I always imagined if I was ever in a multi-spousal situation, that *I'd* be the one with multiple men at *my* service and whim. Not one wife, sharing one mere male with another elf."

"If it's worth anything," I said. "It wasn't exactly what I imagined either."

"When you were a little drow girl?" Aerin asked, chuckling a little as she swallowed her sobs.

I laughed. "I know it doesn't compare. I wanted to marry Layla already. I just hadn't proposed yet or anything. But at least I'm still with the girl I love. I can't imagine how hard it must be to be the third wheel, bound to the marriage, always watching us but never really a part of it. Not romantically, at least."

Aerin shook her head. "I'm so embarrassed."

I cocked my head. "Why would you be embarrassed? You're totally justified to be upset about this."

Aerin sighed. "It's silly. But in our culture, for a woman to pine after a man is shameful. Women are supposed to be able to choose for themselves the men they will marry—males of good stock, likely to produce quality heirs. As a princess, it was always assumed that I'd have my choice of any man. But then there was the prophecy."

"And now you're stuck with me, a human who's in love with someone else." I put my hand on Aerin's back.

She jerked away. "Don't touch me, Caspar. This is too hard as it is."

"Sorry, I didn't mean…"

"You don't feel that? When you touch me?" Aerin asked.

I bit my lip. "I did before. But after everything… I don't know.

I still feel that attraction when Layla touches me. But I felt that before already, so…"

"It's a part of the marriage ritual. An almost irresistible attraction. It's supposed to ensure that we complete the binding."

"So our binding is incomplete until we consummate the marriage?" I asked.

Aerin shrugged. "I don't know for sure. I've never heard of anyone amongst the drow who got married, whose lives were bound together by these rings, who didn't consummate their relationship. Isn't the wedding night supposed to be the best part of the wedding day?"

I scooted over a little. "I had no idea. I felt it before. At the wedding. When you touched me…"

"I felt it too," Aerin said. "And that's the thing. I still do. Do you know how much restraint it takes just to stop myself from ripping off your clothes right now?"

"It's the rings, though," I said. "It's not like you're really attracted to me."

Aerin took a deep breath then wiped another tear from her right cheek. "That's the thing, Caspar. I'm not sure. It's not like you're especially attractive physically. You're not awful looking, but…"

I cocked my head. "Thank you, I think?"

Aerin chuckled. "Look at it from my perspective. I grew up always being told I'd have my choice of men. Then we sensed the magic you were wielding. We suspected the chosen one had come. I knew the prophecy. I was supposed to marry the chosen one."

"So you're saying you're just attracted to the idea of being with the chosen one?" I asked.

Aerin bit her lip. "No. Sure, I mean, there's a certain allure to that. But like I said, I'd always had a choice. Then, suddenly I didn't. I was just expected to marry you. So, like a good drow princess, I did my duty."

"I don't know, Aerin," I said. "Did you really have a choice? You said you almost married King Brightborn once."

Aerin nodded. "He was my choice once. Briefly. He was charming. I know now it was all just an act. He was using me, and I fell for it."

"Did you choose someone else?" I asked. "Before I showed up, was there some other drow man, or woman I suppose, you had your heart set on?"

Aerin shook her head. "No one. Not yet. I'd been looking, hoping… But no one showed up. Then when I realized you were the chosen one, it was like I was fine with it. I don't know why, Caspar. Maybe it's the fact that you're different. Maybe it's because you have a good heart. Perhaps it's because you aren't weak-minded like most drow males are raised to be. Or, I hate to say it, maybe it was because you were with someone else. Wanting what isn't yours, you know?"

I nodded. "The forbidden fruit."

"Exactly," Aerin said through a sigh. "Whatever it was, I fell for you, Caspar. I didn't want to. I didn't plan on it. It took me by surprise. I won't say I love you or anything like that. But I was moving in that direction."

I snorted. "I had no idea. I just thought you were sort of in love with the whole idea of being married to the chosen one. Fulfilling the prophecy, all that."

Aerin shook her head. "Not at all. If anything, I resisted it at first. Not outwardly. No one else knew about my reluctance. It was you, Caspar. But I also knew you were in love with Layla. I couldn't just take you from her. So when she suggested we bind ourselves together, all three of us. Well, she's cute enough. I figured we could all grow to love each other. But then I saw how single-minded you were about saving her when she went back to her father. When she was infected by that blade. I saw how she looked at you, even when she thought she was dying. I realized I couldn't ever have your heart in the way you had mine. That any notion of she and I loving each other, any idea that all three of us might love one another equally wasn't going to happen."

"And it's only gotten harder," I said. "Now that we're here, together. Since our rings are still creating that desire in you, to, you know…"

"That's the thing," Aerin said. "When Layla touches me, even if she brushes my hand, the allure isn't as strong. That's why I think it's more than that. I think it's because my heart was already opening up to the possibility of us. You and me, I mean."

I bit my lip. "I can't imagine how hard that must be. It's not that I'm not attracted to you. It has nothing to do with you at all. If I hadn't already met Layla, and if she and I didn't already have a connection that goes deeper than these rings…"

"I know, Caspar," Aerin said. "I realize that under most circumstances, I'd be way out of your league."

I laughed. "I'm not even going to dispute that. You're gorgeous, Aerin. I'm just sorry you can't have the kind of love you deserve. Everyone deserves to not just fall in love, but to have someone love them equally in return."

Aerin nodded. "This marriage, if that compulsion ever subsides, will be a formality. At least for me. In our culture, it is permissible and even expected that women might take multiple husbands. Perhaps, once this is over, I'll find love. I'll be able to take a second husband."

I cocked my head. "But since we're bound already, does that mean I'd end up married to a dude, too?"

Aerin smiled. "Only as a formality."

"I suppose I can accept that," I said. "Once this is over, there won't be any reason to keep this up. You'll be able to leave if you like."

Aerin tucked her hair behind her ears. "Thank you. For listening, I mean. It's good to get this off my chest."

"Anytime, Aerin," I said. "So long as I'm still around and I don't get arrested or anything. You can tell me anything. You don't have to pretend to be Xena Warrior Princess with me. It's okay to be vulnerable."

"Xena?" Aerin raised her eyebrows. "You're dating yourself with that reference. Besides, Xena wasn't nearly as badass as I can be."

"I believe it," I said.

"One more thing," Aerin said.

"Yes?"

"It goes both ways. If there's anything you want to talk about. I know you have Layla, but if there's something you don't feel like you can tell her, or something's weighing on you and you just need another person to talk to, I'm here for you."

"I really appreciate that, Aerin," I said. "More than you realize. This isn't easy on me, either. Not just this marriage, but the whole situation with the government."

Aerin nodded. "One seal of the elven prophecy has yet to be revealed. Perhaps, once it is, we'll have more answers."

"Where is it, anyway?" I asked.

"In the care of one of my subjects," Aerin said. "It will be brought with the rest of the drow when they arrive this evening."

I cocked my head. "This evening? We still have a lot of tents to set up."

Aerin laughed. "That's why I wanted to help. I suppose after my experience earlier, I'd best leave that task to you and Layla."

CHAPTER FOUR

I wasn't expecting an eighteen-wheeler. The massive rig pulled onto the overgrown gravel road that led from the edge of the property to the farmhouse.

Three large men were squeezed into the cab. The one who was driving, a good-sized man, looked like a dwarf next to Jag, who sat beside him. Jag, who was an aspiring professional body-builder, looked like a shrimp next to Brag'mok, the lone surviving elven giant from New Albion who'd assisted me in more ways than I could count.

The driver stepped out first.

"Dwight?" I asked. I'd only met him a couple times. When Brag'mok first came to Earth, he'd kidnapped the man to take his rig. However, in the process, Dwight had seen so much he couldn't explain that he took a reluctant interest in the cult formerly known as the Order of the Elven Gate.

"Howdy, Caspar," Dwight said, scratching at what looked like a half week's beard sprouting on his neck.

"Glad to have you with us," I said. "After what happened, I wouldn't blame you if you steered clear of all this."

Dwight nodded. "Took some time. But I saw you on the internet, taking out those elementals. Then, Jag told me about the elves and even the government turning against you. Well, they might consider me a traitor for it, but I've been at war before. What they're doing… That's not the kind of freedom I thought I was fighting for."

"Iraq?" I asked.

Dwight nodded. "Two tours there. One in Afghanistan with the corps."

I reached out and shook Dwight's hand. "Thank you for your service."

Dwight pressed his lips together and nodded. "Thank you, sir."

"Just Caspar," I said.

Dwight smiled. "They're all in the back."

"The drow?" I asked.

"Sure enough," Jag said as he hopped out of the rig behind Brag'mok. "Couldn't have done it without Dwight, here, and his truck. Hard to arrange rides for a hundred drow."

"A hundred?" I asked, scratching my head. "We only set up ten tents."

"Looks like you'll have to get a few more," Jag said.

Dwight unlocked the back of the truck and rolled open the door. Layla stepped up behind me and put her hand on my back, and Aerin walked over to the back of the rig.

"Brag'mok," Aerin said. "Mind giving us some assistance?"

The elven giant grunted and stepped up beside Aerin. He extended his hand and helped the drow out one by one.

I'd seen them before, some of them at St. Ensley's, but I wasn't expecting so many.

"Aerin," I said. "Why didn't you tell us this many would be joining us? We don't have enough tents."

Aerin shrugged. "I didn't realize they'd all made it here so soon. I figured most would be joining us over the course of the next few weeks."

"We were fortunate," one of the drow said as she took Brag'mok's hand and hopped to the ground. "Airline tickets were at a good price."

I stood there, with my jaw dropped, as one drow warrior after the next leaped to the ground. All female; there wasn't a dude in the bunch. Each was more attractive than the last. Every one had a long sword either at her waist or in her hand. Like Aerin, they wore long, extravagantly colored dresses.

"What about the men?" I asked.

Aerin smiled. "Our men aren't trained for battle. They had to stay behind to care for our young."

"Dwight," I said. "Mind taking the rig for supplies? We weren't counting on so many."

"I'll go with him," Aerin said. "I'll buy what we need."

"Not a problem," Dwight said. "I've got a pickup tomorrow, though, so I'll need to get back on the road as soon as possible."

"It won't take long," Aerin said.

"There's a Home Depot and a few other stores forty-five minutes or so down the highway," I told her.

Something squeezed my shoulder, and with it, half my chest and back.

I turned around. "Brag'mok! How's it going, rooming with Jag?"

The giant grunted. "Got a place we can go to talk?"

I nodded. "Sure. What's up?"

"I don't want to cause alarm. I'll tell you when I'm sure no one else can hear."

I didn't want to take Brag'mok into the farmhouse. Our floorboards could barely hold my weight, much less his. He was, at a minimum, three times my size and weight. Instead, I led him around to the back of a pile of scrap metal, next to what looked like an old burned-up and charred Dodge Ram.

"Brightborn has been sending assassins after me," Brag'mok said.

THEOPHILUS MONROE & MICHAEL ANDERLE

I shook my head. "We expected he might. But you said you could handle your own, right?"

"It's not just that," Brag'mok continued. "We're also being watched. By humans in suits. Government, I think."

I bit my lip. "Again, I suppose that shouldn't be a surprise."

"It's just a matter of time that they'll come for me, given your government's foolhardy alliance with the elves. One way or another."

"You could stay here," I said. "We'd probably need a bigger tent, unless you'd like to use some of these rusted and burned-out vehicles as shelter."

Brag'mok shook his head. "I've come not because I am trying to hide. I've come because I want to help you do what must be done while I still can. Before something happens to me."

I sighed. "I don't have a clue what to do, Brag'mok. Layla and Aerin thought I should go on some big public relations campaign, perform some healings and get the people on my side. Make it difficult politically for the President to act against me in any way."

Brag'mok scratched his head. "That only addresses one of the problems, Caspar. The problem with your government. But it won't provide you any advantage in defeating Brightborn."

I shrugged. "I don't know. Not being in prison is a pretty decent advantage, don't you think?"

Brag'mok huffed. "Like there's a prison on Earth that could hold you with your power."

I rolled my eyes. "That's what Layla and Aerin said, too. Use my power to break out if they arrest me. But that doesn't seem the right way to go about it."

Brag'mok shrugged. "Why not?"

I bit my lip. I wasn't going to give my giant of a friend a lecture on Biblical principles regarding obedience to secular authorities. But I did have other reasons, ones more pertinent to the elven prophecy. "I'm supposed to be a unifying figure, right?

So long as the government is the authority in this land, I don't think it's wise to set myself up against it like a rogue. It wouldn't exactly set me up in the best position, legally speaking or otherwise, to bring all the races together, like the prophecy says."

Brag'mok nodded. "This is wise, I think. I may have a plan. A way to substantially weaken the elves while also protecting yourself here, making it less likely they might find you."

"What are you suggesting we do?"

"We have to drive a wedge between the elves and the fairies," Brag'mok said.

I sighed. "I don't think we'll be able to win them over to our cause. You saw what they did to Ensley, who was their own king before he helped me until I used magic in a way they didn't approve of."

"We don't have to win them over," Brag'mok said. "We need only convince them that the elves are a greater threat to the Earth's magic than you or humanity in general."

I nodded. "You wouldn't think it would be hard to do. Given the magic that was meant to sustain New Albion was squandered on war."

Brag'mok shook his head. "Under Ensley's command, they turned against Brightborn once before. Back when we went to New Albion and restored magic to the planet's ley lines."

I nodded. "I remember. I thought once Ensley came back to help us that it was clear the fairies were on our side. Seems I was wrong about that."

"They were," Brag'mok said. "Sort of, anyway. Ensley was on your side. The rest, well, they followed his lead. Until they didn't."

"In the forest, back at Pruitt-Igoe, just before they killed Ensley. The new fairy king, Develin, said something about how the Furies had deposed of Ensley and made Develin king instead."

Brag'mok nodded. "This is likely true."

"What are these Furies, anyway?" I asked.

"There are three. Alecto, also known as the unceasing. Megara, the jealous. And Tisiphone, the avenger. According to the legends, they were born from the same event that created my kind."

"And all this really happened?" I asked.

The giant nodded. "I do not expect it is a part of your world-view, Caspar. Nonetheless, as the tale goes, when the Titan, Kronos castrated his father, the blood from his scrotum fell to the Earth and created three races: the giants, the Furies, and the nymph."

"The nymph?" I asked.

"Also known as elemental spirits. You've encountered one of each kind already. In the trials."

I cocked my head. "So you, and these Furies, were created from some god's nut sack?"

"This is the legend," Brag'mok said. "You have your story of Adam and Eve. Did it happen exactly as your tale tells? Who knows. But it is a story to explain your beginnings, and insofar as it does so, it is true, is it not?"

I snorted. "So if I start calling you testicular spawn…"

"I do not see what is so strange about this. Are not all babies born of testicular spawn?"

"Well, yeah. But not like that. They're born from an intimate act. Ideally, one performed in love. What you described, Kronos castrating Uranus, sounds incredibly violent."

"Perhaps that explains why my people have only ever known war, why the Furies are associated with vengeance against those who violate the natural order, and why the elementals are so notoriously difficult to subdue."

"But they were once considered goddesses by the ancients," I said. "Their concern was to protect the natural order, and in turn, to punish those who violate it."

"Legend serves a purpose in explaining history," Brag'mok said.

"What do these Furies have to do with the fairies?" I asked.

"It is the Furies who created the fairies to do their bidding," Brag'mok said. "At least, such is the story as it was told to me as a child. None on New Albion had ever seen or encountered a Fury. They were not a part of our world. I suspect they've been rather inconspicuous here, too."

"Why would these Furies side with elves, then?" I asked.

Brag'mok scratched his head. "Perhaps the Furies believe the elves might be a means to avenge the Earth and punish humanity. Like an ax used by the Furies to cut down mankind only to be tossed into the fire later."

I nodded. "In the Bible, the Old Testament, there's something like that. When the Babylonians conquered God's people, a lot of people wondered why in the world would God use a people so godless to punish his own people."

"Did God answer that question in your Bible?" Brag'mok asked.

I nodded. "His answer was similar to what you suggested. He used them as his instrument to punish. Not for punishment's sake, but so that Israel would see the error in her ways. Then, when Israel repented and was restored, God commenced his judgment on Babylon at the proper time."

"I imagine that something like that is how the Furies must justify deposing of Ensley and replacing him with one more loyal to their plans."

I nodded. "So your plan is what, exactly? It isn't like we can just walk right up to these Furies and ask them to change their minds."

"I agree," Brag'mok said. "If we hope to turn the Furies against Brightborn, to reconsider their plan, we would first need to find them."

I shook my head. "If we found them, what would we tell them?"

"I am the last of the giants," Brag'mok said. "The protection of the Earth was always our sacred duty. It is why we fought to prevent the elves from assaulting this world."

"And as one of three races, along with the Furies and the elementals, born from Uranus' balls…"

"It sounds dirty when you say it like that," Brag'mok said. "But yes, as one of the three races charged to protect the natural order, I may be able to persuade them that the elves represent a more imminent threat than humanity."

"If the Furies, and most of their fairies, were on Earth all this time, you might have a hard time convincing them that humanity is somehow innocent."

"I do not intend to make that case," Brag'mok said. "But I've spent my whole life fighting against the elves of New Albion, convinced that they are the gravest threat to the Earth. I should think they would hear me out."

"From what you've told me, it makes sense. The Furies were never, based on that myth, the sole guardians of the Earth. Your people were, too."

"And you've already subdued the elements," Brag'mok said. "You've partnered with giants, first B'iff, my brother, and now me. What if the prophecy to unite the peoples is meant to begin by uniting the three races originally charged to protect, defend, and avenge nature?"

"That's an intriguing thought," I said. "I think we should talk to Aerin. The drow have managed to avoid the fairies, and by extension, the Furies for centuries."

"They did it by using enchantments rather than magic directly," Brag'mok said.

"Yes, but even enchanting involved some use of magic. I suspect, since they were keen to avoid the fairies all that time, they probably know something about where the Furies might be. You can't easily avoid something if you don't know where it is."

"This is good thinking, Caspar," Brag'mok said, slapping me on the back, almost knocking me over. "They also are the ones who harnessed the nymph, the elementals, and brought them to you in the trials. This leads me to believe that you are correct. The drow princess might know more than I imagined."

"I'm not sure how this is going to keep me out of prison, but I like the idea."

"You are now the one who represents the elements. With you and I standing in unity, the Furies would have to at least listen. If they turn against the elves, perhaps Brightborn will be forced to show his true colors. It may convince your President to rethink this alliance."

CHAPTER FIVE

Aerin had already left with Dwight to get supplies. That didn't mean we couldn't share Brag'mok's idea with Layla.

By the look on her face as Brag'mok explained to her what he'd already told me, she didn't know much more about the Furies than I did.

"So, you're telling me that the giants come from some god's nuts?" Layla asked, raising her eyebrows.

"It's just the myth we were taught," Brag'mok said. "What story do the elves have to explain the origins of the fae?"

Layla shook her head. "Nothing so graphic. We always believed that they had descended from some kind of ancient deity. But I don't think we had any myths or whatever to explain how that happened exactly."

"Not surprising," Brag'mok said. "The story effectively puts the elven kingdom of your ancestors at odds with not just those your people refer to as orcs, but it implies that opposing us is as good as opposing the Earth itself."

"And now my father hopes to use the Furies, the fairies, and the elements themselves, to defeat humanity so that the age of the elves can begin."

"We need to talk to Aerin about this when she gets back," I said. "If I can approach the Furies as the one who represents the elementals, having harnessed their power, and Brag'mok can speak on behalf of the giants…"

Layla nodded. "It makes sense, but you aren't exactly an elemental yourself. Will they even recognize you as anything more than a human?"

I shrugged. "I don't know. Ensley believed in me. If they can be convinced that he had good reason, maybe? I don't know if it will work, but it's worth a shot. So long as your father has the fairies on his side, I can't do much of anything without him knowing it."

"It won't stop my father," Layla said. "But it would certainly remove one of his most significant advantages from the equation."

"It might force your father to take a more aggressive posture," Brag'mok said. "Which could give the government reason to reconsider its position."

"I agree," Layla said. "There's one other thing we should explore."

"What's that?" I asked.

Layla raised her hands. "These rings. Not just the wedding ring, but the other two artifacts that gave me this new power. My father hopes that it will make me the chosen one in the eyes of the legion. I can harness this power, learn to use it. From what I sensed of its potency when Fred was using it, he barely scratched the surface of what this so-called angelic or celestial magic can do."

"You've used it to portal yourself," I said. "That's how you escaped your father. Fred was able to charge those daggers with the magic. That's how he poisoned you."

Layla smiled. "Two steps ahead of you. Already tried that with a few of my arrows. Can't be too careful, though. I'm not sure it's possible to heal someone from that. Not without wearing the rings."

I nodded. "So unless you're going to shoot to kill, probably better to stick with normal arrows."

Layla shook her head. "Not necessarily. There might be other benefits. The way Fred wielded this magic was crude. I need to experiment with it a little. Not like we've had the time."

I took a deep breath and released it. "And with a hundred drow, none of whom probably have any better an idea how to pitch a tent than Aerin, I think we're going to be busy a while."

Layla shook her head. "If she can even find that many tents. I imagine she could buy every tent in stock at Walmart, and it still wouldn't be enough."

I scratched my head. "Not necessarily. They make some big tents that can sleep, like, ten people. Doubt they carry a lot of them at Walmart."

"We'll see what she comes up with. At least since she's doing the shopping, she'll also have to deal with the complaining. These drow women, maybe they're great warriors. But from the looks of them, I don't think any of them have a lot of experience with the great outdoors."

I glanced at Brag'mok. "Any ideas of how we can keep these drow warriors entertained until Aerin gets back?"

Brag'mok grunted. "Looks like Jag has it covered."

I looked around the corner from the pile of junk that Brag'mok was tall enough to look over. Jag was standing in a crowd of drow, his shift lifted while one of them stroked his abs. He was flexing one arm while one of the drow was hanging from it as if he were a jungle gym.

I snorted. "Should've figured. You should head over there, Brag'mok. Compared to you, Jag is small. Think of all the attention you could get."

Brag'mok grunted. "Not interested. I am married."

I cocked my head. "You are?"

"I mean, I was," Brag'mok said. "Before Brightborn."

"I'm sorry, Brag'mok," I said, shaking my head. "I had no idea."

"I had twelve children…" Brag'mok turned around.

"Twelve?" Layla asked, raising her eyebrows at me.

"I do not want to talk about it. What is done is done." He screamed and grabbed the bed of a rusted-out pickup truck. With both hands, he tore it in two and tossed one chunk into another junk heap.

"Holy shit," I whispered to Layla. "Did you know he was that strong?"

Layla nodded. "Crazy, right?"

"I have an idea," I said, seeing a way to help him and everyone else here. "One second…"

I stepped up behind Brag'mok and reached up to put my hand on the small of his back. Any lower, I'd be cupping a butt cheek. That wouldn't exactly send the message I was hoping for.

"If you need to vent your frustration," I gestured to the trash pile, "have at it. But do you think you could build something with all this scrap? I figured, if you're tearing it apart anyway…"

Brag'mok grunted and nodded. "It would be good to do something with my hands."

"I don't know how you'd go about it," I said. "But maybe you could repurpose some of this junk to make some shelters?"

Brag'mok nodded. "I'm sure I can figure something out."

CHAPTER SIX

I sat on an old, abandoned rocking chair and stared off into the distance. All of us had lost something. Aerin had lost her chance at love. Layla had lost the world and the only family she ever knew. I'd lost my vocation. None of us had lost more than Brag'mok. For his entire race, numbering in the millions on New Albion, to suddenly be gone...

How does one even begin to wrap one's mind around a loss of that magnitude? So far he'd been in denial, trying to press on without thinking about his loss. Now, he was in the second stage of grief, anger. Based on the model I'd learned in seminary during the one and only required course that would-be ministers took in counseling, after anger came bargaining, then depression, and finally acceptance.

Knowing Brag'mok, the anger stage would probably last a while. He'd probably breeze past bargaining and come out of his anger in depression. It was normal, but we also had a world to save. I wasn't trying to be insensitive, but the way I figured it, giving him a way to channel his anger productively would have the added bonus of helping him feel useful. It was my hope, ultimately, that this would help minimize the depression that was surely coming.

Watching him work from a distance was impressive. He yanked the hood off an old rusted-out station wagon, bent the edges with his bare hands, and locked it into another piece of metal that he'd modified in a similar way. He clearly had some kind of experience with this sort of thing. Whatever he was building wasn't pretty, and being made of metal, it would probably get hot as hell come the heat of summer, but it was a shelter. At least, it was starting to look something like one.

The old farmhouse wasn't at all luxurious, but it did have a nice country-style porch that wrapped around the front of the house.

Layla was working with Jag to get the drow situated. I needed some time to think. We had a lot of very vague, general ideas. We needed something to do. It's hard to do the next right thing when you don't have a clue what that might be. It was like we were wandering barefoot through the dark rooms of a place we'd never slept in before in the middle of the night with the goal of reaching a bathroom. The immediate goals were clear: avoid getting arrested, convince the Furies to break the alliance with Brightborn, and hopefully gain a few advantages over the enemy. We just didn't know where the bathroom was, what legos might be on the floor that we might step on, or what other surprises might be waiting for us in the dark.

Hopefully, Aerin would have some ideas.

I saw the headlights of Dwight's rig from probably a mile away. It hadn't been dark for long. The drow had scrounged up some tinder and built a fire. They were singing songs and dancing. Not anything I recognized, not even in the English language, but it sounded jovial.

Layla was dancing with them. She didn't know their songs or their dance moves, but she seemed almost at home with the other drow. They were elves, after all. From entirely different worlds, of course. But elves, no less, and elves who were on our side.

I'd never seen so many beautiful females in my life. Sure, they caught my eye as they gyrated their hips and shook their bodies to the songs they were singing. But it was Layla who captivated me as she moved. She wasn't the best dancer of the bunch, by any means. But she was my Layla. It was good to see her smile. Even when shit is hitting the fan and flying all around you, it's good to find opportunities for joy.

I just couldn't get out of my head enough to bring myself to join them. The old me would have grabbed a fifth of whisky, drowned out my anxieties, and joined in the fun. But right now, I needed to allow myself to feel my sense of worry. I needed to be honest with whatever it was that made me uncomfortable. I had to name it, acknowledge it, and then apply the Serenity Prayer—to figure out what things I could and couldn't change and find the courage to do what I could.

With Aerin and Brag'mok grieving in their own ways and both of them placing their hopes in me and my abilities as the chosen one, it didn't feel right to dance and sing.

Besides, if anyone ever saw me dance... My moves usually resembled doing yard work. I had the lawn mower—acting like I was pulling on the rope start. I had the shovel—kicking one foot in front of me as if I was digging into the ground. Then, I had something I called the sprinkler. One arm up in a ninety-degree angle, the other extended horizontally and moving back and forth, bouncing off the other one.

If anyone ever defined every stereotype of white-boy dancing, it was me. I also did a mean Hokey Pokey.

Jag was just standing there nodding his head and making his pecs dance beneath his shirt while one of the drow, one of the more stunning of the bunch, stood at his side giggling and poking at his bouncing chest muscles.

Who needs smooth dance moves when you've got the body of a professional wrestler?

I chuckled to myself. Jag always talked a big game when it came to his desirability amongst the females. This was the first time I'd really seen him put his boasts into practice. I had to admit, in a strange way, I was impressed.

Dwight pulled his rig up in front of the farmhouse, and Aerin jumped out with a wide grin on her face.

"Get everything we need?" I asked.

Aerin smirked at me. "You'll see."

Dwight opened up the back of the truck.

I stood there a half-second with my jaw agape before I could find the words. Several generators, still in their boxes, all stacked up. More than a dozen five-gallon gas cans, all filled. Several portable air conditioning units.

Several pallets of non-perishable foods, one of them stacked with nothing but box upon box of Top Ramen soup. College students, everywhere, were probably protesting the Top Ramen shortage in the wake of Aerin's purchase. There were a bunch of tools, ranging from small hand tools like screwdrivers and hammers to larger power tools like table saws and even an electric jackhammer. There were at least three weedeaters and one John Deere zero-turn mower.

"Holy crap, Aerin," I said. "Did you buy out the whole Home Depot?"

"Almost," Aerin said. "We did buy all the tents at Walmart. Not enough, but all they had. We have about twelve more. We'll have to get some more later when they are back in stock."

I shook my head. "How the hell did you do all this in just a few hours?"

Aerin smiled. "I just told the customer service people what I wanted. Asked them to load it all up. Funny how hard people will work when you throw extra money at them."

"You tipped the loaders at Home Depot and Walmart?" I asked. "I didn't think workers there could accept gratuities."

Aerin chuckled. "Probably not. But it isn't like any of them were going to tattle to their bosses about it. An extra thousand dollars for a low-wage worker will go a long way."

I snorted. "You gave them all a thousand bucks?"

Aerin shrugged. "It's just money. Never saw so many smiling humans work so hard."

"I bet!" I said. "And you two filled all the gas cans yourselves?"

"Nope," Aerin said. "The people who worked at the gas station apparently respond well to cash, too."

"You realize you probably spent more tonight than I used to make in the ministry over a whole year? Hell, you probably spent more than I earned the entire time I was a pastor."

"I'm not worried about it," Aerin said. "Like I said, I have more money than I know what to do with. Besides, what's too much money to spend in the name of saving the world?"

I shrugged my shoulders. "Good point, I suppose. If the world ends, money won't be worth much. It would suck to not have spent it."

"That's the spirit!" Aerin exclaimed.

"I realize this might not be the best time to talk about it, but do you know much about the Furies?"

Aerin nodded. "More than most, but even that is very little. Why do you ask? Are you thinking about trying to convince the fairies to break with Brightborn?"

"It wasn't my idea. Brag'mok said that his race, along with the elementals, share an origin with the Furies. He thought if we could present our case to them, we might persuade them to switch their allegiance."

Aerin bit her lip. "I wasn't aware of that. I knew the elementals were born alongside the Furies, but the giants?"

I nodded. "He thinks if we approach them representing two of the other three races originally created to defend the natural order, we might turn the tide in our favor."

"It's a fine idea," Aerin said. "But trying to evoke the Furies, it's not easy, and it would come with some serious risks."

"Like what?" I asked.

"Think about it, Caspar. We're talking about deities of a sort who embody ideas like vengeance and wrath. Those aren't the sort of beings you just approach on a whim."

"What's the worst that could happen?" I asked.

"Let me put it this way," Aerin said. "Ever heard of Mount Vesuvius?"

"Yeah, isn't that the one that erupted and destroyed Pompeii?"

Aerin nodded. "What you probably didn't know was that it happened after some of Pompeii's citizens attempted to evoke the Furies in the hopes that they might help destroy the Roman Empire. The Furies have a history of turning on those who petition them, punishing those who do so without what they deem to be a worthy cause in devastating ways."

"A history? What other disasters in history can be attributed to the Furies?"

"I suppose we'll never know. I just know if I hear of such a catastrophe, whether it be an eruption, a hurricane, even a pandemic, I always wonder if the Furies were behind it. If maybe someone evoked them out of turn and unleashed their wrath."

I shook my head. "I don't know about them. But if Brag'mok is right, as the last giant, he certainly has a right to say something. I've subdued the elements, too."

"But the trials didn't make you an elemental," Aerin said.

"They didn't. But you'd said before that you believed the chosen one would be able to wield all five elements in unity. I'd be able to at least bring all five elements together, along with Brag'mok, to present our case to the Furies."

Aerin sighed. "The drow have spent centuries trying to avoid engaging the fairies, much less the Furies."

"But whether we like it or not, the fairies are already involved. They are helping Brightborn. What if that's what the prophecy is about? What if, before I can unite all peoples, I have to first unite the giants, elementals, and Furies for the first time since..."

"Since what?" Aerin asked, detecting my hesitation.

"Since they existed as a part of some god's testicles."

Aerin cocked her head. "Is that what Brag'mok said?"

"He said it was a legend that his people inherited. Said one of the Titans supposedly sliced open his scrotum, and when his spooge fell to the Earth, they gave birth to each of the three."

"Greeks have weird myths," Aerin said. "I'm surprised that the giants knew of Greek stories. Most of the giants, I thought, came to New Albion from Britain, the original Albion."

I shook my head. "It's hard to say. Long before the elves, the former druids, and the giants fled to New Albion, the influence of the Greeks had spread far and wide. Ever since the time of Alexander the Great, there wasn't a corner of the known world that wasn't touched by Greek ideas. It isn't impossible to imagine that some of the stories, particularly if they had a peculiar interest for the giants, might have reached them at some point."

Aerin bit her lip. "This is possible. In truth, we do not know if the giants had always called the British isles home. There are stories of giants in many cultures."

"In the book of Deuteronomy, King Og of Bashan is described as the last survivor of the giant Rephaites, and it says he had a bed that was nine cubits long. That would be about thirteen feet, roughly Brag'mok's size. If they were the same race as Brag'mok, it makes sense that they were probably numerous in other parts of the world as well. Not to mention, the Bible speaks of the Nephilim and describes them as giants. I can't prove that these people were the ancient ancestors of the giants who ended up on New Albion, but it's possible. From what we do know of them, at least in the Bible, they were defeated. Since history is usually written by the victors, it isn't exactly surprising that we wouldn't know much more about these people."

"All speculation," Aerin said. "But it doesn't matter. If there is truth to Brag'mok's story, and he's right that he represents the last of a race meant to guard the world alongside the Furies and the elementals, there might be something to this plan."

"So you know how to call upon the Furies?" I asked.

"Not exactly. I mean, sort of. I know someone who has done it before. It just didn't turn out so well for him when he tried it."

"Who is it?" I asked.

"My father," Aerin said. "Only he's not with us. He's been in exile since I was just a girl. I'll just say, as you might have guessed by the fact that he once tried to evoke the Furies, he didn't agree with the tradition of restraint. He believed that the drow should embrace magic fully. Not be limited to enchantments."

"So when he did this, when he called on the Furies, what happened?"

"They abducted my mother," Aerin said. "It's why I'm the current reigning monarch despite being still just a princess. Not until my mother dies will I officially become queen."

"So if they abducted your mother, who sent your father into exile?"

Aerin sighed. "I did, Caspar. When he dies, as the sole female heir to the throne, I will assume power. It was necessary to exile my father, which adds a layer of difficulty to this whole plan."

"You don't think he'll be inclined to tell you how to do it?" I asked.

Aerin shook her head. "He won't. Why would he? I sent him into exile for doing the very thing we'd be asking him how to do."

"Into exile where?"

Aerin pressed her lips together. "I sent him here."

"To the United States?" I asked, raising an eyebrow.

"Not just to the United States. He's here in St. Louis. It's where he wanted to go. He said that all things were going to come to a head here, so I allowed it."

"After all that's happened, you haven't gone to see him?" I asked. "He hasn't reached out?"

Aerin shook her head. "Like I said, I don't think he wants to see me. And I wasn't exactly keen on looking him up before."

I scratched my head. "Well, at least it's convenient. Since we don't have much time to respond to the President's ultimatum, I'll call that a small victory."

CHAPTER SEVEN

Brag'mok, Jag, and Dwight made short work of unloading the rig. Brag'mok saw lifting heavy things as another opportunity to take out his frustrations. Jag made it a point to roll up his sleeves as he carried one heavy item after the next out of the truck, presumably to impress the drow woman he'd taken an interest in. Dwight...well, he directed traffic.

Brag'mok had assembled a number of metal shelters made mostly from truck beds, the hoods of abandoned cars, and other pieces of scrap. The drow gathered to watch as Layla and I assembled one of the tents, then picked up the rest and duplicated our efforts.

Dwight drove off, leaving Jag and Brag'mok behind. I shook my head. Jag didn't live here. He had his own apartment, and Brag'mok had been living with him. Did they really expect me to give them a ride back? It wasn't like Brag'mok could fit in the Eclipse, anyway. Jag would probably fit uncomfortably.

Of course, the junkyard probably had enough car parts between all the broken down vehicles that had been abandoned there that a good mechanic could put something together that might be more accommodating to larger-than-average passengers.

Jag wasn't exactly a professional mechanic, but based on the fact that he was looking under the hood of an abandoned farm truck he gave me the impression that he knew at least a little.

"What are you doing?" I asked. "Why didn't you go back with Dwight?"

Jag shrugged. "Not really safe there for Brag'mok. The way I see it, if Brightborn sends any assassins after him, they won't hesitate to do the same with me. After all that has been happening, I'm just not sure it's safe for either of us to go back. Not now, anyway."

I nodded. "What are you doing with this old truck?"

"It's not in awful shape," Jag said. "Rebuilt a truck sort of like this one with my dad when I was a kid. Just a little curious, honestly."

"Think you could get it working?" I asked. "I don't think either you or Brag'mok could fit comfortably in my car."

Jag nodded. "Might just be something simple. Don't have a key. I'll have to hotwire the thing to see what happens when I try and fire it up. Looks like all the parts are here, though. Not sure they're all functioning, but maybe I can dig up replacement parts. This isn't the only farm truck of this vintage abandoned here. Maybe between all of them, I can put together one functioning vehicle."

I smiled and slapped Jag on the back. "I'd hoped as much. You guys have a place to sleep?"

Jag nodded off into the distance at one of Brag'mok's makeshift shelters. It looked, to me, like another pile of scrap. "You sure that'll do? You really don't have to stay down here with us if you don't want to."

"I *do* want to, Caspar," Jag said. "Only thing I'll miss here is the gym. I'm sure I can figure out something. Maybe I'll find a Prius to bench press or something."

I snorted. "You can't bench a Prius."

"Can, too!" Jag nodded, pressing his lips together. "At least, I think I can. Haven't tried."

"It's a whole car," I said. "It has to weigh at least three thousand pounds."

Jag grunted. "No, it couldn't be that much. It's so small."

"I'm sure you can find something to lift. I mean, we've got some tires and wheels. Put those on the end of a long pipe or something, and you'd have as good as an Olympic bar."

Jag pinched his chin. "Not a bad idea, Casp!"

"Is everything in order at St. Ensley's?" I asked. "I'm sure there will be more government agents there next Sunday, expecting me to say something in support of the President's alliance with Brightborn."

Jag nodded. "Provided we can get there, sure. I still have all the equipment there to live-stream whatever it is you want to do. I'm sure that your friend Cecil and the rest of them will be there too."

"We're working on a plan," I said. "I'm still reluctant to use St. Ensley's. With the government on my case and the elves probably looking for us, I don't want to subject the people there to danger."

"Whatever you decide," Jag said. "Just let me know how I can help."

"Thanks, Jag. It means a lot. Besides, it's nice to have another human here. Nice to know I'm not the only one on our side of this whole thing."

"We aren't the only ones," Jag said. "There are others, all those who gathered at St. Ensley's before, just waiting and ready to help in whatever way you might ask."

"That's the thing," I said. "I don't want to get more people wrapped up in this than is necessary. At least not so long as my whole future is in question."

"It will work out," Jag said. "I believe in you. You'll find a way through this mess. I know it."

I slapped Jag on the shoulder. Not in an aggressive way. It was a gesture meant to communicate solidarity. "Again, I really appreciate everything you're doing and your vote of confidence."

"Goodnight, Casp," Jag said, turning and making his way toward the makeshift dome that Brag'mok had constructed for the two of them to share. I half wondered, with two such massive men in one shelter made of scrap metal, how loud it would be when they started snoring.

I yawned and turned back toward the farmhouse.

One of the generators was already running. It was on the porch of the farmhouse, and a cord was strung inside.

"You set up air conditioning inside?" I asked Layla as I walked through the door. She had been waiting for me, rocking on a chair on the porch.

Layla bit her lip. "Not exactly."

I followed the cord inside and found it leading to Agnus' self-cleaning litter box. I looked at Layla with a blank stare. "Seriously? The litter box was a priority?"

"Agnus wouldn't stop bitching about it," Layla said. "I figured it would get him out of our hair."

I chuckled and shook my head. "Well, at least it shouldn't pull a lot of electricity."

I put my arm around Layla. "I'm beat. Ready to hit the sack and start again fresh in the morning?"

Layla took a deep breath. "Yeah, I'm tired, too."

As we walked into the bedroom, I found the air mattress that Layla and I had been sleeping on was totally flat. Agnus was curled up on one of the blankets in the middle of it.

"Agnus," I said. "What happened to the mattress?"

Agnus looked at me, licked his paw, and ran it over his head. "Sorry, Casp. Claws. What can I say? With all these blankets, I just couldn't resist kneading them. Then there was a pop, and…well… it was like bubble wrap but with only one big pop."

I snorted as I reached into a duffel bag of various supplies I'd packed when we moved out of the apartment and pulled out a roll of duct tape. "Where's the leak, exactly?"

"Here and there," Agnus said. "When the air came out, it felt good. It's too muggy in here!"

"I'll get him some tuna," Layla said. "Maybe we can patch it up if he's not putting any more holes in it."

Agnus' ears responded to the word "tuna," and after his ears, the rest of his body perked up, and he scurried out the door.

I tossed the blankets off the deflated mattress and onto the floor. On my hands and knees, I found the holes I could locate and taped them over. I wasn't sure how well the duct tape would hold, especially once we got our weight on the mattress, but I was hoping it would at least hold enough air to last the night.

Of course, what would be the chances that I'd find all the holes on the first try? The mattress had a manual pump, but it also had an electric one. I unplugged Agnus' litter box and plugged in the pump. As the mattress partially inflated, I ran my hand across the top, looking for more leaks. Altogether, I found about a dozen claw-sized punctures. Once I had them patched, I put the blankets back on the bed and tucked myself in.

Layla joined me, spooning behind me, and we fell asleep.

CHAPTER EIGHT

When I woke up the next morning, the bed had deflated. We were lying on the hard floor. I wasn't sure how long it had been that way, but at least I'd been able to sleep through it.

Layla was still sound asleep. Somehow. Agnus sat at the foot of the bed, staring at us.

"What are you looking at?" I asked. "Looking for a can of morning tuna?"

"I'm fine," Agnus said, cocking his head. "But you... Ever since the trials, when you sleep... It's getting worse. I think you need release."

I cocked my head. "What sort of release? Just yesterday, Layla and I..."

"Not that, you perv," Agnus piped back. "Not that you don't have an embarrassing case of night-wood most of the time. But that's not what I was referring to."

I scratched my head, then grabbed my pillow and put it over my lap. Stuff like that wasn't embarrassing before my cat could talk. But now...

"What were you talking about, Agnus? Since the trials, what?"

"Ah yes," Agnus said. "Sorry, I was distracted. Didn't your mom tell you it's not nice to point?"

I rolled my eyes. "Just answer the question, Agnus."

"I can barely touch you when you're sleeping. It's almost like electricity, and it gets stronger every night. It's like you're all pent up. We know what happens when you don't take matters into your own hands—when you don't give yourself a release."

"We're still talking about magic, right?" I asked, raising an eyebrow.

Agnus looked at me blankly. "Of course. What else would I be talking about? I'm just saying, if you don't find an outlet, a way to use your magic, you might inadvertently fire off at an inopportune moment."

I bit the inside of my cheek. "Good to know. If we're going to do something like that, we need to get as far away from the ranch as possible. So Brightborn doesn't find out where we're at."

Layla rolled over and put her hand on my back.

"Holy crap, Caspar. You're hot! Like, burning up."

"Burning up?" I asked. "I don't think I'm sick. Doesn't feel like I have a fever."

"It's fire magic," Agnus said. "It's not the worst element trying to get out. I'd hate it if you broke wind or wet your bed."

Layla snickered. "If it was Earth, you might wake up getting your rocks off."

"Stop it," I said, shaking my head. "This is serious. If this magic gets out, all of this we're building here will be at risk."

"I know," Layla said, standing up and quickly throwing on a t-shirt and slipping into a pair of yoga pants. Not because she was planning to do any exercise, but because she wore yoga pants like some people wear sweats. She found them comfortable. I didn't mind. Her butt looked amazing in them.

I still wasn't quite in as good of shape as she was. I was getting there, but a few months of even the best training wasn't going to completely reverse years of Twinkie and Pizza binges. I didn't even have a six-pack yet. I had two little abs right on top that sometimes peeked out. Then they disappeared again as if they'd seen their own shadow.

Six more weeks of cardio hell.

At least, that's what would have happened before we were living on the ranch. Most of the workouts I got in here were tied to actual manual labor.

"What are you doing?" Layla asked.

"Sitting on my ass. Why?"

"We need to get you out of here, Caspar. Before you shoot your magical load all over the ranch."

I huffed. "That was…a disturbingly graphic image."

"If you find the idea troubling, imagine being on the receiving end. All the people here, the drow, even Jag and Brag'mok who believe that this place is safe."

I sighed and stood up. The blood rushed from my head, and I wobbled.

Layla grabbed my arm. "Caspar, are you okay?"

"I don't know. I mean, I think so. Maybe I stood up too fast."

"We don't know what all that magic might do to your body if it builds up too much. Come on, I'll drive."

"But you don't have a license. I mean, not a legal one."

"You aren't in any shape to drive, Caspar," Layla said. "Besides, say you got pulled over, and they ran your license. You really think the government wouldn't notice?"

I sighed. "Good point. I'm seeing double, as if I'd been drinking."

Layal took me by the arm and led me out of the farmhouse.

"Where are you two going?" Aerin asked. She was standing on the porch, evidently taking in the morning air.

"It's Caspar," Layla said. "Something's wrong. We think it's his magic building up. I need to take him somewhere he can release it safely."

"I know a place," Aerin said. "I'll come with you."

"You know a place?" I asked, raising my eyebrows as I saw two Aerins looking back at me.

Aerin nodded. "We were talking about going to visit my father anyway. Might as well do it now."

"So you can show off your magically charged husband?" I asked as Layla opened the passenger side door for me. "Chivalry isn't dead after all," I said–, almost bumping my head on the roof as I lowered myself into the passenger seat.

Aerin shook her head as she opened the back door of my Eclipse. "When we exiled him, we knew he'd be using magic. We figured he'd incur the wrath of the fairies eventually and give it up. But shortly after we came to St. Louis, I decided to check it out."

"I thought you said you didn't go see him," I said as Layla started the ignition. Felt a little bit like my car was cheating on me. I know, with my wife. It's weird. But I'm possessive about my car. I couldn't remember the last time I allowed someone else to drive it, apart from the mechanics who pulled it in and out of the shop, anyway.

"I didn't go to see him. I went to observe. He'd set up a ring of stones, like those the druids used to use in Northern Europe. I saw him casting different kinds of magic inside. It was like the stones contained it. They prevented the power from escaping, hiding him from the fairies. He'd always insisted that there were ways we could use magic without upsetting the fae, but such things were unthinkable according to drow custom. We were taught from a young age that the only kind of magic we could dare wield was through the medium of enchanted items."

"So if we go there, to his stone circle, I can release all my magic without consequences?" I asked.

"Theoretically," Aerin said. "I mean, yes. It should work."

"In theory, or yes? Which is it?" I asked.

"All I know is what I saw my father do. He can't wield all the elements. I can't guarantee that whatever method he used there with the stones would work in your case. But I can sense the magic in you, Caspar. My father is our best chance. If you release it anywhere close to here, you'll give the elves a place to start looking."

I nodded. "All right. But you said before you weren't sure he'd want to see you."

Aerin bit her lip. "He might not. But once he knows what's at stake, he'll help. My father's views are not, how can I put it, what you'd call orthodox. But he isn't a bad man. He always intended to do good. If he realizes you are the chosen one, that you're Naayak Nightshade, I can't believe he won't help."

"And if he's willing to teach us how to summon the Furies, all the better," I said.

Layla grunted. "I don't know. We don't have Brag'mok with us. We shouldn't attempt it without him."

"We're not saying we're actually going to do it," Aerin said. "Only find out how to do it. If he's inclined to share, that is."

CHAPTER NINE

The junkyard ranch was just a few exits past Six Flags off I-44. By "off the Interstate," I mean, quite a ways off it, down a series of country roads. The closest few roads that we had to take to get to the ranch were all poorly kept gravel.

It meant my Eclipse was destined to be covered in dust. It didn't matter if I washed the car unless it had rained recently. A single trip to the ranch was enough to make it look like it hadn't been washed in months. As we left the gravel and hit the first paved road, I reached over and pulled the lever that triggered the release of windshield wiper fluid and the wipers to clear Layla's vision.

"Thanks," Layla said. "Wasn't sure how to do that."

I nodded and reclined my seat back. My head was still spinning. I closed my eyes.

Aerin stroked my hair from behind me. Layla glanced in my direction briefly before fixing her eyes back on the road. She didn't say anything, but I could tell she didn't appreciate Aerin's gesture. Since I knew that when Aerin touched me, she had... urges, I wasn't sure what to make of it myself. But I was too out of sorts to care.

Alternating waves of heat and cold coursed through my body. A sense of gritty heaviness in my gut and an airy sensation in my lungs. That accounted for four of the five elements. Only aether, or spirit, wasn't producing any discernible sensations.

I closed my eyes. It helped a little. I wasn't sure if it was the elements inside me or a simple case of car sickness exacerbated by my otherwise disoriented state of mind. However, with all the other sensations swirling around my body, minimizing visual stimuli calmed my nerves.

Cool air blew against my face. I didn't remember the Eclipse having such a powerful air conditioner.

I opened my eyes.

I was staring down at the top of the Eclipse, hovering over the car. I shrieked. I wasn't in my body. Not completely. A golden tether of some sort ran between me and my body. Was I an astral projection or something? I'd read a little about astral projection. Cool idea. Never thought it was real. You know, like other things that weren't supposed to exist, like elves or magic.

I focused my mind and forced my consciousness back into my body. The other sensations, those produced by the other elements, immediately returned.

"Doing all right?" Layla asked.

"You didn't see that?" I was trying to catch my breath.

"See what?" Layla asked.

"I was outside of my body, hovering over the car. I think all the elements in my body are going haywire."

"They need a release," Aerin said, "some way to manifest. The elementals within you are not just powers; they are entities. They need to be regularly expressed."

"Like walking a dog?" I asked.

"Or letting children out to play," Aerin said. "Can't coop them up too long without them getting restless."

"How close are we?" Layla asked.

"Just a few more miles down the highway," Aerin said. "I mean, I think. I only went there once before, and I had a driver."

I snorted. "So you don't know for sure how to get there?"

"I think I do," Aerin said. "Just keep driving, Layla. I'll recognize the turn when I see it."

I was too focused on trying to keep myself inside my body to worry about directions. The women would figure it out, I assumed. But what if fire got out while we were all cooped up in the car? Even water, or air, and certainly earth, could be devastating in their own way.

"I don't know how much longer I can contain all this," I said, clenching my fists.

"Right there!" Aerin said, pointing at an exit sign through the front window. "Exit there and turn right."

Layla pulled off the highway and followed a series of turns that Aerin said seemed familiar. Hopefully, her sense of direction was better than mine. I often make wrong turns when I'm in places I don't know well because something—a tree on a corner, a little sign, whatever—looks somehow familiar. We couldn't afford to get lost right now.

I just hoped Aerin's dad didn't hold a grudge and that his stone circle would work to harness my magic.

We pulled onto a dirt road. Not even gravel. With the ruts in the road, I wasn't a hundred percent certain that the Eclipse wouldn't bottom out. They must not have been as deep as they seemed. If it had been raining, though, we wouldn't have made it without getting stuck.

The road was mostly covered by the trees on either side, the branches forming a canopy above us.

"Right here," Aerin said. "Just through those trees."

"I don't see anything," Layla said.

"It's there," Aerin said, getting out of the car. She opened my door and, taking me by my arm, helped me out and onto my feet.

I wasn't just seeing double. Maybe triple. With so many trees around us, it felt like they were closing in as we walked down the narrow path between them. Like the forest was swallowing us.

Layla came up from behind and took me by the other arm. "I've got him," she said.

Aerin stared at her briefly before nodding and releasing my arm.

A cat fight was probably brewing. It was just a matter of time. But the tension between the women was the last thing on my mind. For the moment, given all the other sensations swirling in my frame, the tension between them was just a mild annoyance by comparison.

I didn't have the mental resources to waste worrying about it. It took every bit of focus I had to keep from exploding into a mushroom cloud of elemental magic.

We reached what looked like a makeshift cottage. I'd seen tool sheds bigger than this place before. Aerin knocked on the door.

"Here goes nothing," Aerin said. "I half expect he'll just slap the door in my face."

The door swung open.

"Aerie-berry!" the aged drow man who opened the door exclaimed. He had a long, white beard that nearly reached his waist. He was slight of build, his arms so thin if I was seeing them correctly that I thought I might be able to wrap my whole hand around them.

"Hi, Dad," Aerin said.

The man enveloped Aerin with a hug. "It's about time. I wondered how long it would take before you came looking for me."

Layla and I exchanged awkward glances.

"Princess Brightborn, I presume," the man said, nodding at Layla. "And Naayak Nightshade!"

I snorted. "How did you…"

"I saw the trials. I might live a simple life out here. But I'm no neanderthal. I have the internet on my phone."

"Dad," Aerin said. "I'd love to catch up. But we really need your help."

"Of course you do," the man said. "Name's Elrand, by the way. Elrand Nightshade."

"Nice to meet you," Layla said.

I nodded. "Yeah, me too."

"You're my son-in-law!" Elrand said. "I presume, based on that ring on your finger, Princess, that you're my daughter-in-law, too?"

"Something like that," Layla said, looking to the side. "Please, sir. We don't have much time."

"Naayak's power is overwhelming him," Aerin said. "I know you have a stone circle you've been using to prevent your magic from being detected by the fairies."

Elrand bit his lip. "Been spying on me, daughter?"

"Just one time," Aerin said. "I was checking up on you."

Elrand nodded. "Come with me."

We followed Elrand down another trail that led from the back of his cottage farther into the woods. Layla held onto my arm as I stumbled behind Elrand, focusing my eyes on the man in an effort to find my balance.

"I presume you've also come to summon the Furies," Elrand said.

Aerin, walking beside her father, turned and looked at me. I shrugged. "How did you…"

"The entrails of an opossum revealed it to me," Elrand said.

"You can't be serious," Aerin said. "Examining entrails to tell the future?"

"It's a well-known practice, daughter," Elrand said. "Well attested to by the ancients."

"I just didn't know that it really worked," Aerin said.

"Of course it does! How else would I know why you came? Everything is already prepared. Once Naayak releases his energy, the Furies will pay us a visit in the stone circle."

"Wait," Aerin said. "We aren't ready for that yet."

"I know, I know. There's a giant you hoped might also come and appeal your case to the Furies," Elrand said. "But no worries, daughter. Once we've evoked them, we'll have a full cycle of the moon to make our appeal before they judge our case."

"Our case?" Aerin asked. "Dad, I appreciate your help. But this isn't a matter that concerns you."

"Of course it does, daughter! I've been preparing for this day ever since you sent me here."

Aerin grunted. "I thought you'd be upset about it. I wasn't sure you'd even want to see me."

Elrand laughed. "Baby girl! I could never be angry at you for doing your duty. All those things happened to prepare us for this very moment in time!"

Everything they were saying, I had to admit, was quite fascinating. I didn't have a lot of thoughts about it. Mostly because I didn't have any mental faculties to spare. It took everything I had to both stay upright and put one foot in front of the other while also holding myself together. The elements were all coursing through me, giving me several sensations at once. I couldn't discern one from the next. Extreme heat from the fire, the ice-cold sensation of water, the heaviness of earth, and the lightness of air. They all melded together into one giant sense of incredible discomfort, like my body was being ripped apart from the inside out.

"Have you evoked the Furies before?" Aerin asked.

Elrand laughed. "I couldn't, until now. Without all five elements, it's simply not possible. The only elements I can wield are earth and aether."

"But now Naayak can…"

"Indeed, my girl. Such is what I believe the chosen one was always destined to do!"

"To unite the peoples," I said, managing to get a few words out. "Means to first unite the three guardian races."

"Precisely!" Elrand exclaimed. "I like this one, Aerin! You did well!"

Layla firmed her grip on my arm. "Are we almost there?"

"Yes, Princess. Just through the clearing ahead."

We stepped through an opening in the trees. Five stones—which looked like ten to me on account of my double-vision—were arranged in a perfect circle.

Still holding onto my arm, Layla helped me into the middle of the circle.

Elrand stepped to the perimeter. "Come, both of you. He is the only one who can be within the circle when the elements are released."

Layla put her hand on my back. "You've got this, Caspar."

I nodded and stumbled into the middle of the circle.

"Now, Naayak. Release the elements! Each one will settle on its corresponding stone, and the Furies will appear!"

Once everyone was outside the circle, I exhaled, relaxing my body. The power pulled my hands skyward and five, distinct energies poured out of my fingers. Blue, red, green, white, and golden power blasted into the sky.

The elemental powers swirled together in a tornado of unrestrained energy.

The cyclone of power surrounded me and pulled me off of my feet.

As I hovered in mid-air, spun by the magic, each element left the tornado one by one. The element of fire flowed to one of the stones first, turning the entire stone red to match the color of its magic. The others followed suit. As each elemental power left the tornado, it slowed, gently setting me back on my feet as the last element, aether, settled on its respective stone.

I looked down at my feet, ensuring that I had a good footing on the ground. Then, I looked up.

Three identical women stood there. They were tall, at least seven feet in height. Their hair was golden in color. Not blonde, literally golden, and their skin radiated with white light.

I shielded my eyes with my hand.

"Tell us," the three women demanded, speaking in unison, "why you, human, have dared to call upon the Furies?"

CHAPTER TEN

I looked around. The five stones glowed so brightly that I couldn't even see Layla, Aerin, or Elrand standing beyond them.

"I am the one they call Naayak," I said. "The chosen one of the elven prophecy."

"We know who you are," the three Furies responded in concert. "Or at least, we know who you claim to be."

"Then you know why I'm here," I said. "I represent the elements and also the giants. I come to beg you to reconsider the alliance between the fairies and the elves."

"Your race has become a parasite on the Earth," the Furies replied. "The elves are your just judgment."

I shook my head. "The elves seek to use the Earth's magic for war. In their world, that's all they've known. They've turned the power of life toward destruction and bloodshed."

"It is not the elves who have polluted our waters and skies. It is not they who have done violence to our forests and lands or have used the power of fire to destroy. Humans have lost touch with aether. They are no longer true to their own spirits."

"The elves will do far worse if they take control of this world,"

I said. "If you need proof, just consider what they did to the giants."

"What are you speaking of, human?" the Furies asked.

"They killed them! All of them! Only one still survives, and he is the one who told me I should summon you to beg your reconsideration."

The three Furies exchanged glances with one another. "How can we know that what you say is true? You would not be the first human to invoke us and attempt to persuade us with lies."

"I can bring him to you," I said. "He'll tell you himself what the elves did."

"If this is your end, why do you approach us in the company of elves?"

I shook my head. "They are not aligned with the elven king, the one who hopes to destroy us. They are here to help."

"Then why does one of these harness the power of celestial beings?" the Furies asked. "Such power was meant to be attained by the chosen one."

I sighed. "I gave it to her to save her. Her father, the elven king, would have allowed her to die otherwise. I had no choice."

The Furies all looked at me, furrowing their brows. "Then she is the one the elven king believes to be the chosen one."

I shook my head. "He knows the truth. He's trying to convince the elves that Layla is the chosen one. He had her stabbed with a blade charged with this…angel magic in order to force my hand, to use me to kill a man who'd stolen the rings that contain this power and to give it to her instead."

"You did what?" the second of the Furies, the one in the middle asked, speaking for the first time on her own.

"I had no choice," I said. "The elven king forced my hand."

"But a man has died by your hand no less," the same Fury responded.

"But it was the elf who acted in jealousy," the Fury on the far right said. "Not the human. Had it not been for the king's envy, his desire to name the chosen one himself, Naayak would not have had to act in turn."

"Then it seems," the Fury on the left said, "that to decide to whom we should declare our loyalty falls to me. I am Allecto the angry. The king, I believe, acted in anger. This human acted out of love. Although the elf who holds the angel power is the king's daughter, he was moved by love above all else."

"That's two to one, right? So you will side with me?" I asked.

"We will not," the three responded, again in unison.

"But two of you took my side."

"The Furies do not act if our will is divided. We require unanimous consent."

I looked at the middle Fury. "What can I do to prove that I had no choice?"

"I am Tisiphone, the Fury who avenges murder. What does choice have to do with whether a man is guilty of bloodshed?"

"Everything," I said. "Murder has to be premeditated. I did not want to kill the man. Because my life is bound to Layla's, and also Aerin's, the princess of the drow, if I allowed Layla to die, we all would have died. It was either kill Fred, the man who'd stolen angelic magic, and one life would be tragically lost, or all three of us would have died."

Tisiphone cocked her head. "If you three had died, the guilt would have fallen on the king."

I sighed. "If I am guilty, then I took that guilt upon myself in order to save two others."

"You did it to save yourself, as well," Tisiphone said.

"But as the Fury of jealousy and pride," the Fury on the right said, "I sense it was his love for the elf who holds the magic now that he acted. Not for his own sake."

"You may have assumed guilt for the sake of love," Tisiphone said, "but you cannot claim guilt without also bearing the consequences. More, you used the magic of the elements to accomplish the deed."

I scratched my head. "You're right; I can't justify what I did. Sometimes, I believe, we are forced to make unfortunate choices in this broken world. We must sometimes choose the lesser of evils, even if it means we must bear sin in our souls. But you three, you were made by another. I don't know if you were really created from Uranus' testicles, but I believe in a God who is above all of us. A God who believes in redemption and atonement. I believe in a God who gave His own Son as a sacrifice so guilt would not forever stain our souls."

The three Furies stood, again, in silence. They all three narrowed their eyes as if looking into my soul. "Tell us what you propose to offer to atone for your guilt."

I sighed. "I believe we are saved by grace through faith."

"We are not speaking of your eternal salvation or damnation, human," the Furies said. "We are speaking of your guilt and its consequences. You must still endure the punishment prescribed for your guilt in your mortal life. Tell us, human, would a man who killed another be exonerated of his crime in your human courts merely because he'd done good deeds before or after he committed the offense?"

I shook my head. "He would not. Though sometimes, in human courts, if such an action was out of character, or if extenuating circumstances left him without a choice, and he took responsibility for his actions, a jury of his peers might acquit him, or the judge might impose a lesser sentence. Once he completed the sentence, he would be free."

"This is how human authorities exact justice?" the Furies asked.

I nodded. "Yes, and this would be according to God's will. In my faith, in the Bible I believe in, it says that all people should be subject to the governing authorities, for there is no authority except what is given by God, and those that exist have been instituted by God. For rulers and authorities, the Bible says, are God's avengers."

"We do not dispute your holy book," the Furies said.

"What if I turn myself in?" I asked. "If I allow the human authorities, the avengers appointed by God, to judge my case? Since you three are also born of God, created to preserve the natural order, would you accept their judgment?"

"We would be bound to do so," the Furies said.

"But if what you say of the elven king is true, that he has slain the giants, we also require the testimony of the surviving giant."

"So if I do this, if I face the justice of our courts and bring Brag'mok to you, will you agree to order the fairies to disavow their support of Brightborn and the elven legions?"

"We must confer amongst ourselves regarding your proposal before we give consent to this agreement," the Furies said.

I nodded. The three Furies turned their backs to me. If they were speaking at all, they were doing so through some kind of inaudible speech, or perhaps on a spiritual plane. Whatever they had to deliberate took longer than I expected. I stood there, tugging at my shirt, my knees shaking, for what felt like an hour or more. It may have been much shorter than that, but my nervousness and anticipation made time slow down.

Finally, they turned around, and the Fury on the left began speaking.

"I am Allecto, unceasing in anger. I do consent."

"I am Tisiphone, avenger of murder. I too consent," the middle Fury declared.

"I am Megara the jealous. I agree with my sisters and consent in kind," said the third.

"So that's it?" I asked. "I turn myself in and bring Brag'mok back to you?"

"Our agreement will expire within a single lunar cycle," the Furies said in unison.

"One month?" I asked. "It takes a lot longer than that for human courts to decide anything, much less a murder case."

"These are our terms, human," the Furies said. "Should you

71

not return, having been judged by your courts, with the giant in one lunar cycle, we will respond to your summons with wrath."

"What kind of wrath?" I asked.

"Many of your kind will suffer if you do not succeed, Naayak. For where we stand, there is a great fault nearby. The earth will shake with a fury never before known if you fail."

CHAPTER ELEVEN

I knew what the Furies meant—the New Madrid fault. I'd learned growing up in Missouri that a quake in the early eighteen hundreds had been so violent that it caused the Mississippi River to run backward. If the Furies unleashed the fault on a scale like they said, one that had never before been known, I couldn't imagine how much devastation it would cause.

I stood in the stone circle in silence after the Furies disappeared. The energies illuminating the five stones faded.

Layla, Aerin, and Elrand were still standing there, outside the circle.

Layla ran up to me and put her hand on my back.

"What happened?" Aerin asked.

"The Furies agreed to his proposal," Elrand said.

"That's fantastic!" Layla said. "So the fairies have broken ties with my father?"

I grunted. "Not exactly. Elrand is right, though. They did agree."

"How did you know that?" Aerin asked her father.

"Again," Elrand said. "The entrails portended it would be so."

"What exactly did they agree to?" Layla asked.

THEOPHILUS MONROE & MICHAEL ANDERLE

"I thought the whole point was to convince them to stop backing my father?"

I nodded. "They agreed with certain terms."

"What terms, Caspar?" Layla asked.

I shook my head. "I have to turn myself in."

"Turn yourself in? To who, for what?" Layla asked.

"To the government. I have to face their judgment for the murder of Fred."

"You can't!" Layla protested. "You can't save the world from prison, Caspar! How can you fight my father if you're in jail?"

"How can I fight him if he still has the fairies on his side?" I asked.

"We'd find a way! You can't do this!"

Aerin put her hand on my shoulder. "But he must."

"Why the hell must he?" Layla asked.

"Because," I said. "If I don't, and if I cannot come back within a single cycle, they'll unleash an earthquake that will completely destroy St. Louis and probably half of the Midwest."

"Those are horrible terms with dismal odds of success. Why would you agree to that?" Layla asked.

"The consequence of destruction was a given once the Furies were evoked," Elrand said. "That Naayak has found terms to pacify the Furies' wrath should be considered an opportunity."

"Going to prison," Layla said, turning her back to us and folding her arms across her chest. "What a fantastic opportunity."

"We don't know that I'll be convicted," I said. "Two of the three Furies already agreed with my position. It was only the one who has some hang-up about murder who insisted my guilt be properly adjudicated and my sentence satisfied before she would grant her consent to the idea I proposed."

"That's two out of three!" Layla shouted. "Why does this one Fury have a say over the others?"

I shook my head. "They aren't a democracy. They only agree to anything by unanimous consent."

"Well, that's a shitty way to do things," Layla said. "Can you imagine if your government required unanimous decisions?"

I shrugged. "Juries have to convict criminals unanimously. If even one can be convinced that I should be acquitted, we'll be fine."

"And the chances of that happening in one cycle of the moon?" Layla asked. "I've seen how your government works. It's like the whole damn country is run by a bunch of sloths and snails."

I snorted. "Donkeys and elephants, actually."

"Not much better. You're saying it's run by jackasses and giant beasts who look big and strong but get easily frightened and end up trampling over everything."

I shrugged. "Interesting political commentary, actually. Technically speaking, our constitution grants the accused the right to a speedy trial."

"But one lunar cycle, Caspar?" Layla turned back toward me, her hands on her hips. "Not *that* speedy."

"Perhaps we should stick to the original idea," Aerin said. "Create a swell of public support. Do something amazing. Use your magic in a way that people can't deny. Then, turn yourself in and dare the government to convict you."

I shook my head. "It doesn't work that way."

"But your government also grants the accused the right to an impartial jury, does it not?" Aerin asked. "What if you do something so great, so amazing, that there isn't a single person who could be found who'd be impartial?"

"I need an acquittal or a conviction with a sentence that I can serve by the time the month is over. The latter isn't likely at all, no matter what. There isn't any sentence for a convicted murderer that can be satisfied in a month. We need to get a good lawyer. We need to find and produce such compelling evidence that they'll legitimately find a reason to acquit me of the crime. Which won't be easy, considering I am guilty."

"No, you aren't, Caspar," Layla said, shaking her head.

"Layla, I didn't just agree to do it. I was the murder weapon. Literally. You can't say I'm not guilty."

"Guilt is about more than who did it, Caspar. It's about who is responsible. The only reason you had to kill Fred was to take back a power that was yours by right, one he'd used already against me. He nearly killed me, and even then, he only did it because he was brainwashed by my father. Both Fred himself, and my father, were more responsible for Fred's death than you."

"Somehow, we'd have to convince a jury of that," I said. "Which will be even harder since the second we start talking about magic powers and elves—"

"Again," Aerin interjected. "If we bring everything out into the open and you do something to prove who you are and what you can do. Make it so public, so undeniable, that any jury will have no choice but to consider the mystical elements of the case."

"It's still not going to happen in a month," Layla said, shaking her head.

"It might," I said. "Once I start rallying the public's support, it'll piss off the President. I can offer to turn myself in on the condition that my trial is expedited."

"But still, even if that's possible, to complete it in one lunar cycle," Layla said.

"If the President wants me to turn myself in, if he wants to silence me, he'll have to agree to pull whatever strings he can to make it happen."

"Naayak will be successful," Elrand said.

Layla rolled her eyes. "Opossum intestines tell you that?"

Elrand shook his head. "I've seen nothing in the entrails concerning this matter beyond the invocation of the Furies. Their actions and decisions cannot be foretold. But I do believe in the prophecy. I am surprised, Princess, that it is you who lacks belief."

"I believe in the prophecy," Layla said. "I believe in Caspar. I just don't trust human governments."

"It is a foolish man," Elrand said, "who puts his faith in princes or presidents. But how can you have faith in the ends while doubting the means? If you believe that Naayak will indeed fulfill the prophecy once all the seals are revealed, why such trepidation now?"

Layla shook her head. "Like I said before, I just don't trust this world's governments."

"Do you imagine that these governments are so powerful that they might thwart an ancient prophecy?" Elrand asked.

"Of course not!" Layla said.

"Then have faith, Princess," Elrand said.

"I have faith," Aerin interjected with a single nod. "I believe this will work. I know it will."

Layla narrowed her eyes. If her new celestial powers had allowed her to shoot lasers out of her eyes, she would have destroyed Aerin in that moment.

Thankfully for all of us, Layla didn't have that ability.

CHAPTER TWELVE

It was certainly an odd way to meet Aerin's father. But it was better than the first time Layla introduced me to hers. At least Aerin's dad *approved* of me. Sure, he was an exiled drow, not an otherworldly elven king. Earning his approval, I suppose, was a relatively low bar to clear. It wasn't like Aerin and I were a *real* couple. I suppose it would be more numerically accurate to say that our trio was something of an illusion. Layla and I were the ones who were together. Aerin had joined us as a formality, even if she did have feelings for me on account of the rings that bound us.

I didn't tell Layla that Aerin had a desire to jump my bones. Nothing good would come of that. Aerin had confided in me, and in the end, it was just a side-effect of the rings that bound us together. But the way Aerin went out of her way to touch me... When she'd caressed my hair in the car or when she put her hand on my arm or on my side. Given what it did to her, I had to wonder how hard she was resisting her desires.

The last thing I needed on my hands at the moment was relationship drama. I'd be lying if I didn't admit that the notion of two insanely hot elves competing for my affections wasn't flattering. It was good for my ego. Even if it *was* just on account of those damned rings and not because, as Right Said Fred once put it so eloquently, I'm too sexy.

"We need to figure out a plan," Aerin said, sliding into the passenger seat.

Layla sighed and rolled her eyes. It was her turn to sit in the back, now that I was fit to drive. I looked at Layla in the rearview mirror. She pursed her lips and turned her eyes away.

I shook my head. Why was she acting like this? What choice did I really have with the Furies? I had to offer something. All things considered, it wasn't the worst thing I could have offered. I couldn't think of any other way to convince Tisiphone, "avenger of murder," to change her vote. Would Layla have preferred I let the Furies unleash an earthquake on the city without trying to appease them?

I fixed my eyes forward. Aerin was right. We needed a plan. I'd talk to Layla about it later. She clearly wasn't in the mood to express her feelings at the moment, and if she did, she wouldn't be honest about what she felt. Not in front of Aerin.

"Thinking of another healing service?" I asked.

Aerin shook her head. "If we do that, people will know where you're at. Not just the elves. The government would probably show up at St. Ensley's to stop you."

I gripped the steering wheel. "I think I still have clergy credentials at all the local hospitals."

"Clergy credentials?" Aerin asked.

I shrugged. "For some hospitals, you have to be approved and added to a list. For others, if you just sign your name on a sheet and say you're a minister, they'll let you in to visit patients. Pretty incredible. If I'm wearing a clerical collar, I can pretty much go anywhere I want in a hospital, and no one will think twice about it."

Aerin cocked her head. "That doesn't sound safe."

I nodded. "I've often wondered that, too. I mean, anyone can pick up a clergy shirt at the local clerical supply."

"That's a thing?" Aerin asked. "I mean, I've heard of military supply stores."

I chuckled. "Yeah, there are a couple places in town. There's a Catholic Supply store on Chippewa and a Lutheran one at their publishing house on Jefferson."

"So pretty much anyone can just walk into one of those places and buy a collar?" Aerin asked.

I nodded. "Well, Jag bought ordination credentials from the internet. So, yeah. Come to think of it, you can buy clergy shirts and pretty much anything you'd want if you'd like to dress up a like real-life minister online."

"And if you're wearing one of those shirts, you can just walk in and go wherever you want in a hospital?" Aerin asked.

I nodded. "Most people can go just about anywhere in a hospital, even without a clergy shirt. But with the collar, hell, I've walked right into the ICU, and no one has questioned me. I can get into the mental health ward fairly easily. They don't even frisk me like they might some of the other visitors. I've walked right into the maternity ward, to the nursery and everything, at a few of the hospitals, and no one even asked me my name."

"That's frightening as hell!" Aerin protested.

I nodded. "I agree. Most of the hospitals will at least check your identification if you are going onto a floor where there are children. But when you're wearing that shirt and collar, it's not hard to get through. Show them a driver's license, and combined with the collar, you can get in pretty much anywhere. It's not totally insecure. They do have security cameras everywhere."

"Still," Aerin said. "I'm just surprised wearing a collar like that gets you such a pass."

I chuckled, reached into my pocket, and pulled out my driver's license.

"You wore that collar for your driver's license photo?" Aerin asked.

I nodded. "I think that's the last time I wore it. I hate those shirts. But I've gotten out of several speeding tickets because of it."

Aerin laughed out loud. "Seriously?"

I smiled wide. "You should hear the officers. They're all like, 'Sorry for the bother, Father! We'll let you go with a warning. Could you just try and watch your speed a little more carefully in future?'"

"So lame!" Aerin protested, laughing.

"Yeah," I said. "I'm always, like, 'bless you, my child,' as the officer smiles at me before walking back to his car."

"So, what are you thinking?" Aerin asked. "Just go from hospital to hospital and heal people?"

I shrugged. "Why not? They won't know where I'm coming from. By the time people hear about it happening and the doctors confirm the healings, I'll be on to the next one."

"Still risky," Layla piped up, breaking her silence. "The fairies will still sense it if you do magic. You'll have to move from place to place pretty quickly. Keep them chasing your tail."

"Good point," I said. "I'd say I'd fly from place to place, but we need someone filming this stuff and broadcasting it."

"You flew with me before," Aerin said. "When we escaped the forest."

"Like Superman and Lois-fucking-Lane," Layla quipped.

I raised my eyebrow as I glanced in the mirror. "First, I don't think that's Lois' middle name. Second, It's not like we'd be taking a romantic trip across Metropolis, Layla. What's the problem? Did you stick a corn cob up your—"

"Stop talking, Caspar," Layla said. "I didn't do anything of the sort, and you know it."

"You're welcome to fly with him instead," Aerin said. "If you'd prefer?"

"Ideally," I said. "Someone would take the Eclipse. Not that I'm thrilled about allowing someone else to drive my car. But you know, desperate times and whatnot. It would be helpful if someone would go ahead to the next hospital and find someone who needs to be healed. We can give whoever is doing that one of my clergy shirts. Text me a room number and a name, then go to the next. I'll fly with one of you, and you can live-stream the healing. Hopefully, if we get our timing down, whoever is scouting the next hospital will have a good name and room number elsewhere waiting for us by the time we finish."

"And since I'm the only one with a license, even if it's a fake one, I guess that makes me the scout," Layla said, rolling her eyes.

I shrugged. "I mean, it's just an idea."

"Looks like you get to fly with Caspar again, after all, Aerin," Layla said, crossing her arms over her chest and sinking into her seat.

I tried to lock my eyes onto Layla's through the rearview mirror, but she wouldn't look back at me. Seemed pretty damn childish. If she was serious about pulling this off, you'd think she'd set aside petty jealousies for the sake of the greater good. It wasn't like Layla had any reason to envy Aerin. I wasn't in love with Aerin. At the end of the day, this whole polygamous marriage thing was *her* idea. Whether we liked it or not, we needed each other.

Our lives were bound together.

CHAPTER THIRTEEN

Once we arrived back at the ranch, Aerin took off to see how the drow were settling in. Layla didn't waste any time stomping into the farmhouse. The second I shifted the car into park, she was off, moving with purpose, making it clear to me that following her wasn't a good idea.

I've never been good with female psychology. To me, her storming off meant she wanted to be left alone. But if she wanted me to come after her, and I didn't, I'd probably hear about it later. It was one of those "damned if you do, damned if you don't" situations. I could go after her and risk getting my head bitten off, or I could give her space and hear about how I was insensitive and not there for her when she needed someone to listen.

I decided to err on the side of being too attentive. At least, in that circumstance, while I might end up headless, at least she wouldn't be able to accuse me of being heartless.

I nodded at Jag as I walked past. He was hunched over the opened hood of the truck he was working on.

"Hey, Casp!" Jag said. "Making good progress!"

"You almost have it running?" I asked.

"I think so," Jag said. "Give me to the end of the day, and we'll have ourselves a working pickup truck!"

"Awesome, Jag," I said. "Really incredible."

Jag's grin split his face from ear to ear. He was clearly proud of what he'd accomplished. It was a good thing because if by some miracle of miracles I managed to pull off an acquittal for murder, we'd still need a way to transport Brag'mok to the Furies.

"Thanks, Casp! Just looking to help out any way I can."

I smiled and nodded. I was just about to turn to follow Layla inside when an idea occurred to me.

"Hey, Jag," I said.

"Yeah, Casp?"

"You wouldn't happen to know a good defense attorney, would you?"

"I've got a guy who helped me get out of a few speeding tickets," Jag said.

I shook my head. "Not a traffic court lawyer. I mean, a serious defense attorney. Someone who could help defend someone who was accused of homicide."

Jag reached over and grabbed a rag that he'd draped over the truck's bumper and wiped off his hands. "I knew what you meant. I was just giving you shit. I actually expected you might need one, and I hope you don't mind; I took a few liberties."

Jag reached into his back pocket and pulled out a business card, and handed it to me.

I grabbed it. It was moist to the touch, soaked by Jag's sweat.

"Dude," I said.

"Sorry," Jag said. "It's just butt sweat."

I almost threw up a little in my mouth. I pinched the card, extending my hand as far as I could from my body while I examined it. "Collin Law?" I asked. "You seriously found a lawyer whose last name is Law?"

Jag shrugged. "Might be a pen name."

"I don't think lawyers use pen names. At least, if they do, they don't call them that."

"I met a Chiropractor once whose last name was Bone. I remember seeing on the internet a gyno whose last name was Beaver."

"A proctologist whose last name is Butts?" I asked.

Jag shrugged. "I wouldn't doubt that there is one, somewhere. The funniest part is that the gyno's first name was Harold."

"Harry Beaver?" I asked. "You have to be making this up."

"I'm totally not," Jag said. "Google it!"

"Know anything about this lawyer?" I asked. "Like, is he any good?"

Jag smiled wide. "Dude, they say this guy could get anyone off."

I snorted. "You might want to rephrase that."

Jag cocked his head. "What do you mean?"

"Never mind." I shook my head. You'd think, being a former minister, I wouldn't have such a juvenile sense of humor. But if there's an off-color way to interpret something, chances are I'm giggling about it secretly inside of my head.

"You should check out this guy's Yelp reviews. People love him and hate him. Those who hired him think he's the best thing since sliced bread. All of them were probably guilty. But not when Collin Law had their backs. Then, of course, the families of their victims don't care for him too much. Say he clings to legal loopholes and technicalities and prioritizes winning his cases over real justice."

"And you think that's what I want?" I asked.

Jag shook his head. "I think it's what you need. The fate of the world might rest on this, Casp. We can't take any chances with a lawyer who has principles."

"This guy expensive?" I asked.

"I'm sure he is," Jag said. "But won't your sugar momma elf take care of it?"

"Aerin?" I asked. "I thought I was the only one who thought of her in those terms."

Jag laughed. "Everyone knows it's Momma who brings home the bacon in your house. You should have seen how she was throwing money around at the store last night. I hadn't seen anyone make it rain like that since the last time I went to the strip club."

An image of Home Depot employees twirling their orange aprons over their heads while Aerin tossed dollar bills at them crossed my mind. I quickly refocused my thoughts. "I'll give her the card. Thanks for looking into this, Jag."

"Always have your back, buddy," Jag said.

I pocketed the lawyer's sweat-moistened business card and went inside. Layla was pumping up our air mattress again while scratching Agnus behind the ears.

"Want to talk?" I asked.

"What?" Layla asked, raising her voice to talk over the sound of the electric air pump.

"Want to talk?" I asked again, almost shouting my question.

Layla nodded and turned off the pump. She sat on the edge of the mostly inflated mattress.

I sat next to her. "I'm sorry, Layla. If I could have talked to you about this before I agreed to it with the Furies, I would have."

"I'm sorry, too," Layla said. "I'm not usually the jealous type. It's just to see Aerin being so nauseatingly supportive."

"You realize the whole reason she isn't as upset about this as you are is that she isn't in love with me like you are?"

Layla shook her head. "I'm not so sure about that. I've seen the way she looks at you."

"I have a nice butt. What can I say?" I asked, smirking.

Layla backhanded me on the shoulder. "You do. But I think it's more than that."

"It might be," I said. "But no matter what she's feeling, she hasn't overstepped. She hasn't even so much as tried to kiss me. Not since the wedding, anyway."

Layla shook her head. "I'm glad I didn't see that."

"It was all for show," I said. I wasn't lying, exactly. When Aerin kissed me at our wedding, we both felt the attraction that the rings had sparked within us. There was passion in that kiss, but it was carnal passion. Not the same kind of passion that came from love, and nothing like I felt when Layla and I kissed.

"I know I'm being petty," Layla said. "We've got bigger issues. I don't blame you for agreeing to what you did with the Furies. I know you didn't have a choice."

I nodded. "Still, if I could have talked to you about it first, I would have. I'm sorry if I was defensive about my choice. I wasn't sensitive to how you were feeling."

Layla put her hand on my back and rested her head on my shoulder. "We'll get through this, Caspar. I *do* believe in you. More than *she* does, I'd wager. She trusts the prophecy, but I don't know what I think about that damned prophecy anymore. Every turn we take, it seems we find out that the prophecy isn't as straightforward as I was taught to believe."

I reached into my pocket and retrieved the lawyer's business card. It was pressed against the card the President had given me. The one with the number I was supposed to call when I'd made up my mind about whether I was going to support his alliance or turn myself in for Fred's murder. It came out, stuck to the card Jag had given me.

"We have two numbers to call," I said. "Jag found a lawyer for us. I'll have to talk to Aerin about paying for it. We'll need his help. Then, we'll have to call the President. But I think before we do that, we need to go on our healing spree. It'll be interesting to hear how he responds after that."

"Should probably hire the lawyer first," Layla said. "Since we're short on time, he'll probably need time to prepare his case."

I nodded. "Who knows how in the world he'll react to it.

Elves, magic, all that stuff. Not exactly the sort of case he's probably accustomed to taking."

Layla stood up and extended her hand. I grabbed it and stood up. Not like I needed her help to stand. I was half inclined to grab her hand and pull her back down onto the bed with me, but the clock was already ticking.

As I stood up, Agnus nuzzled my shin. I reached down again and petted him from head to tail.

Agnus meowed. "I don't want you to go to jail."

I looked at Layla. She looked back at me, pressing her lips together. It was the first time, I think since I started talking to Agnus, that I detected any real sense of fear or vulnerability in his voice.

"I know, buddy," I said. "I don't want to go, either. But Layla is here. She'll take care of you until I get back."

CHAPTER FOURTEEN

The lawyer said he didn't have any room on his schedule for us until Aerin took the phone and started talking money. Miraculously, he found an hour later in the afternoon when he could see us. Funny how that works.

We didn't have much time. Our trip to see Elrand and the incident with the Furies had taken up most of the morning. So much had happened that it felt like it should have been evening already, but it was barely noon. The lawyer said he could see us around one-thirty. Technically, it was only a forty-five-minute drive, but traffic in St. Louis is notoriously unpredictable. Even in the middle of the day, there was a good chance that once we got into the city, we'd face at least a brief traffic jam at some point.

I didn't want to risk it, so we left straight away. This time, Layla got to ride shotgun.

We arrived thirty minutes early.

"Caspar Cruciger," I said, introducing myself to the lawyer's secretary. "Here to see Mister Law."

"Have a seat," the secretary said. "I'll let him know you're here."

No sooner did she pick up the phone and tell him I'd arrived than a tall, thirty-something blond-haired man appeared. He was wearing a white dress shirt with his sleeves rolled up and a paisley-patterned tie loose around his neck.

"Mister Cruciger," the lawyer said. "Collin Law."

I nodded. "Thanks for seeing us on short notice."

Collin shrugged. "What can I say? Money talks."

I snorted. "Well, at least you're honest about that."

"No one goes into law because it's such a fascinating subject," Collin said. "Don't let anyone tell you otherwise. We're all in it for the cash."

I nodded. I glanced at Layla, who shrugged. "This is Layla and Aerin. Technically they're my wives."

"Wives?" Collin asked. "You realize you can't have more than one, legally speaking."

"Well, we never filled out the legal paperwork. Just had the ceremony."

"Then technically, legally speaking, neither of these women are married to you."

I nodded. "I guess that's right."

"If we're going to talk candidly," the lawyer said, "I have a few forms to sign. Just ensures that what we talk about will remain confidential. You know the deal."

"Not really," I said. "But if you can defend me, I'll sign whatever. There's nothing you could say to me that you can't say in front of Layla and Aerin."

We followed Collin into a small room. There was one rectangular table in the room. The chairs arranged around the table were all padded with leather.

We took our seats and signed a bunch of forms. Stuff that, more or less, allowed us to talk. And of course, Aerin paid him for his hour.

"So, murder, huh?" Collin asked.

"Potentially," I said. "I need to turn myself in."

Collin shook his head. "I wouldn't do that."

"I have to," I said. "I need to clear my name, and I need to have it all resolved within a month."

Collin dropped his pen and stared at me. "You really haven't had any experience with the legal system before, have you?"

I shook my head. "Not really. But I realize things don't usually move that quickly. I think this situation might be different, though. The President is involved."

Collin stared at me blankly. "Why would the President be involved in a murder case?"

"He gave me a choice. He wants me to either help support an alliance he's forged with some bad people who *really* want to take over the world. Or, he said, he has witnesses who could testify that I murdered someone."

Collin snorted. "Sounds like this is a political matter, not a legal one. Not yet, anyway."

"Except for the fact that I don't intend to do what he wants," I said.

"Because these people he wants you to support want to take over the world... Yeah, you told me that."

"Doesn't sound like you believe me," I said.

Collin shrugged. "Doesn't matter if I believe you. I'll pretend to believe anything you're going to pay me to believe. What's important is that whatever judge hears your case, and more, a jury, if you don't take a plea, will believe you."

"Who is the victim?" Collin asked.

"Fred," I said.

"Just Fred?" Collin raised an eyebrow.

"Fred Rogers," Layla piped up.

I looked at Layla. "His last name is seriously Rogers? I'm being accused of killing Mister Rogers?"

"Not the same one, I presume," Collin said. "*That* Mister Rogers died several years ago."

I nodded. "Yeah. The name is just a coincidence."

"So tell me the whole story. What happened, and what dirt do they have on you? It's important you tell me everything. If there's anything I don't know and the prosecution brings it up, I won't be prepared. I need all the facts."

I explained everything, from start to finish. I told him about the elves. Layla and Aerin even showed him their ears to prove the point. I told him about what happened at Pruitt-Igoe, and how Brightborn had given me no choice.

Collin was taking notes, but from the way he was smirking as he wrote, I was pretty sure he thought I was talking out of my ass.

"Now," Collin said. "Why don't you tell me what really happened? Because what you just said seriously sounds like you've taken Mister Rogers' trolley to a land of make-believe."

"I'm telling you the truth," I said. "All this shit, I wouldn't have believed it myself a few months ago. But I swear, it's true."

"So, you're telling me that you used magic to kill this guy, right?"

I nodded. "Exactly. But I only did it because otherwise, Layla would have died."

"Right," Collin said. "Because she was infected with... What did you call it? Celestial magic, right?"

"We can prove it to you," Layla said. "If you don't believe us."

Collin grunted. "You're going to prove to me that magic is real?"

Layla nodded. "Let me see your pen."

"Layla, don't do anything that the fairies will be able to track."

"Don't worry about it, Caspar," Layla said. "They can't sense this kind of magic."

Collin clicked his pen, retracting the ballpoint, and slid it across the table to Layla.

Layla picked up the pen and, holding it in front of her, channeled purple celestial magic into it.

The whole pen glowed.

"Now," Layla said. "If I were to stab someone with this, they'd be infected the same way I was."

"An interesting trick," Collin said. "Do you have anything better than that?"

Layla forced more magic into the pen and it exploded, the ink splattering all over the table. "That enough for you to believe?"

Collin stared at the ink splatter, wide-eyed. "That's...interesting."

"Have a phone?" Aerin asked.

"Of course I do," Collin said.

"If you want to see what Caspar can do, it's all on video. Just Google his name. It's gone viral. Shouldn't be hard to find."

"All right," Collin said, tapping at his phone. Someone had apparently taken the video of my trials and put it on a second-rate news site. As Collin watched the video, his jaw was practically on the table. "This is incredible," Collin said. "I'll watch the rest later. But say I believe you, how do you expect me to present this stuff to the court?"

"It doesn't matter," I said. "You're the expert. I just need to make sure I get a full acquittal."

"I'm going to outline the legal situation," Collin said. "This could be tackled in a couple different ways. Either way, we have an angle we could use. Under normal circumstances, I'd strongly prefer one option to the other. But given your apparent urgency and the fact that the President is involved, it changes this dynamic significantly."

"So what are we looking at?" I asked. "Let's hear both approaches to the case."

"Granted, some of this depends on how the prosecution would handle the case," Collin said. "I'm guessing that with the President involved, they'll want to prosecute this in federal court. There are several factors that might warrant that legally, but I'll try and keep this simple."

"Please do," I said.

Collin nodded. "The best course for a full acquittal would be to argue that the action was committed under duress. You wouldn't deny that you did the deed, but we would make the case that it was the king's efforts that forced your hand and that the loss of life and other consequences of not doing what he demanded would have been worse. You have a pretty sound case in this respect."

"That's perfect!" Layla exclaimed. "That's exactly what happened."

Collin nodded. "It's a case that could be made, but on the surface, it's not a strong defense. There might be another way to tackle this."

"What is it?" I asked.

"We'd present this similar to a hitman case. Sure, you weren't hired to commit the murder, but you did have a vested interest, namely the recovery of your powers. The victim had stolen something from you and also attacked your girlfriend, so you'd have a motive. However, this Brightborn character also had a motive. Namely, to spare his daughter. In this case, we could argue there was a conspiracy to commit the murder. Just coming together with someone else with the intent of planning a murder is a crime in itself, a felony. By establishing the conspiracy, it would mean that the courts would have to consider two guilty parties, both you and Brightborn, for two felonies—the conspiracy to commit murder and the murder itself."

"But if we did that, I wouldn't be acquitted. Brightborn and I would both be charged."

Collin nodded. "The issue is that in this case, it might be easier to prove a conspiracy than it is to prove duress, given the apparent motives involved. In either case, we have leverage that can be used."

"Leverage?" I asked.

"You said that the President gave you a choice. I'm not even going to go into the legality of the quid pro quo you say he presented you. It would be hard to prove. But it's not nothing. Consider the politics of the situation. The President has unilaterally tried to forge an alliance with an alien interest without the consent of Congress and has threatened an individual—you— who he believes could impact the success of this alliance with felony charges if you do not do as he asks."

I nodded. "Could he be charged with something, too?"

Collin shrugged. "Charging a sitting President with a crime is a disputed topic, and it's outside my expertise. But I imagine at the very least, his actions might be impeachable."

"Let me get this straight," Layla said. "You're saying we use our leverage on the President to get him to back down?"

"Not necessarily," Collin said. "Particularly given your irrational insistence that you receive some kind of adjudication on your case."

"An acquittal," I said.

"We'll get to that," Collin said. "Like I said, arguing duress, I'm reasonably sure if we could gather enough evidence, including the testimony of you three as witnesses, that we could get an acquittal. The problem is, to present this case, we'd have to plead not guilty. Just getting a plea hearing, much less taking it to court, would take more than the thirty days you are insisting on."

"What if I turned myself in, contingent on an agreement that the case be brought to trial before my time is up?" I asked.

Collin shook his head. "It doesn't work that way. Legally speaking, if you turn yourself in for a felony, the judge is not bound by agreements made with any other party."

"Not even the President?" I asked.

"Not even the President," Collin said. "The judge might consider his recommendation, but no judge is bound to any order from the President. Division of powers."

"So, what exactly are you suggesting?" I asked.

"The 'hitman' case has the advantage over the other one in

that while it wouldn't result in your acquittal, most likely it would require the conviction of Brightborn."

"Even if he's not a citizen?" I asked. "From what I understand, he has asylum."

Collin nodded. "Since there isn't a place where he could be extradited, it would likely be handled in the US legal system. Needless to say that any alliance forged between the President and Brightborn would be suspect and likely nullified by Congress. Furthermore, if there is a record of the President's trip to St. Louis to meet with you *after* the crime was committed, and since you did meet with him in Washington beforehand, there's enough smoke there to at least rouse suspicion that the President was involved."

"So, how exactly do you suggest we proceed?" Aerin asked.

"Make your public spectacle if you'd like. More eyes on you means more potential eyes on the case if it gets processed. Your refusal to acquiesce to the President's ultimatum is important, and if possible, it would be advisable to record the call."

"Is that legal?" I asked. "Don't both parties have to consent?"

Collin shook his head. "Under federal law, only one-party consent is required. With that, we'd have the quid pro quo in our back pocket. At the very least, a conversation where the President is trying to basically blackmail a person into supporting a decision of his administration would be a bombshell for his political opponents."

"And then what?" I asked.

"Turn yourself in as a suspect. We'd probably approach the feds on this rather than local authorities. I'd walk you through this process. The important thing is not to answer any questions. If the bag is out on the President, if the notion of his involvement is already out there on paper, we'd lose our leverage."

"Our leverage for what, exactly?" I asked.

"To convince the President to issue a pardon," Collin said.

I raised my eyebrow. "A pardon? Is that as good as an acquittal?"

"Legally speaking, yes. It is a total exoneration from the crime."

I bit my lip. Technically, if I was pardoned, I'd be alleviated of responsibility for the murder by the government. That was what the Furies agreed to accept. "Are you sure that the President would agree to it? Wouldn't it look bad for him to pardon a murderer?"

Collin smiled. "This is why I like your idea about all these spectacles, these healings. Presuming you can do it, and it gets plenty of public interest, we should be able to pin your indictment after you turn yourself in on an overzealous prosecutor or something. This would give the President the opportunity to swoop in and appear to be the hero for a hero. While I don't know the President personally, he's a politician. I'm not sure that he could resist the temptation to earn that much public favor."

CHAPTER FIFTEEN

I think Aerin paid Collin enough money that he could probably afford to buy a small country. The key to it all, he made clear as we left his office, was to exercise my right to remain silent. When it came to the case, he'd handle all the talking. I'd just have to say what he told me to say when he told me to say it.

I wasn't a hundred percent certain I liked the idea. Sure, the President was basically blackmailing me. We were going to attempt to blackmail the blackmailer. I still didn't like it.

When you're slithering with snakes, I suppose you have to get in the mud. That doesn't mean you have to enjoy it.

The plan was to hit several hospitals in a row right along Interstate 64. I knew my way around most of them. A lot of people don't realize how much time ministers actually spend in hospitals. Hardly a week went by when I didn't have someone to visit. Sometimes it was a joyous occasion. When a mother gave birth to a child, for instance. Usually, though, my visits to the hospital were to sit and pray with people who were sick, having surgery, or dying. Through the years, I've spent more than a few nights with families in waiting rooms. Not every minister does that. Some only make hospital calls when the situations are dire. Some never go at all.

My years of visits to the hospitals were going to pay off. I knew where the ICUs were. I had credentials at some of the hospitals, and at those where credentials weren't required, I knew each one's protocol for signing in, signing out, and the like.

I texted a list of the hospitals and where the ICUs were to Layla as we sat in my Eclipse. Layla and I changed into black clergy shirts with clerical collars. You don't see a lot of women wearing them because, well, Catholics don't have female priests. But there were high church denominations that wore collars and also ordained women, so it wasn't a complete oddity. If anyone asked, I told Layla to tell them she was an Episcopalian.

The idea was to get in and out. Find the direst cases, people on their last breath, then save their lives and bail before the nurses and doctors figured out what I was doing. We'd have the video up to show what happened, ideally, before anyone had a clue what had happened.

People would start putting two-and-two together. I had to move fast because the fairies could portal to wherever we were if they sensed me using magic.

From what Ensley had told me, though, the fairies didn't know exactly where magic was used right away. They'd sense that magic was used somewhere in the general area, but they would only be able to track it once the magic that was used settled into the aether. He'd also told me that the fairies needed a good visual of the location to create portals there. That meant we'd probably have enough time to at least get one or two "miracles" done at each ICU before moving to the next.

The plan was to start with three hospitals on Kingshighway, just north of the Interstate. One major hospital and two children's hospitals were situated right next to each other. Aerin and I were going to choose a few random people to heal in the ICU at the first hospital while Layla located some especially worthy cases in the children's hospitals. She'd text us the names and room numbers and leave, heading down the road to the next hospital, which was just off Clayton Avenue, a few miles up the road. After that, there'd be more of a drive to the next hospital, which was several miles away. By then, if all went according to plan, Layla would have enough of a head start to make it before we did. While I could fly, and that meant I could avoid St. Louis traffic, I wouldn't be able to fly as fast as she could drive. Especially not with Aerin on my back.

What if people saw us flying? I suppose it would just add to the superhero mystique of the narrative we were hoping to put forward. My healing service had made the news before. This would for sure.

As Aerin and I walked through the halls of the first hospital, several people smiled and nodded at me when they spotted my collar. I smiled back. So far, so good.

I knew where I was going. We took the elevator to the third floor and followed the signs to the cardiac ICU.

From my recollection, there were about fifteen rooms in the unit. Any of them would do. I wanted to heal everyone. I could. But we had to move fast. Perhaps, someday, when all this was over, I could make this a regular thing. The possibilities...just to think how many lives I could save.

The key was to walk with a purpose. We had to look like we knew where we were going. The nurses were always ready to help, but they'd certainly ask if they could help me find whatever room I was looking for if I looked at all lost or aloof.

We stepped into the closest room. A sleeping woman, prob- ably in her sixties, was reclined on the hospital bed. She wasn't on a ventilator or anything, but she had a number of wires attached to her to measure her heart rate, breathing, and what- ever else it was they tracked.

"You ready to record this?" I asked.

Aerin nodded as she raised her phone. "We're live-streaming now."

I looked at the phone camera. "My name is Caspar Cruciger," I said. "Some of you have seen me on this channel during the elemental trials. I've never met this woman, but she is in the intensive care unit at a local hospital. I'm going to heal her."

Aerin nodded at me. I put my hands on the woman's chest and inhaled, gathering the power of aether, or spirit, at the forefront of my consciousness. I visualized what this woman might look like healthy, on her feet, full of life. When I'd healed people before, that was what I did. I focused on the ends, not the means. I trusted that the magic would do what it needed to do to make it happen.

I released my magic. A golden glow enveloped the woman's chest.

The woman gasped.

Then she opened her eyes, looked at me, and cocked her head. "Where am I?"

"You're in the hospital," I said. "And you're going to be fine."

The woman furrowed her brow. She was still disoriented, and she was confused.

I smiled at Aerin, and she stopped recording.

We left the room and quickly made our way back out of the hospital.

We repeated our efforts at the children's hospitals nearby.

I had a little badge that I clipped on my shirt, but we couldn't get as far as the children's ICU without raising suspicion due to security, especially since Aerin didn't have any credentials. Layla texted that there were several young people in physical therapy on the first floor. Most of them were there on an outpatient basis, and several of them had injuries and conditions that would be more visibly obvious when I healed them.

I wanted to do more. I wanted to visit the cancer ward. But

this would have to do. Not to mention, healing any of the children in the hospital would have a profound impact on their lives.

There was a waiting room where a mother was sitting with three children. Two of them were healthy, playing with the various toys that the office kept in the waiting room. But the third was in a wheelchair.

"Hello," I said, greeting the mother.

She smiled at me politely. "Hello, Father."

When someone addressed me like that, it didn't necessarily mean they were Catholic or religious. But it did usually indicate that they had a certain respect for the clergy.

"Mind if I ask what your son's condition is?" I asked.

"Cerebral palsy," the mother said.

"Does the therapy help?" I asked.

The mother sighed. "A little. Progress is slow, but it's very hard for David to do much. He can barely hold a toy, much less a spoon. But we're trying to remain optimistic."

"Would you mind if I prayed for him?" I asked.

"I'd appreciate that," the mother said.

I nodded at Aerin. She took the cue and opened her phone. It wasn't obvious she was recording, one of the perks of having cameras on phones. No one would think much of her having her phone out. She just had to be inconspicuous about how she was holding it. We didn't want it to be obvious that we were taking video.

"Hi, David," I said. "My name's Caspar."

David looked at me and smiled. He had one of those endearing smiles that touched your soul. A child suffering so much who was smiling really made me think. If he could be happy despite what he was facing, what were my troubles really worth?

"I'm going to pray with you, David," I said.

He continued smiling and raised one hand.

I took his hand in mine.

I inhaled again, bringing the power of aether to mind. I visualized this child's hand, firmly gripping mine. I imagined him standing from his chair, playing with his siblings on the other side of the room.

The magic I released filled his body. David grabbed my hand tightly. He started kicking his legs.

"Momma?" David asked.

The boy's mother stepped over to her son. She looked at me, her eyes wide with wonder. "What did you do?"

"He'll still need therapy to regain his strength," I said. "But he is healed, ma'am."

"Did you say…"

I nodded. "Yes, ma'am. I've healed your son," I said.

Aerin pocketed her phone again, and I turned to leave.

The woman grabbed my arm. "You said your name is Caspar, right?"

"Yes, ma'am," I said. "God Bless you."

The woman stood there speechless. I wasn't sure she believed me. It took a lot to imagine a child suffering as David was to be suddenly and miraculously healed. But she'd see that it was true.

Aerin and I exchanged smiles.

"This is incredible," Aerin said. "I wish we could do this all day, every day."

I smiled. "Me, too. One day, perhaps, we'll be able to."

CHAPTER SIXTEEN

All in all, we healed eight different people at various hospitals around St. Louis. Aerin rode on my back as we flew from place to place. Of course, that meant she had to touch me. She didn't say anything. Not exactly. But I could see the desire in her eyes. All that physical contact, plus the thrill of what we were doing.

Nothing I'd ever done felt more rewarding. I couldn't get past the look on David's face when he squeezed my hand. He knew he was better. He knew he'd been healed. I could see it in his eyes. The gratitude, the hope for what his future now held, and the utter sense of wonder and surprise.

And of course, he had that smile. It didn't change.

Aerin and I met up with Layla when we were done at the last hospital. Layla was already driving, so I sat shotgun, and Aerin slid into the back of the Eclipse.

"How'd it go?" Layla asked.

"He was amazing!" Aerin exclaimed before I could answer. "You should have seen him. So much grace. The expressions on people's faces when they realized they were healed was incredible to see."

"Are the videos getting any views?" Layla asked.

"Let me check," Aerin said. "We've been so busy going from place to place and recording more I haven't even looked at the numbers."

Layla pulled back onto the highway. "I suppose we should go back to the ranch?"

I nodded. "Let's do that. Once we are sure that this worked and that people are talking about it, we'll go ahead and give the President a call."

"Remember," Layla said. "Collin said to record the call."

I nodded and pulled out my phone. "I'll have to see if there's an app for that."

"I'm pretty sure there is," Aerin said as she scrolled down the screen of her phone. "Looks like our views are strong. Already a couple million."

"A couple million?" I asked.

"I think since we already had an audience with the trials, it helped," Aerin said. "Let me see if I can find any more buzz. I included a hashtag in the description for the live-stream.

"That's smart," I said. "Will help it go viral, hopefully. What was the hashtag?"

"Hashtag healz4realz."

"Like, all one word?" I asked.

"Yes, and with z's rather than s's, and the number four rather than the letters."

"With 3s instead of Es?" Layla asked.

"Ugh," Aerin said. "I hate when people do that. No, for some reason, the letter Z is cooler than the letter S."

"Not quite as cool as the letter X, though," I quipped.

"True," Aerin said, giggling. "Add an X to something, and suddenly it's three degrees cooler."

"Doesn't work with every letter," I said. "Not like you could do that with a Q and have the same effect. The X-games, that's awesome. Not sure the Q-games or the P-games would spark the same interest."

Aerin chuckled. "The P-games. Sounds so nasty!"

"Hey," I said. "Peeing for distance is a real hillbilly sport. Don't have to go much further south than the junkyard ranch, and I'm sure you'd find regular leagues."

"I'd totally win that event," Aerin said.

"You'd win a peeing for distance contest?" I asked, raising my eyebrows. "I'm half inclined to challenge you just to see if you can put your money where your mouth is… Or your…well, not your mouth. You know what I mean."

Layla rolled her eyes. "I get it. Aerin is cool. Healz with a z; it's badass and all that. But will people take it seriously? Sounds kind of juvenile."

Aerin smiled wide as she continued scrolling on her phone. "Considering the fact that the hashtag is now trending, I'd say it worked."

"Sweet," I said. "Now it's just a matter of hoping some news outlets pick up on it."

"Hopefully, this doesn't work *too* well," Layla said. "Even if you turn yourself in, if they don't want to indict you, they just won't. It isn't like they're going to present you with a menu of options. Not until you get to decide on a plea. If they don't have any evidence other than what the President might leak to them to suggest you're guilty."

I shook my head. "I'm probably the first person in history who was worried about *not* getting indicted for murder. But you're right. If I'm not indicted, I can't be acquitted or pardoned."

"And if you can't do that, the Furies won't accept that you've fulfilled your part in the agreement," Aerin said.

I scratched my head. "We'll see what the President says. I'm going to be pretty firm about the fact that I won't, for any reason, support his alliance with Brightborn. Hopefully, he'll get the wheels turning to expedite the indictment. I still have some leverage. He knows I won't be easy to capture, much less keep in custody. But if I'm willing to comply on the condition that he does this quickly, he might get things moving faster."

"Won't he be curious why you want it done fast?" Layla asked.

I nodded. "Probably. But I don't think he's going to guess it's because I have a deadline with the Furies and that one of the nation's major cities, not to mention a lot of the region, might be compromised otherwise."

"You could tell him," Aerin said. "Let him know what's at stake."

I shook my head. "Can't trust him. Not now that he's in league with Brightborn. The last thing we need is the elven king getting wind of our agreement with the Furies."

"I wonder how he'd act if he thought his time with the fairies on his side was limited," Layla said.

"That's an advantage that Brightborn would hate to lose before any battles are actually fought," Aerin said. "There might be something to that."

"I think he's hoping to avoid having to fight any battles at all," Layla said. "That's why he's schmoozing the President. If he can convince the government to endorse his armies and they gradually ceded him power..."

I shook my head. "I just can't believe that the government would do something like that."

Layla shrugged. "It depends how desperate the situation is. Trust me, my father has something else up his sleeve. He's doing more than buying time with the President. He's setting things up. I imagine he has something planned. Something awful. Knowing my father, he's going to rise to the occasion like the hero at the ninth hour. When the government has no other options, he'll be there, ready to assume the 'burden' of power in order to save the nation."

I nodded. "Another reason why we need to do this quickly. If Brightborn still has the fairies, he'll use them if I try to use my magic to stop whatever it is he has planned. The last thing he wants is for me to rise up and appear to be the hero. He won't want me to steal his thunder."

"Looks like your healings are getting some national play," Aerin said. "There's a story from the AP now, so it's just a matter of time before the other networks pick up on it."

"What's the story?" I asked.

"Miracle Working Preacher is Back—But Is He for Real?" Aerin said, reading the headline out loud.

I smiled. "What's their determination? Do they answer the question?"

Aerin shook her head. "Not directly. They haven't had a chance to talk to any witnesses yet. But I'm sure they will as soon as they can. Then they'll see that these people were really healed and the doctors don't have an explanation."

"Once that happens, once the evidence is out there and the stories can't be easily buried. Then, I'll call the President."

CHAPTER SEVENTEEN

All three of us were glued to our phones. Our pay-in-advance plans only allowed so much data. Perhaps we weren't being efficient given our limitations. Getting this news out there was important for a variety of reasons. It was hard to say how public opinion might shift once the news came out that I was being accused of murder. At the very least, it would make my arrest public enough that the powers that be couldn't just sweep it under the rug and drag their heels.

Besides, I had more leverage than that. Because, as Layla and Aerin had reminded me many times, the government didn't have any way to really disarm me, magically speaking. The President could probably get me indicted and arrested. Holding me, though, required a certain degree of compliance on my part.

I was inclined to comply regardless. I was raised to believe that, as a Christian, so long as the government doesn't require me to disobey a command from God, I'm nonetheless duty-bound to obey earthly authorities, even if their actions are unjust. Of course, the President didn't know that. One thing that Collin made clear was that, at this stage of the game, leverage was everything. My best shot to meet the thirty-day window was a pardon rather than an acquittal. That meant, above all else, exercising whatever leverage I had with one man—the President of the United States.

I shook my head as I stared at my phone. Calling the fucking President? I hadn't even voted for the man. It wasn't long ago when he'd had me brought to the Oval Office, with Brag'mok and Ensley already there, to strategize about how to prevent the elves from coming to Earth. But now that the elves were here and they'd shown how powerful they were, and since they'd offered to lend that power to the government in exchange for asylum— which was a cover for the elves to get a foothold here so they could launch their campaign of world domination—the President suddenly found himself kowtowing to Brightborn.

My goal was to complicate that position. I wasn't sure if I'd be able to convince the President to rethink his alliance with Brightborn, but perhaps I could raise some questions in his mind. If I was more willing to go to prison than to support his alliance, that might at least give him a moment of pause. How many accused murderers would refuse to give a little speech and endorse a President's policies to avoid conviction? Probably not many.

But when the fate of the world was at stake and the burden for saving it fell squarely on my shoulders, that was what I was duty-bound to do.

The major networks had picked up on my story. It was viral on social media. It was time.

Aerin and Layla were standing outside on the porch, still scanning their phones for more news. I wanted to be alone. It's hard to have important conversations when people are lurking around listening in. I was recording the conversation, anyway. I'd downloaded an app for that. They could listen to it later.

Agnus curled up in my lap. I suppose being "alone" didn't necessarily exclude my cat from my present company. Sure, now that we could communicate, I didn't have the same sense of privacy when he was around that I used to. Even changing clothes in front of him had become awkward. But having him in my lap while I made the call was comforting.

"Time to face the music, buddy," I said, scratching him behind the ears.

"I was going to ask if I could have the TV," Agnus said. "But no internet here except for your dumb phones. So, what's the point?"

I snorted. "Glad you're concerned about the things that really matter."

"For what it's worth, I think this is a mistake."

"Why do you say that?" I asked.

"Politicians are like Siamese Cats."

I raised my eyebrow. "Not sure I follow."

"Pretty on the outside. Everyone thinks they want one. They parade around, showing off. Then you meet them, and they're total bitches."

"So you're telling me that the President is a bitch?"

"Pretty much," Agnus said. "I mean, how quickly did he turn on you in favor of Brightborn?"

"Politicians change their views with the wind," I said. "I'm just hoping to change the direction of the breeze back in my favor. More or less."

"If it comes down to it, you'll have to come back. You can't let the Furies unleash that earthquake."

I scratched my head. "You really think I could stop them? If I can't get exonerated of the crime, they won't agree with me."

"You have the power of the earth, right?" Agnus asked. "If they're planning on an earthquake, they're relying on the element of earth. You have the power to thwart them."

"I'd rather not do it that way," I said. "The goal is ultimately to convince them to break faith with Brightborn. If I'm turning the elements against the Furies, I'll end up dividing the three guardian races rather than uniting them."

"A lot of people are going to die if they unleash that fault line,

Caspar," Agnus said. "You might have to choose between saving lives and fulfilling the prophecy."

"That's why I have to do this," I said. "It's the only way to stop the earthquake and also stop Brightborn."

"Do you think this lawyer you hired is going to handle the President for you?" Agnus asked.

I shrugged. "He seems to think we have an argument."

"Everyone has an argument," Agnus said. "Not to mention, he wants Aerin's money. It isn't like he's going to tell you straight up that your case is hopeless."

"I realize that," I said, scratching Agnus' belly as he rolled over in my lap. "But you've watched enough football with me, Agnus. Tell me, if the game comes down to a Hail Mary pass, wouldn't you take it? The success rate of the Hail Mary is very low. But if it's the only chance you have to win the game, you take it."

Agnus looked up at me and cocked his head. "You realize there's more than one way to end a game with a win than completing the Haily Mary, right?"

I cocked my head. "Sure. Technically if there's a penalty call. Defensive pass interference. It's a spot foul, and even if the clock runs out, by rule, the game can't end on a penalty."

Agnus looked at me. "That might be how you win this, too, Caspar."

I bit my lip. "I'm not sure I follow. What penalty could there be that would give me an out if the President won't give me a pardon or I can't get acquitted?"

"I don't know for sure," Agnus said. "But in football, a defender usually commits that penalty if he thinks that the other player would score otherwise. When you talk to the President, you need to be confident about your victory. He needs to sense it in your voice. Only then might he feel the pressure and grab onto your jersey."

"So you're suggesting I lure the President into an interference penalty?" I asked.

"It's a spot foul," Agnus said. "If he does that, he might set you up with one play at the one-yard line. All I'm saying is that you need to have a play ready. If the President panics, if he gives you an opportunity to score with no time left on the clock, you need to be ready to take it."

I chuckled. "You know, Agnus. You've been paying closer attention to all those football games I've been watching through the years than I realized."

Agnus snorted. "One big play can change a whole game, Casp. So can one bad call. You can go for the big play. You can even win a game benefiting from bad officiating. Maybe you win because even though you fucked up the game plan, the other team fumbled the ball at the wrong time. At the end of the day, a win counts the same no matter how you got it."

I nodded. "All true. Just not sure how the metaphor applies specifically to this situation."

"I'm just saying," Agnus said, nuzzling his head into my palm, "there may be more than one way to come away from this with a win. Don't get so focused on the plan that you miss an opportunity."

I chuckled. "I almost forget, sometimes, that you're a part of all this prophecy stuff, too."

"I was one of the first parts of the prophecy that was fulfilled," Agnus said. "And I wouldn't be doing my job if I didn't give you advice."

"Have any more gems for me before I call up the President to turn myself in?"

Agnus looked at me and cocked his head. "Don't drop the soap."

CHAPTER EIGHTEEN

I set up my app to record the conversation, pulled the card out of my pocket with the direct line to the President printed on it, and dialed the number.

The phone rang twice.

"About time you called," the President said on the other end of the line.

"Yeah, well, I've been busy."

"I see that," the President said. "Putting on quite the show, it seems."

"I can't support your alliance with Brightborn," I said. "I know you were hoping I could speak up, convince those who were a part of the Order of the Elf Gate to back your position, but I just can't. You realize that Brightborn is using you, sir."

There was a brief moment of silence before the President started speaking again. "I realize that, Cruciger."

"You do?" I asked. "Then why…"

"Caspar," the President continued. "When Brag'mok and Ensley were in my office, they told me all about him. How Brightborn wiped out the giants. Their mistake, the giants' mistake, was to try and take him down through battle. I'm taking a more diplomatic approach."

"He's just buying time," I said. "He's going to turn on you."

"Maybe," the President said. "But I'm counting on the fact that we still have more to learn about him and his legion than he has left to learn of us. If we try to resist him, fight him now, he'll have every advantage."

"I'm sorry," I said. "But I have to turn myself in."

The President snorted. "You certainly aren't making things easier for me, Caspar. It won't look good if you're facing a federal indictment the day after you made national news for literally saving people's lives."

I chuckled. "Then, perhaps, you'll have to pull some strings to get me off."

The President sighed. "I have to give Brightborn the impression, at the very least, that I've stuck to my end of the bargain. If I don't keep you in custody, Caspar…"

"You realize you can't keep me in custody. I could escape at any time."

"I understand that," the President said. "But I'm hoping you'll play along. We need to get as much information and power from the elves as possible. No matter what you do, you'll either be a prisoner or you'll be a fugitive. If you're going to go the route of playing the fugitive, well. Let's say that harboring a fugitive is a serious charge, and there are several people associated with St. Ensley's church staying with you on that old farm where you're at currently who might not fare so well if they try to resist arrest."

I sighed. "How do you know where we're hiding?"

"I'm the government," the President said. "Do you really think that using a few burner phones and staying off the grid would be enough? We have our ways, Caspar."

"None of these people did anything wrong," I said. "Leave them out of it."

"They haven't yet," the President said. "But if you intend to escape custody and any of them help you in even the slightest way..."

"I get it," I said. "Aiding and abetting a fugitive. But you are just the President. Isn't this the sort of thing that the FBI would do? Maybe local law enforcement?"

The President laughed. "Who appoints the director of the FBI, Cruciger?"

"All right," I said. "Fair point. But I'm not confessing to the murder, sir."

"You don't have to," the President said. "All you need to do is turn yourself in. How you plead and how you try to handle things after that? Well, let's hope it doesn't come to that."

"I'll agree to comply," I said, "and I won't run. But I want a pardon or acquittal in less than thirty days."

The President laughed in my ear. "I'm not sure we could even get this in front of a grand jury in thirty days."

"You're the President," I said. "You really expect me to believe that you couldn't make that happen if you really wanted to?"

"Here's the thing," the President continued. "If I get you indicted quickly, if you're either acquitted or pardoned, I lose all my leverage. I don't see any reason why I should do that for you."

"Right now, you're eager to see me speak out to support your position with Brightborn," I said. "But soon, you will be more eager to see me as an ally to defeat him. Trust me, Mister President. It's just a matter of time before he turns on you."

"Do you think I made my way to the top without out-maneuvering snakes like Brightborn?" the President asked.

"With all due respect," I continued. "Brightborn is not your run-of-the-mill garter snake. He's a fucking anaconda."

"My anaconda don't want none..."

"Yeah, yeah. I know the lyric. Unless you got buns, hun. The point is, he's already destroyed one world in pursuit of his goals.

You think he wouldn't destroy this one in his effort to take it over?"

"Take over the world?" the President asked. "He's powerful. I'll grant him that. But he hardly has the manpower to take over the whole world."

"He doesn't need manpower," I said. "We don't know for sure how many elves he's already brought to this world. All we know is what he's shown us. I'm warning you, sir. You don't want to underestimate him. By the time you come to your senses, once you realize you need my help. Well, it might be too late."

"Too late? I have my own plans and my own timeline for things, Cruciger. I'll tell you when we're out of time."

I bit my lip. "Sir, this isn't like you. When we met before. You were so certain about standing up for our freedom, for the American way. It makes me wonder what Brightborn might have on you."

"You don't know what you're talking about, Cruciger!" the President shouted, raising his voice for the first time since we started our conversation.

"What does he have on you, sir?" I asked.

"He's got nothing on me! I'm the President of the United Fucking States! What do you think he could possibly have on me?"

The President's tone said it all. I'd struck a nerve. The truth was that Brightborn, apparently, *did* have something on the President. I wasn't going to get him to tell me what, of course. Not when he was so defensive at even the suggestion that the elven king might be blackmailing him.

I took a deep breath. "I need a pardon in thirty days or less."

"Turn yourself in today," the President said. "I'll have agents meet you at that church you call St. Ensley's. And I promise I'll spend the next twenty-nine days considering it."

CHAPTER NINETEEN

From the junkyard to the swamp of Washington politics. I couldn't believe the President was so presumptuous as to think that he had the upper hand in his relationship with Brightborn. Still, I had the conversation recorded on my phone. Aerin would make sure Collin got it. It helped in the swamp to have a creature of the lagoon at your side. At least Collin would be in his element.

The fact that the President got so angry when I suggested that Brightborn might have something on him was interesting. You don't react that strongly to something like that if there isn't any truth to it. But what could it be?

I stepped out of the front door of the farmhouse and onto the porch. I handed Aerin my phone. "Make sure the lawyer gets this."

Aerin nodded. "What did the President say?"

I shrugged. "Not a lot. You can listen if you'd like. He got especially upset when I suggested that Brightborn might have something on him. Something damaging."

"Knowing my father," Layla added. "He certainly has something."

A loud rumble stole my attention.

I looked up. Jag had apparently managed to get the truck running.

"Well, that's good timing," I said. "Might be helpful to have another set of wheels once I'm gone."

"When do you turn yourself in?" Layla asked, scratching the back of her head.

"I need to do it immediately. The President said he'd have someone waiting for me at St. Ensley's."

"Immediately as in, *we have to go now?*" Layla asked.

I nodded. "I'm sorry. But we have to get the ball rolling on all this. If we have any shot at all, now's the time to take it."

"We'll drive you," Aerin said. "I mean, Layla will drive. But I'll come along."

"You don't have to come," Layla said. "You could stay here with the drow. I think they still need some direction."

"All right," Aerin said, nodding. "Just make sure to take the phone to Collin. He'll have to get to work right away. If he needs any more money, just let me know."

"You can count on that," Layla said, rolling her eyes.

"That you'll let me know? I figured…"

Layla laughed. "That he'll want more money."

Aerin shrugged. "Whatever motivates him to get the job done."

I chuckled. "You say that like throwing cash at the lawyer is akin to throwing treats to a dog."

"I suppose it is a bit like that," Aerin said, tucking her hair behind her ears. "But I think he has a good plan. You just focus on keeping your head down. Don't do anything dumb. I don't think you'll go to prison right away."

I shrugged. "Not really sure how that works."

"I think they'll probably hold you in a local jail before trial. Probably in the county. They won't transfer you to a federal facility until you've been sentenced, which, technically speaking, we're hoping to avoid entirely."

"Well, it's a good thing that I'll be local, I suppose. Once I'm released, presuming all goes according to plan, we might not have much time left before I have to meet up with the Furies. Just make sure that Brag'mok is ready, too. He has to come along."

"We'll handle it," Layla said. "One way or another, we'll have you out of there before the month is up."

"One way or another?" I asked. "Layla, remember it has to be by acquittal or pardon. The Furies won't accept anything else."

Layla rolled her eyes. "I know, Caspar. That's obviously the goal."

I nodded and stepped down from the porch. I walked over to Jag and patted him on the back. "Nice work, man."

Jag smiled from ear to ear. "We have a truck, Casp!"

"I see that," I said. "I'm going to be leaving for a while. You seen Brag'mok?"

Jag nodded. "He's in the camp, sparring with the drow."

"Sparring?" I asked. "Seriously?"

"I think he's really in his element. Fighting, elves, you know?"

I chuckled. "Yeah, I can see that."

Jag squeezed my shoulder. "You'll get through this, Casp."

I took a deep breath. "I hope you're right. I don't think I've ever been so nervous about anything."

"Whatever you do," Jag said, "remember, if you get down on yourself, look at yourself in the mirror…"

"And call myself a pussy?" I asked.

"This isn't the gym," Jag said. "I was going to say to remind yourself that you're a hero."

I shook my head. "Hard to feel that way, you know, locked up facing a murder charge."

"The truth is on your side," Jag said. "We'll be ready when you get back."

I nodded and extended my hand.

"I'm not shaking your hand as if this is a goodbye," Jag said. "I don't know a lot about going to jail, but from what I understand, it's a mental game. Sort of like when you're tackling a workout. The moment you allow doubt to creep in, it's over."

"Your faith in me," I said, shaking my head. "It's encouraging. I appreciate it."

Jag nodded. I nodded back. Because that's what men do. We nod at each other. I'm not sure what the nod meant. But it was comforting. "I won't let you down."

"I know you won't," Jag said. "You never do."

I smiled and walked back to the tents. The drow were gathered in a circle in a clearing behind where the tents were pitched.

Inside the circle were three drow warriors with pieces of burlap tied around their blades to prevent them from cutting their opponent on one side, and Brag'mok on the other without so much as his broadsword in hand. All three charged him.

Brag'mok stood there, ready. As they circled him, he grunted, and with a sweep of his leg, took out the first drow who came after him.

The second one jumped on his back, bringing her sword around his neck.

He flipped her over like a rag-doll. The drow warrior landed on her back.

The third charged at him and dived low to sweep at his leg.

Brag'mok jumped high, missing the sweep, then grabbed the drow warrior by her shirt and lifted her over his head.

"Nice try," Brag'mok said. "Try another approach."

I laughed as I stepped into the circle.

"You guys practicing?" I asked.

Brag'mok smiled, his lower incisors curled over his upper lip. "These drow haven't faced a giant before. Not that they'll be facing any others. But the way I see it, they need to know what I'm capable of once we end up in a battle with the elves."

I nodded. "Smart. You ladies all right?"

One of the drow, the one Jag had taken a particular interest in, the one they called Rina, smiled and nodded at me. "We'll take him down eventually."

"I'm sure you will," I said, chuckling.

"You have a minute, Brag'mok?"

The giant nodded. "Give me a moment," he said to the drow warriors.

Brag'mok followed me back toward the rear side of the farmhouse.

"If I don't get out," I said. "You'll need to lead them. You're the only one who has ever fought the elves, and you might be the only hope our world has."

"Stop talking like that," Brag'mok said. "The prophecy would not have brought you this far to leave you languishing in jail, Caspar."

I nodded. "I know. I want to believe that. But just for my sake, whatever happens, I need to know that you'll be prepared to fight."

Brag'mok cocked his head. "I'm always ready to fight. These warriors are better than you'd think."

I snorted. "Could have fooled me, the way you threw them around just a second ago."

"They won't be fighting giants," Brag'mok said. "And they won't be shielding their blades in battle. Their weapons are enchanted."

I nodded. "But they don't wield magic the same way the elves do. You're the only one here who has faced the elves that way."

Brag'mok put his massive hand on my shoulder, his thumb spreading halfway across my chest. "We'll be ready when you return."

"How are you doing with everything?" I asked.

Brag'mok grunted. "I'm still angry. Furious. But the time for battle will come."

"It will," I said. "I just need you to be ready. I'm going to need you to testify."

"In court?" Brag'mok asked.

"To the Furies," I said. "Even if I can't get out, if I can't get acquitted, they need to know what Brightborn did to the giants."

Brag'mok nodded. "They will know my tale. But I am not inclined to approach them until you return, Caspar."

"I know," I said. "I'm just saying, in case I don't get back in time. You have the best chance to convince them to change their minds."

Brag'mok snorted. "You can count on me, Caspar."

CHAPTER TWENTY

The US marshals were waiting for me on the steps of St. Ensley's. Layla lifted her hand to my cheek and kissed me softly.

"One way or another," Layla said, "we'll get you out of there."

She put her hand on my shoulder. "Remember, you *can* use your magic if you have to. The elves will already know where you are, so if push comes to shove, shove back."

I nodded. "As a last resort, of course. But I need to try and do this by the book."

A tear fell down Layla's cheek. I caught it with the back of my hand. "Someday, we're going to laugh about this."

"I can't wait until we can," Layla said. "But right now..."

"I know," I said, nodding. "It sucks."

"Understatement of the century." Layla sighed.

I stepped out of the car and approached the marshals. They were the sort of men who fit every law enforcement stereotype you might expect. I could see that they were wearing bulletproof vests beneath their black jackets. Not that the vests would do much against my abilities, but I suppose they had a protocol to follow.

"Come with us, Mister Cruciger," one of the marshals said. "We'll have to put you in cuffs for transport."

"I'm not going to fight," I said.

"Still," the marshal said, "it's standard procedure."

I nodded.

The marshal recited my Miranda rights, the ones you hear on all those crime television shows about the right to remain silent and all that crap. When it came to my case, I didn't plan on talking. I had the right to an attorney. Had that one covered.

Riding in a car with your hands cuffed behind your back isn't comfortable, not to mention I had an itch on my cheek.

Couldn't scratch it.

I rubbed my cheek against the seat instead.

I tried to engage the marshals in small talk. I know I had the right to remain silent, but hell, what harm would there be in a little harmless chat about the unseasonably pleasant weather? Apparently, despite the universal interest in the topic, the marshals didn't care. One of them made brief eye contact with me through his oversized rearview mirror.

"So, how about those Cardinals?" I asked. "Think we've got a shot at the series this year?"

They weren't having it. No reply. These guys were like drones, on task. If they had any humanity, they weren't showing it. Of course, the Cardinals had *no* chance in the series this year. Perhaps my topic choice just fell flat.

"You guys watch football at all? I heard the Chiefs are really overhauling their offensive line. All about protecting Mahomes. I can't wait to see how good he'll be behind a proper line. Can you imagine?"

Again, nothing. Not even a glance in the rearview mirror this time. You never know how people will react to football chatter in St. Louis. Since the Rams left town, people either had no interest in the NFL at all, they gravitated to the Chiefs as the only other team in the state of Missouri, or they were downright bitter that the team they once stole from Los Angeles decided to go back home to a more lucrative market.

"Did you guys see what Britney did?" I asked.

No response. Britney hadn't done a lot in a long time. But it used to be a regular conversation starter a decade or so ago. "What about Miley?"

These guys were unshakable.

All a part of the image. The act. They were probably regular dudes when they were off-duty. I was just trying to distract myself. Silence is deafening. Meaningless small talk would, at least, keep my mind off the reality of what I was facing.

They pulled up next to the Thomas F. Eagleton United States Courthouse. The building was a modern monstrosity that had been designed without any thought of saving the taxpayers money. One of those new federal courthouses, it doubled as a number of other offices dealing with federal law enforcement.

I imagined the unnecessary flourishes meant to communicate the "majesty" of the feds was also meant to be intimidating. When you're being dragged into that building, where I believed most federal court cases in the region were held, it was hard to imagine yourself as anything other than one more bug ready to be squashed by the almighty government.

Of course, I probably wouldn't be held there. Not for long. The place wasn't a jail, strictly speaking. Though, as I soon found out, the marshals did have cells.

Processing was a slow process.

Fingerprints.

Photographs. Face forward. Turn to the side.

At least they hadn't made me put on one of those orange jumpsuits. I supposed that would come later when the indictment was confirmed.

Bend over and cough.

Pretty much all the crap that I'd seen a hundred times on *Law*

& Order. Of course, this time, I was dealing with the feds. If you thought local law enforcement was pretentious...

These guys didn't even pretend to be my friend. I was sure some nice guy, acting super casual, would show up later to question me about Fred's murder. He'd act like he was my friend.

I knew, no matter how nice he might pretend to be, that he *wasn't* my friend. These guys were pros. Intimidate the hell out of you in the booking process, then try to act like they're on your side so you'll talk.

There was a lot of waiting. Sitting in a cell by myself, still cuffed, while the marshals did whatever. Surfed the internet. Played solitaire. All a part of the process, I imagined, to break me down. After so much waiting and boredom, I'd be more liable to talk.

Or, at least, that's what I imagined they were thinking.

"Just so you guys know in advance," I said. "My lawyer is Collin Law. I won't be talking about my case until he gets here."

Two marshals exchanged exacerbated looks. "That's your right, I suppose," one of them said. "We really just need to make sure you're not a threat before we can let you go."

"Let me go?" I huffed. Another tactic, I imagined. They don't let people who are accused of murder and arrested by order of the President—although I doubted these marshals knew the President was involved—just walk after a few questions.

The marshal nodded. "Right now, we don't really have enough evidence beyond the fact that you apparently communicated with the authorities a willingness to turn yourself in to hold you on charges. So, I suppose it's your lucky day. If you can, just clarify a few questions for us."

"All right, I'll answer anything you ask."

"Good to hear," the marshal said.

"Once my lawyer is here."

The marshal stared at me blankly. "Of course. But that might take some time. Can't guarantee he'll be able to make it here today."

"Excuse me?" a familiar voice asked.

"Mr. Law," the marshal said, rolling his eyes as Collin Law walked in with his assistant. Apparently, my lawyer had a reputation even with the feds. He'd also spoiled the marshal's plan to get me to talk by suggesting that I might, heaven forbid, have to stay the night in the cell.

"I'd like a few moments with my client," Collin said.

Two of the marshals exchanged glances. "We'll have an agent here shortly for questioning."

The marshal led me to another room that had a table in the middle and a mirrored wall on one side that, if my extensive experience with crime shows was accurate, was two-way glass.

"Can they listen to us in here?" I asked.

"They're not supposed to, and they know that if they tried something like that, I'd see to it they were reprimanded," Collin said, closing the curtain on the mirrored wall. "Violating attorney-client privilege is serious business. If they did commit a violation, we'd have reason to push for dismissal. Besides, my assistant will make sure they're not listening."

"So, are we going to get an indictment like I wanted?" I asked.

Collin nodded. "I think it's in the works. I've been in conversation with the US Attorney. He's hesitant to move forward based on a lack of evidence. But apparently, he's being pressured from above to make it happen."

"From above," I said, rolling my eyes. "Did you get the recording?"

"Your conversation with the President," Collin said. "I've got it."

"Anything there you can use?" I asked.

"Not in court," Collin said. "But before that, yes. We have a lot of leverage here. If those comments got out, it wouldn't look good for him. He basically admits that he was blackmailing you into supporting his political agenda."

"So you can get him to issue the pardon once the indictment comes through?" I asked.

"Probably," Collin said. "But this isn't exactly the usual way of going about things. Your phone also has the direct line to the President that you called. Push comes to shove, I can always use that. Hopefully, he'll pick up."

"Are you sure that's a good idea?" I asked. "I mean, is it safe for you to confront the President like that?"

Collin smiled. "Not my first rodeo, Cruciger. Granted, it's the first time I've had to deal directly with the President of the United States. But I've dealt with powerful people before. I'll just say this, everything I have is on a drive, actually multiple drives, in several secure locations, ready to be sent to the news media if I don't check in regularly and pass several security measures to prevent the e-mail from going out. Anything happens to me, or to you while you're in here… I'll just say I don't think the President wants any of this out there."

I shook my head. "You're good at what you do. I'll give you that."

"I'm not just good, Cruciger. I'm the best."

I nodded. "I certainly hope so."

"They're going to bring in an interrogator from the FBI. Just let me do the talking. I'll let you know if you can or should answer. I've dealt with most of these guys before. They're schmoozers. No matter what they tell you, they're just looking for something to use against you. At the end of the day, if there's solid evidence against you, it will be harder to convince the President to issue a pardon. As embarrassing as it might be for him if this information goes out, it certainly would raise questions if he pardoned someone who was clearly guilty."

"I'm not guilty," I said. "I mean, I am. But the facts show that Brightborn is *more* guilty."

Collin raised his hand. "That's exactly the kind of thing we can't have you saying when the agent is in here. If you're convicted, they just say 'guilty' or 'not guilty.' There isn't a conviction that says 'he's guilty, but not as much as the other guy.'"

"I get it," I said. "I'll keep my trap shut."

"Not easy for a former preacher, I get it. But you have a right not to incriminate yourself. Remember that. Don't admit anything. Don't lie, either. Just tell them that you're exercising your fifth amendment rights. Especially if they try to talk to you again after I'm gone."

"Got it," I said. "Thanks, Collin."

CHAPTER TWENTY-ONE

The interview with the agent was uneventful. He asked several questions. Collin answered most of them on my behalf. All I said was that I had nothing to say about the incident and was exercising my fifth amendment rights. The agent was visibly perturbed, but based on how quickly he gave up, I imagined he expected it. From the way he and Collin bantered back and forth, it was clear that they'd dealt with each other before.

"You'll probably be staying here tonight," Collin said. "They can't hold you indefinitely unless you're formally charged. If they move you to County, I'll know it, but I anticipate, based on my conversation with the US Attorney, that the indictment is forthcoming. I'm doing everything I can to expedite the process. I'll handle things with the US Attorney. Hopefully, I won't even have to communicate with the President. When he sees the facts and learns that this Brightborn character will have to be charged alongside you, I imagine the President will relent. If not, well, then we move to plan B. Releasing recordings. Dirty pool, maybe. But I don't mind throwing a little mud in the pool when he's already pissed in it."

"Got it," I said. "I think you're mixing metaphors about different kinds of pools. But I get it. Thanks again."

"You can waive your right to a grand jury indictment, which normally, I wouldn't suggest. But since you want to resolve this quickly, that's what I'd advise. By law, they have seventy days from indictment to go through discovery, basically gathering all the evidence, before trial."

"I can't wait seventy days," I said.

"I realize that's your position," Collin said. "I'll do what I can to expedite this. Like I said before, the best way to avoid that is to get the President to intervene with a pardon before things get that far."

I sighed. "Just be honest with me. What are our chances?"

Collin shrugged. "Depends how stupid the President is."

"So, you're saying our chances are good?" I asked, smirking.

"I'd say so." Collin laughed. "He isn't as smart as he thinks he is. Certainly not as smart as I am."

"And just as arrogant?" I asked.

Collin laughed. "It's not arrogance when you can back it up."

"So, tomorrow?" I asked.

"They can't hold you for longer than forty-eight hours without charges," Collin said. "They might let you stay the night here, but they'll probably move you to County in the morning. I'm going to try to get something done before that happens."

I nodded. "Thanks, Collin."

My lawyer stood up, gathered his paperwork into his briefcase, and left.

A few minutes later, one of the marshals came and escorted me to the cell where I imagined I'd be staying the night.

It was a dull evening. They had a Bible there. The only thing I could read. One open toilet and a bed, if you could call it that. Just a platform and something that resembled a pillow. Certainly not the most comfortable thing in the world. It was like a tarp stuffed with a filling that had long since flattened from use.

One of the marshals brought me a peanut butter and jelly sandwich.

"Mind ripping off the crust for me?" I asked.

The marshal stared at me blankly. "Eat the damn crust or rip it off yourself. I don't give a shit."

Apparently, they weren't so nice now that they realized I wasn't going to talk without my lawyer present. Go figure.

At least they were generous with the peanut butter. The jelly, not so much. But it filled the hole. If I'd thought about it, I would have stopped by O'Donnell's for a Reuben sandwich before I turned myself in. I'd probably be hungry again in a couple hours.

I made the best I could out of the bed they had in my cell and figured I'd try to get a little shut-eye. Not easy for a variety of reasons. Besides being the most uncomfortable combination of bed and pillow I'd ever had, they kept the lights on. Presumably, their cameras could see through the dark. I imagined they just didn't care to bother. Or, it wasn't nighttime yet. I didn't have a clue what time it was. I couldn't see a clock from where my cell was.

I turned on my side and threw my forearm across my face to block the light. A little light got through, but it was enough. I figured I would be able to get to sleep.

If I could turn off my overactive mind.

So many thoughts were racing through my head. My brain just wouldn't shut up.

I was obsessing over Collin's tactics, the legal arguments he'd make, the ways he'd pressure the President to issue a pardon. It had to work, didn't it? I wasn't so sure. What if it didn't work?

I don't look good in orange.

If I got convicted...

It wasn't just a matter of having to endure a life sentence. If things didn't go well in the next month, there was no way I could get back to the Furies and prevent them from unleashing their wrath via the New Madrid fault.

I wondered what Layla and Aerin were up to. Were they training with Brag'mok and the drow? What about Jag? He was probably taking his new truck for a joy ride.

Agnus was probably cleaning himself, sitting on my deflated air mattress, and licking his junk. Because that was his favorite thing to do.

Damnit. I couldn't clear my mind enough to sleep. I wanted to do nothing more than sleep. It wasn't like any of my thoughts were particularly productive. Obsessing over everything that was happening outside my cell wouldn't do anything for me. At the moment, I was at the mercy of other players—Collin doing his job, the President bending to his pressures, the legal system moving fast enough to get the indictment through.

I flopped over on my opposite side, using my other arm, this time, to block the light.

Had someone turned more lights on? I wasn't aware there were more lights, but it seemed brighter than before.

I sighed and opened my eyes briefly.

A gold halo had formed just above me in my bunk.

"Shit!" I shouted.

I knew what it was. It was a fairy portal, and it was being pressed over my body.

Where it was taking me, I wasn't sure. But I had a good guess who it was taking me to.

I found myself lying on a carpeted floor. It was a clean, luxurious carpet.

Where the hell was I? I looked around. I was in an older home, one of those turn-of-the-century mansions probably built in St. Louis around the time of the world's fair.

Two elven legionnaires stood guarding the only exit from the room, spears in their hands, but with regular Earth clothes, jeans and plain white t-shirts.

"What am I doing here?" I asked.

The two elves didn't acknowledge my question. They stood

there, stiff and stoic as if they were the guards that tourists like to screw with at Buckingham palace. And I thought the federal marshals were dense.

I walked toward them, and predictably, they crossed their spears in front of me to block my path.

"You guys realize I have enough power I could get through if I want, right?" I asked.

The two legionnaires held their spears steady. I wasn't joking. I had no reason to hold back my powers anymore. I was in the enemy's lair. I didn't have to hide from the fairies because they had brought me here, albeit likely at Brightborn's command.

I saw a flash of light on the wall surrounding the doorway that the elves were guarding.

A reflection.

I turned around—another fairy portal.

King Brightborn stepped through it. In contrast to the guards he had posted in the room, he was wearing traditional elven regalia: a long, purple robe with a golden cincture around his waist. No crown on his head. I imagined that wearing a crown, while important in some situations, wasn't comfortable. Most monarchs, human or elf, probably didn't wear their crowns any more than necessary. He had a long blade sheathed at his side.

Develin, the fairy king who'd killed and replaced Ensley, was perched on his shoulder.

"Hello, son," Brightborn said.

I cocked my head. "Son?"

"You married my daughter, did you not?" Brightborn asked.

I nodded. "Yeah, but..."

"Then whether you or I like it, you are my son."

I snorted. "Why'd you bring me here, Brightborn? You need to send me back."

The king cocked his head. "A simple thank you would suffice. I just broke you out of jail, Caspar."

"I turned myself in!" I protested. "I can't believe you

141

convinced the President to side with you. Does he have any clue what you're really planning?"

The king smiled and put his hand on my shoulder. "Do you have any clue what I'm really planning, Caspar?"

I shrugged. "World domination. You know, the same thing that most of history's psycho rulers dreamed about."

"Humanity's rulers," Brightborn said, shaking his head. "I'm not like any king or emperor this world has ever known."

"Of course not," I said. "I mean because the genocide of an entire race is totally beneficent."

The king cocked his head. "You speak of the orcs?"

"The giants, yes," I said. "You wiped them all out!"

"Is that what your orcish friend told you?" Brightborn asked. "Wouldn't that confound your whole scheme with the Furies if it turned out that it wasn't true?"

I cocked my head. "What are you talking about, Brightborn?"

Develin was cackling to himself on the king's shoulder. "The fairy king is aligned with me, son. Do you really think he wouldn't know if his position was being challenged or that he wouldn't tell me of it?"

I shook my head. "You're bluffing. You killed the giants, Brightborn."

"I certainly couldn't have you turning yourself in and fulfilling your side of the agreement. Or, perhaps, the whole matter was simply intended to root you out so I'd know where to find you."

I clenched my fists. "If I don't fulfill my side of the deal, the Furies are going to level the whole region!"

"Yes," Brightborn said. "An earthquake, wasn't it? It's a shame we don't know someone who has power over the element of earth."

I shook my head. "You aren't the first to suggest that. But I don't know if I have the strength to stop something of that magnitude once a fault line is released. Not to mention, it would set me at odds with the Furies indefinitely. Sounds to me like that's exactly what you'd want me to do."

Brightborn shrugged. "What I want is irrelevant. You are the one who invoked the Furies to begin with. For one so intent on taking responsibility for the death of that miserable cultist, you seem hesitant to take responsibility for the disaster that you've nearly unleashed."

"Fred only died because you set it up that way," I said. "I might have pulled the trigger. But you forced my hand."

"You had a choice," Brightborn said.

"To let Layla die?" I asked, shaking my fist. "That was no choice, and you knew it! You're the one who commanded Fred to throw that dagger into her back. That you'd risk your daughter's life like that, it's disgusting!"

"To save the world," Brightborn interrupted, "one must be willing to risk loss. Is it not part of your religion that God Almighty sacrificed his only begotten Son in order to save the world? Your God not only risked His child's life but forced Him to endure a torturous death. Yet, you worship this God while you despise me."

I grunted. "You're comparing yourself to God? You realize how fucking conceited that is?"

Brightborn laughed. "I wasn't comparing myself to your deity. The analogy, though, still applies. Why would you consider your God's sacrifice an act of love for the world but think my own to be an atrocity of the worst kind when I knew you'd choose to save her in the end?"

"Because you didn't do it out of love for the world," I shouted. "You did it because you want to dominate the world!"

The elven king smiled, turned to Develin, who was still on his shoulder, and winked at him. "Domination is such a harsh term, Caspar. You've suggested that you imagine I hope to usurp your President in time."

"Don't you?" I asked. "You have something on him. I could tell, just talking to him.."

Brightborn shook his head. "I'm not the one trying to black-mail him. I have no issue with human governments so long as they are willing to submit to my greater rule."

"What are you talking about?" I asked.

"One-world rule," Brightborn said. "For one who thinks he's the one meant to unite all the peoples, according to prophecy, I'd think you'd be more open to the idea. There's nothing in the elven prophecy, in fact, that demands the chosen one fight against me."

"You're talking about a single world government? A New World Order?" Even as I asked the question, visions of Hulk Hogan in his black-and-white NWO tank top from the late nineties flashed through my mind. Brightborn, though, had much more on his agenda than playing the heel of a professional wrestling soap opera.

The king placed his hand on my shoulder. "Think of the possibilities, Caspar. Human governments know how they're devastating the planet. But even those governments willing to change their behaviors won't do so because it sets them at a competitive disadvantage against nations who won't comply, who will continue to rely on fossil fuels."

I shook my head. "That's not necessarily true. There's an economic incentive in innovation. Countries that embrace green technology will have an advantage eventually."

"In time to reverse the course of climate change?" Brightborn asked. "From what I've seen, even if every government ceased carbon emissions today, without a way to remove carbon from the atmosphere, all you'd succeed in doing is delaying the inevitable consequences of global warming."

I sighed. "How do you know about all this? No one really knows what's going to happen."

"I've seen the models," Brightborn said. "Thanks to the

research and information that Layla has brought us over the years. But if we worked together, Caspar, with your abilities and my rule, I could force the world into compliance. You, if you refined your skills, could actually clean the air. We could save the world together, Caspar."

I scratched my head. "What would you do to those governments not willing to bow to your power?"

"They would be forced into compliance."

"Forced, how?" I asked.

"By whatever means necessary. We're talking about the salvation of this world, and now that New Albion is no longer habitable, it isn't just *your* world anymore."

I shrugged. "We've recharged New Albion before. We could do that again. We could make you a whole new world, with a new fantastic point of view."

"It was never our intention to make New Albion our final home," Brightborn said, clearly unfamiliar with the song from *Aladdin* that was running through my mind. "It was always meant that we should return and assume a rightful place as the guardians of this world."

I shook my head. "You weren't cut from Uranus' testicles."

Brightborn furrowed his brow. "Excuse me?"

"The elements, the Furies, and the giants. These were the three races established by God to protect the planet."

"According to whose myth?" Brightborn asked. "Is this a tale you learned from your orc?"

I grunted. "Yeah. So?"

"Tell me, Caspar. If the orcs were meant to protect this world, why did they fight against our return? Why did they insist on remaining on New Albion? It seems to me, if their race was ever meant to protect this world, they long ago abandoned their calling."

"They were protecting us from *you*, Brightborn," I said. "They

THEOPHILUS MONROE & MICHAEL ANDERLE

were willing to stay there indefinitely if it meant keeping you from bringing your legions here."

"Again, you prove my point," Brightborn said. "I've told you my intentions. I have the ability to rescue this planet from humanity's abuse."

"What's the long game here, Brightborn? Once you've solved the climate crisis, do you really expect me to think you'll just sit back and let the world govern itself?"

King Brightborn chuckled to himself. "One problem at a time, Caspar. This is just one example of the plague that humanity has become on this planet."

"And your answer to these other problems is what, exactly? Comply with your dictates or suffer?"

"Humanity has brought enough suffering upon itself," Brightborn said. "They must endure my hand of discipline that they might learn to stop destroying themselves."

"Your hand of discipline," I said, rolling my eyes. "I've heard what your idea of discipline is."

"From your orc," Brightborn said.

"Exactly!" I shouted. "From my *friend*. Tell me, Brightborn. What did you do to the giants? If you didn't wipe them out, you certainly killed millions of them. Those who remain, where are they? And what of the elves? Did you just let the rest of your own people die on New Albion when you took all of its magic with you and your legion?"

"Bring my daughter back to me," Brightborn said. "That she might be seen as the chosen one for my legions. Do that, and perhaps, I'll share with you the truth. Until then, I don't think you'd blame me for keeping their locations and status to myself. I must maintain my strategic advantages."

"Of course," I said. "But you can't blame me for asking. How can you expect me to trust you to govern humanity benevolently if, for all I know, you committed genocide not only against the giants but perhaps even your own people?"

"Why don't you give it some thought?" Brightborn asked. "Make yourself at home, here. I'll see to it that you are treated like my own son."

I shook my head. "Send me back to the feds. I'd rather rot in jail."

Brightborn laughed. "I can't do that, Caspar."

"Then let me go!" I shouted.

"I can't do that, either."

"You said you'd treat me like your own son!" I protested.

"And you've been a bad boy, son. You're in time out."

CHAPTER TWENTY-TWO

The room where I was being held was more like a formal living room than a dining room. Antique couches, chairs, tables, and even a large crystal chandelier decorated the room. None of it looked remotely functional, much less comfortable. When I was growing up, my parents had a formal dining room that we hardly ever used. I always wondered why we had fancy stuff in one room if we only used it on special occasions. The way I saw it, if you're going to have nice stuff, you might as well get some use out of it. Like the set of china my mom had inherited from my grandmother. I think we used it once when my parents had a reception at their house to celebrate my engagement to my former wife. Other than that, the set was displayed in a giant curio cabinet. Right next to a gaudy set of Precious Moments statuettes.

This mansion, and all its furnishings, were on a whole other level of fancy. Brightborn said I should "make myself at home," but given the options I had, I wasn't sure I was allowed to even take a seat, much less kick off my shoes and relax like I would if this place really was my home.

Of course, given the condition of the junkyard ranch and our current lack of accommodating furniture, I suppose sitting on my ass on the hard wood floor wasn't a far cry removed from sitting on my popped inflatable mattress. It certainly beat my temporary jail cell.

So I found an empty space on the wall and sat down, leaning against it. The room had a few windows. The glass was likely original. It offered a slightly skewed view of the surrounding neighborhood due to its imperfections. I wasn't sure where we were. Based on the fact that all the other mansions around this one were also made of red brick and reflected a similar vintage, I guessed we must've been in one of the wealthier, older areas of the city. Perhaps around Clayton or the Tower Grove neighborhood.

The two elven guards still stood their post at the only entrance to or exit from the room—not counting the windows, of course. I suppose I could have tried to escape, but first, I wasn't exactly inclined to throw my body through the old glass, and second, even if I flew out of there, chances were all it would take for Brightborn to catch me again would be a fairy portal or two.

I'd barely had the thought when, as coincidence would have it, I spotted two glowing circles forming right over each of the guard's heads.

The portals both fell over their heads, and they disappeared.

I chuckled. "What the hell? I guess this is my chance."

I stood up and headed for the hallway.

I didn't make it far. Another fairy portal formed just in front of me in the direction I was moving.

I shrugged and stepped inside it.

I wasn't sure what fairy was working to help me escape, but I wasn't going to question it. Whoever it was, or whatever fairy might be risking his glittery ass to break me out, was probably worth trusting.

I reappeared in the stone circle—the one near Elrand's place.

I looked all around. There was no sign of Aerin's father. Each of the stones, though, still glowed in colors corresponding to each of the five elements.

I felt a tap on my shoulder.

I turned around quickly.

One of the Furies stood there, smiling at me more kindly than any of them did the last time we met.

"What is going on?" I asked.

"I took it upon myself to bring you here," the Fury said.

"Thanks," I said. "I mean, I think… I was trying to do what we said. I turned myself in and everything."

"I understand," the Fury said. "But given what you told us before, I've taken it upon myself to investigate matters related to the elves."

"You and your sisters?" I asked.

"Just me," the Fury said. "I am Tisiphone."

I cocked my head. "The avenger of murder? The one Fury who wasn't inclined to agree with me before?"

Tisiphone nodded. "I've been watching you. Listening to you. Your plan with your lawyer. Even your conversation with the elven king."

"Watching and listening?" I asked. "But how?"

"The elements within you, Naayak."

"You can call me Caspar," I said.

"I'd rather not," Tisiphone said, dismissing my attempt to make things more personable and casual. "Only when you wield your magic will the lesser fairies sense your activity. But with the essence of the elements within you, I know all your thoughts, all your actions."

I snorted. "Well, I suppose that's convenient."

"I've heard enough to realize that what you told us before was true. The elven king has, indeed, wielded the sacred power of earth to kill. It was he who manipulated you to kill the one you call Mister Rogers."

I nodded. "Well, it's a beautiful day in the neighborhood, after all."

"You must still answer for your role in the murder," Tisiphone said.

I snorted. "Okay. Well, perhaps it's a slightly overcast day in the neighborhood, then."

"But you must bring it to trial in such a way that the elven king's guilt is also brought forward to the authorities. If he is convicted, in your courts, it will no longer be tenable for your President to maintain his alliance with Brightborn."

I shook my head. "There's just no way we can get this to trial in one lunar cycle."

"I am willing to convince my sisters to forestall our plans to unleash our wrath on your land, provided you can do us a service in kind."

I nodded. "Anything. What do you need me to do?"

"You must do as prophesied. You must unite the three guardian races."

I nodded. "Well, I have the elements. If you are willing to help, I'd certainly appreciate it. Plus, I can bring Brag'mok to you."

"He is just one giant," Tisiphone said. "I need you to rescue them all."

"Rescue the giants?" I asked. "Brightborn suggested they might still be alive. But I don't even know where to start."

Tisiphone pressed her lips together. "From listening in on the elves' conversations, I've discovered that a remnant of the giants managed to preserve a small amount of magic that is sustaining them on New Albion. I cannot take you to them. But I can open the gateway to New Albion. You must take your wife, the one who possesses the power of angels, and the giant Brag'mok with you, and bring them here that they might unite with us to protect your world."

I scratched the back of my head. "I'll do it. But Layla, her power...why do we need her with me exactly?"

"There are creatures on the planet you call New Albion, hostile entities that are impervious to both elemental magic and physical attack. The celestial powers she wields preclude all words. You will need her to survive the trek through New Albion to reach the giants."

"Brightborn just broke me out of federal custody," I said. "They're going to be looking for me."

"Then I'd suggest you complete this mission sooner rather than later. I will shield you from the other fairies. Do what you must to ensure that this is done."

I shook my head. "But breaking out of custody...that's not going to go well for me with the courts."

"That may be," Tisiphone said. "That is a matter of secondary concern."

I huffed. "One day at a time, I suppose."

"And one challenge at a time," Tisiphone said. "This is an opportunity I've never once afforded a mortal, a chance to assuage the Furies' wrath. I advise you to make the most of this chance."

CHAPTER TWENTY-THREE

Tisiphone teleported me back to the junkyard ranch.

"What the hell are you doing here?" Agnus asked as I appeared beside him on my deflated air mattress.

"Sorry, buddy. I suspect you were looking forward to becoming the man of the house?"

Agnus nuzzled his chin against the top of my hand. "How's the butthole doing?"

I snorted. "I didn't get locked up with anyone else, so it's doing just fine."

"Good to hear," Agnus said. "I was worried about that."

I chuckled. "Well, I'll probably be going back eventually. It's a long story."

"Caspar!" Layla exclaimed as she walked through the front door of the farmhouse and saw me. She ran to me and jumped into my waiting arms.

"Hey, babe!" I said before pecking a kiss on her lips.

"They let you out?" Layla asked.

I shook my head. "Not exactly."

"Caspar, I thought you said you wouldn't use your powers?"

"I didn't," I said. "Your father broke me out. Turns out he was just waiting for me to get locked up so he'd know where to find me. He used a fairy gate."

"And he just let you go again?" Layla asked.

"Again… Not exactly… Where's Aerin? I need to find her and Brag'mok. The situation has changed."

"They're both outside training," Layla said. "You'd never believe how smooth these drow women are with a sword."

"Not as good as you are with a bow, I'd wager," I said, smiling.

"Of course not," Layla chuckled. "But still, they're pretty formidable."

I nodded. "We'll be needing them sooner than later, I suspect."

"So, what exactly happened? Tell me everything."

I detailed how her father confronted me and everything he'd said. I told her how Tisiphone broke me out of Brightborn's mansion and what she revealed about the giants in New Albion.

"We need to tell Brag'mok," Layla said. "He needs to hear that there might be survivors."

I nodded. "That's why I asked you where he was."

I followed Layla out of the house and across the grass to where Brag'mok and the drow were training.

The second Aerin saw me, she came running. Brag'mok sauntered behind her. He wasn't much of a runner. Not that he couldn't move quickly when he had to, but when you're that large around a crowd of others not half your size, I suppose you have to be more careful with your steps.

"Caspar?" Aerin asked.

"Going to need you to call the lawyer," I said. "There have been a few complications."

"What brings you back here so soon?" Brag'mok asked.

"Aerin," I said. "Layla will update you on what's going on. Brag'mok, let's go somewhere to talk."

Brag'mok nodded, and he followed me back around to the back side of one of the many piles of junk that littered the property.

"I don't know how to tell you this," I said. "But I have good news."

"Good news?" Brag'mok asked. "Something you had to tell me privately?"

"You might not be the last giant alive," I said. "Brightborn tried to abduct me from jail. He succeeded, actually. While we were talking, he suggested that there might be some giants still alive. One of the Furies confirmed that it's true."

"I don't understand," Brag'mok said. "The magic on New Albion; it's gone."

"After Brightborn abducted me," I explained, "one of the Furies came and helped me escape. She said that there was a small pocket of magic that some of the more adept giants managed to hold on to. She told me I needed to take you and Layla to New Albion to rescue them."

Brag'mok stared at me blankly, and a single tear fell down his massive cheek. "Yes, we must go now."

I nodded. "Get whatever you need. We're bringing Layla with us. Tisiphone, the Fury who helped me, said she'd take us to New Albion but that we'd have to traverse some lands that aren't exactly habitable anymore."

Brag'mok grunted. "We'll have to face the *torwyr nos*."

"The what?" I asked.

"The nightcrawlers," Brag'mok said.

"The native inhabitants of New Albion?" I asked.

Brag'mok nodded. "They are intelligent, but they have no tolerance for lands vivified by Earth magic. During all the centuries we were there, however, the majority of the planet remained in its natural condition. That is where the *torwyr nos* dwell. It is said that to encounter one is to die. There's no way to kill them."

"Except with celestial power," I said. "Tisiphone said that Layla's power would work against them."

Brag'mok cocked his head. "How curious. And fortunate, I

should say. But even with her power, presuming the Fury told you the truth, the nightcrawlers move silently and quickly. They're nearly impossible to see, and once you see them, you might have just a few seconds to react. Only a few have ever survived an encounter with the *torwyr nos*, and it is from these few accounts that we know what we do."

"Have you ever encountered one?" I asked.

Brag'mok shook his head. "I have not. Though, my brother once did."

"B'iff?"

Brag'mok grunted. "When we were but children. He ventured beyond the living lands into the shades."

"Why would he do that?" I asked.

"On a foolish dare," Brag'mok said. "B'iff was smaller than most of our kind. As such, he was subject to…what is it you all call it here, bullying?"

I nodded. "They dared him to go into those lands?"

Brag'mok nodded. "One can barely survive an hour out of the living lands. This is why I was certain that my kind had vanished. With no magic left… But if what you say is true… Do you know how many giants have survived?"

I shook my head. "I wasn't told. Only that there is a small but significant number who'd managed to live."

Brag'mok shook his head. "If they live, still, they shan't for long. Whatever magic they preserved is likely barely enough to sustain a small area of living land. It certainly isn't enough that they could make it to a portal or gateway. We'll need to use your power to try and sustain us through the shades."

Layla and Aerin approached us together.

"Did Layla tell you?"

"Yes," Aerin said. "I want to come with you."

Brag'mok shook his head. "It is not wise. It will take all that Caspar can do with his elemental powers to sustain just the three of us. To add another life, and if one of you does not survive or is attacked by the *torwyr nos*…"

"Brag'mok is right," Layla said. "You're needed here to help Caspar's lawyer sort out his legal situation."

"Not to mention," I added, "if we don't make it back for whatever reason, the drow will need you to lead them. You'll be the only thing left to resist Brightborn. He has designs of some kind of new world order. He thinks he can save our planet from human destruction, global warming, and shit."

"He probably could," Aerin said. "But after that…"

I nodded. "That's what I said when he told me his plan. He insisted that he'd allow human governments to remain intact, but, well."

Layla shook her head. "It would be as it was after the eighth world war."

"You had eight world wars on New Albion?"

"We had dozens of them," Brag'mok said. "But the eighth gave the elves temporary dominance over the planet. At first, the king at the time allowed the giants to govern themselves, but when we did not do what the king demanded—"

"There was a rebellion," Layla interjected. "Leading to the ninth world war. Eventually, the giants regained their independence."

"At the cost of nearly half of our population," Brag'mok said. "It took two centuries of our kind hiding, reduced to nomadic tribes, before we could rebuild our numbers and organize into a force able to thwart the elves again."

"My father's plan is certainly to reduce humanity to a primitive state," Layla said. "He may allow human governments to operate for a time. But without any technology, any power that they can wield to resist him… It would mean the end of human civilization."

"There's another thing," I said. "Brightborn did suggest that there are elves who have survived, too. I can't say for certain, but they may be living in a similar condition on New Albion as the other giants. I believe he intends to bring them to Earth eventually."

"If I show up as their princess," Layla said, "they might follow us. If we could recruit them, bring them to Earth and convince them to resist my father's vision…"

Brag'mok shook his head. "Just rescuing the giants will be hard enough. To try and find the elves, too, could be more than we can handle."

"If my magic can only sustain a few of us, just trying to get the giants back to the Earth portal would be difficult."

"But not impossible. We have to try," Layla said. "It could mean the difference in the war. Think about it, if elves rise up against my father and his legions, it will give us a chance."

"That's a big 'if,'" Brag'mok said. "Can you even be certain they would follow you instead of your father? Bringing them to Earth is a risk. What if they align with Brightborn?"

"It's a risk worth taking," Layla said. "The other elves, much like me, didn't know what my father's plans were until he left them there. They have reason to be angry, to oppose him. If they're led by the chosen one…"

"To unite the peoples," Aerin said. "Not just the original protectors of the Earth. Not only the Furies, elementals, and giants. But to bring the elves together, united with the drow and the giants to defend humanity? This must be what the prophecy predicted."

"I don't know." Brag'mok shook his head.

"We'll do it," I said. "This could be the key to finally defeating Brightborn. He and his legions might be powerful. But he can't possibly stand against all of us united."

CHAPTER TWENTY-FOUR

Aerin called Collin to inform him that the pursuit of the pardon was now off the table. We wanted an acquittal. We'd plead not guilty and pursue what he originally told us was probably the best case to begin with—that I acted under duress and that Brightborn is solely guilty for the crime.

Of course, the President would probably pardon Brightborn in the end. Not without political consequences, of course, but if Brightborn became the "emperor of the world" like he wanted, I doubted that the President's position would continue to be determined by vote and the electoral college.

I'm no expert in foreign policy or anything, but I imagined the vast change in platform and policy that can happen every four years in the United States made any long-term agreements with foreign nations, not to mention global emperors, tentative at best. Despite Brightborn's insistence that he'd allow humanity to govern itself, I doubted he'd have much tolerance for democracy.

But Tisiphone had been clear. We had to at least *attempt* to bring Brightborn to justice. I imagined the Fury was a little naive about how the American criminal justice system actually worked.

Especially when politics got involved.

Apparently, my "escape" didn't help the case. Sure, they probably saw on camera that some kind of magic was involved. They likely saw me trying to wiggle out of the way when the portal was dropped over me. But would they even want that footage aired in court? Collin hoped they'd drop the whole "escape" issue since, ultimately, they didn't have any authority to hold me beyond the forty-eight-hour maximum, anyway. But if they pressed the issue, and if it was revealed that Brightborn broke me out, then it would be harder to argue that I'd acted under duress. It would give the impression that he and I were co-conspirators from the start.

Aerin said she'd told Collin to "work his magic" and figure it out. Ironic, perhaps. But I suppose calling him a master of illusion, a legal magician, wasn't entirely off base. I was pretty sure that Collin's legal briefs were manufactured by Fruit of the Loom because most of his legal arguments came straight out of his ass.

Didn't mean he wasn't effective. Just full of shit.

My legal case was so convoluted at this point that I was almost beyond any hope that truth would prevail. Superman wasn't real. Not a lot of people stand for truth, justice, and the American way. These days, at least in my situation, the "American way" didn't have a lot to do with truth, and justice had even less to do with it.

"What is truth?" Pontius Pilate had once asked. He hadn't been concerned with justice either. The "Roman way" was about power and the authority of the emperor. I suspected, especially with Brightborn asserting himself, that was what my legal situation was about too. Only a thin marmalade of justice spread across a piece of burned toast; that was the truth of my case. It was all about power and eliminating me as a threat.

I'd think about all that crap later. I had to get myself ready to trek across a devastated, uninhabitable world filled with creepy creatures that only Layla had the ability to kill and fulfill an agenda with odds of success even worse than my legal case.

Brag'mok had re-dressed in his armor. I'd only seen him wear it a couple times before. When he strapped on his massive pauldrons and breastplate, the giant looked even larger and more imposing.

"I thought you said we'd be defenseless against these nightcrawlers?"

Brag'mok nodded. "We can't kill them with blades. But a good set of armor can at least buy you some time."

I snorted. "Armor. That's one thing I don't have, and there is no time to remedy the situation."

"You can stay behind us," Layla said. "Brag'mok is the biggest target. Hopefully, he can lure the nightcrawlers out of hiding, and I can take them out with my magically infused arrows."

I glanced at Layla's quiver. Her arrows were glowing violet, like Fred's daggers had glowed when he'd had the power. As frightening as he had been when I thought he was a trained elven assassin before I realized who he was, Layla was far better with a bow than he'd ever been with his knives. Fred, I imagined, had refined his knife-throwing skill as a larper at the local Renaissance festival. Layla had trained with a bow her entire life.

I'd seen her in action before. Though, in truth, we'd only had a few situations that called for her to go into full Robin Hood mode since we met. A part of me was excited to finally see her in action against a real threat.

I'd been to New Albion before when the planet was barely hanging on magic-wise, barely habitable. But now, most of what we were going to encounter was *completely* devoid of magic. The planet would be in its original and natural condition before the old druids who became the elves went there and vivified the place with Earth's power.

I changed clothes before we left. I was still wearing the suit I wore when I turned myself in. Since I'd only been in one cell while going through processing, the feds hadn't put me in an orange jumpsuit. That would have come, more than likely, if I'd been there long enough to get transferred to County or, eventually, if I couldn't get acquitted, to prison.

I wasn't entirely sure why I'd dressed up so nicely to just turn myself in. I'd imagined that I might be brought before a judge at some point. I didn't realize, until Collin educated me a bit on the whole process, that it could take days before I was even arraigned on charges, even with him trying to expedite things.

As inappropriate as the outfit ended up being for what I was doing, it was even less fitting now. I still had a good pair of combat boots I'd bought at the local Army Surplus, along with a pair of camo cargo pants and a form-fitting t-shirt.

"How cold is it going to be there?" I asked.

"You might want more than a t-shirt," Layla said, taking a long black cloak—one of a few elven clothing items she still had in her wardrobe—and draped it over her form-fitting black leather top. "It won't be the temperature that's the problem. The suns on New Albion are intense. Even in the shades, where we'll be, it can get relatively warm. But the sand storms can be brutal."

I shrugged. "I hear exfoliating is good for the complexion."

"Exfoliation, sure," Layla said. "But sand blasting, not so much."

I reached into my closet and pulled out a hooded, khaki Carhartt jacket. I didn't wear it often, mostly in the winter when clearing snow off my car. It had been a score at Goodwill and had the name "Roy" embroidered on the breast. Probably something that Roy, whoever he was, used to wear on the job. It was one of only a few items I bothered to unpack and hang in my closet in the farmhouse. Since I was likely to have to do some outdoor work, and we'd have to get by without a great heating system once we got into the colder seasons, I figured I'd leave it hanging in my closet so I'd know where to get it.

"All I need is my Rambo headband," I said.

Layla rolled her eyes. "You'll be fine without it. Come on, commando."

CHAPTER TWENTY-FIVE

Tisiphone listening in on everything I did and said was an unexpected consequence of subduing the elements. Having the arch-fairies, better known as the Furies, listening in on what I did at all times wasn't a part of what I signed up for, but in this instance, it came in useful.

Why only Tisiphone heard me and not her sisters was something I hadn't thought to ask. Perhaps it was simply that she was the only one who'd *chosen* to listen to me. She was the one, after all, who was concerned that I get myself acquitted of murder. The other two had already decided in my favor.

"Tisiphone," I said out loud, standing in front of the farmhouse with Layla and Brag'mok. "We're ready."

I waited a moment. I wasn't sure if she was going to just appear in front of us or if, as she'd done before, she'd present a portal for us to run through. She was more aggressive than I expected. She *did* present a portal, but this time she formed it over our heads and dropped it down over us.

Usually, when I used a fairy portal to travel to different places on Earth, it was a pretty painless process. You go through the portal and appear where you're going. But Tisiphone was transporting us across worlds. I found myself flying through a tunnel. Was she using the old gateway at the confluence of the Mississippi and Meramec rivers, or was this something else entirely?

The force pressing against me was so hard it took everything I could to tuck my head down. I held my eyes shut. The lights flashing around me were blinding. Presumably, Layla and Brag'mok were experiencing the same thing.

I crashed, face first, into the ground. A cloud of dust billowed around me. I coughed, rubbing my forehead as I struggled, disoriented back to my feet.

"You guys make it?" I asked, squinting as I peered through the debris. A gold circle, the gateway Tisiphone had made for us, hovered about a foot off the ground behind where I stood.

"I'm here," Brag'mok said, waving his hand through the dust to clear the air.

"Yeah," Layla said, coughing. "We're all here."

When the dust settled, it appeared we'd arrived in the middle of a dried-up river bed.

I could barely breathe. The oxygen was thin. I extended my hand and released the element of air. A subtle glow of white energy swirled around us. I took a deep breath.

"That helps," Layla said.

"I'll do what I can to try and maintain it," I said. "I don't think we have a lot of breathable air."

Brag'mok shook his head. "Whatever oxygen is in the air is just what remains from before. If we'd come much later, I suspect we'd have suffocated on arrival."

"Any sign of nightcrawlers?" I asked.

Layla retrieved an arrow from her quiver and nocked it. "I don't see any. But they aren't exactly easy to spot. I'll be ready if any show up."

"They're here," Brag'mok said. "Even if we can't see them, you can be certain that they see us."

"Probably just waiting for an opportunity," Layla said. "Nasty buggers."

"Nasty but smart," Brag'mok said. "They'll wait until they believe we're most vulnerable."

Several dead trees with bark that had turned black stood around us. "It looks like this place used to be full of life."

Layla nodded. "This river valley was once one of the most fertile places on New Albion. It's crazy how quickly such a lush place can become desolate in the absence of Earth's magic."

"Any idea where we'll find the surviving giants?" I asked.

Brag'mok grunted and pointed off into the distance. "If they're anywhere near here, they'll be that way. There was a small contingency of giant priests and sorcerers who lived in a small village about three miles that way. If anyone could have held on to any of Earth's magic and survived, it would have been them."

"Getting to the elves, if they're here, will be harder," Layla said. "They'd be in the opposite direction."

"How far in the opposite direction?" I asked.

Layla shrugged. "On foot, a good half-day's journey."

"Can you fly there?" Brag'mok asked.

"I think so," I said. "Doing that while keeping the air swirling around us so we can breathe might be difficult. I imagine, if the atmosphere is like Earth's, the breathable air up there will be even thinner."

"Take me to the giants first," Brag'mok said. "You can't fly with me, but Layla can ride on your back like you flew with Aerin before."

I nodded. "We should be able to do that. I don't think Tisiphone can create new portals for us here. We'll still have to find a way to get back to the portal."

"If we can convince them to come with us," Brag'mok said, "the sorcerers should be able to use whatever magic they've saved to help them move. But it will mean leaving everything behind. Once they use that magic, there won't be anything left."

"Likely the same for the elves," Layla said. "Though maybe you can add your magic to what they have, Caspar. Either way, while we can fly there to find them, we'll have to travel with them to bring them to the portal."

A high-pitched screeching sound echoed in the distance. I instinctively covered my ears. "What the hell?"

"The *torwyr nos*," Brag'mok said. "They know we're here. Unfortunately, that sound came from exactly the direction we need to go to reach the giants."

I sighed. "Well, that's fantastic."

"Come on," Layla said. "We'll face them when we have to."

"Based on that sound," Brag'mok said. "We won't have just two or three to deal with. That sounded like a swarm."

I shook my head. "You said that they are repelled by Earth's magic. Perhaps I can use the elements to try and at least give us a path through."

"Repelled by it," Brag'mok said. "But it won't stop them. Not completely, and not in those numbers. If they realize you're the one channeling the earthen magic, they'll come after you first."

"It's just three miles," I said. "Do you think we can make it?"

"Three miles isn't a far distance if you're taking a hike through the woods. But this won't be a stroll across the countryside. We'll have to fight every step of the way. We'd best make our way toward them quickly. Cover as much ground as we can before we have to deal with them."

CHAPTER TWENTY-SIX

Wielding all five elements at once is challenging but not impossible. I just hadn't had much practice with it. I'd barely acquired these abilities, then I wasn't able to use them since we were hiding from the elves and the fairies.

The trick, I was learning, was to get one working at a time. Make sure it's under control, then unleash the next. We didn't need all of them, strictly speaking. Air was enough to keep us breathing. But a little water helped humidify the air, and a little fire gave us light to spot the nightcrawlers. The power of earth kept down the dust, and with aether, all of my senses were more acute.

None of that settled the nerves churning in my gut. I wasn't exactly sure what these nightcrawlers looked like. I couldn't imagine, based on the shrill pitch of their shrieks, that they were even marginally cute. Something that sounded like that could only be hideous.

The only nightcrawler I'd ever encountered before was an earthworm. We used to get styrofoam canisters of them from the bait and tackle shop whenever we went fishing when I was a kid. They didn't make any noise at all. So, I was pretty sure that the translation of whatever it was Brag'mok had called them into "nightcrawler" was coincidental.

Layla had her arrow ready to fire. The violet-colored magic coursing through her arrow gave us a little light in addition to what the tongues of fire swirling around us provided.

Brag'mok had his broadsword in hand. A sword like that, if a human wielded it, would require two hands. However, he swung the thing around with ease one-handed, as if it was a rapier.

His sword wouldn't kill a nightcrawler. I wasn't entirely sure why. I couldn't imagine anything surviving a strike from his blade. At the very least, though, he seemed to think that it might help fend them off.

The farther we went, moving briskly, the louder the shrieks became.

At first, they were ahead of us. But soon, it sounded more like they were coming at us from all sides.

These things hadn't just stayed at a distance, waiting for us to enter their domain. They'd circled around us. I suspected it was just a matter of time before they pounced. How Layla would be able to take them out when they started charging us from various directions, I wasn't sure.

The one advantage we had, of course, was that these night-crawlers didn't know her arrows could kill them. A few key shots and they'd be a little more hesitant about coming after us, I hoped. Brag'mok said these creatures were intelligent. In this case, I figured it was better for our sake that they were smart. If they were pure beasts, operating solely on instinct and rage, they wouldn't think twice about coming after us no matter how many of their number fell to Layla's arrows.

These were the strategic thoughts that passed through my mind as we readied ourselves for an attack. I might have been overthinking it, desperately trying to come up with some reason why we stood a good chance to survive. Otherwise, I wouldn't have been able to convince myself to keep pressing forward. We *had* to get to the giants.

In the parlance of World of Warcraft—a game I'd often played addictively post-divorce—this wasn't an optional side-quest. It was absolutely essential. Not just because they were the last giants apart from Brag'mok, but because Tisiphone had made it clear we had to bring the giants back with us if we wanted the aid of the Furies.

"So, has anyone ever killed one of these things before?" I asked.

Layla laughed. "You don't kill nightcrawlers, Caspar. You avoid them."

"So the answer is no?"

"It's a no," Brag'mok said. "If these celestially powered arrows actually work, there's no way to know how they'll respond."

"Did you notice?" I asked. "I think they went silent."

"That's not a good thing," Brag'mok said.

"Definitely not," Lalya added, spinning around in anticipation of the first attack as we moved forward. "They're only quiet now because they're close. They don't want us to know where they're coming from."

"Why do I have a sudden urge to cry for my mommy right now?" I asked.

Layla chuckled. "You aren't alone. But I don't think any of our mommas could handle these things."

"My mother would slap me silly for even considering putting myself in this position," Brag'mok said. "But she'd be proud too, knowing what's at stake."

"Can they understand us?" I asked.

Brag'mok shook his head. "They're smart. But no one has ever spent enough time with one to teach them language."

"So I imagine taunting them is off the table," I said. "Thought, you know, since we were on the topic of mothers, I could maybe throw a yo momma joke their way and get them to act carelessly."

"Caspar, would you just shut up," Layla said. "I need to concentrate."

I snorted. "Sorry. I get chatty when I'm anxious."

"We know," Brag'mok said.

"One of your more endearing qualities," Layla said. "When our lives aren't on the line."

I pressed my lips together, doing my best to stop myself from interjecting another quip. She was right. I was just distracting them. Hell, I probably needed more focus myself. But once I had the five elements working around us, it was all sort of on auto-pilot.

Three rapid shrieks sounded successively from a distance.

Were they really counting to three to attack?

I didn't have to answer my own question.

A shadowy figure jumped at us from our right. I didn't even get a good look at it before I saw a second come at us from the left, then a third from behind.

Layla pivoted and fired one arrow, quickly nocked a second and fired it, and then a third.

"Damn!" I said, putting my hand to my chest to feel my heart race. "That was impressive."

I glanced at the dead nightcrawlers as the purple magic from Layla's arrows spread through their bodies. They were like a hybrid of a spider and a squid and as black as night, their bodies slick and smooth. They didn't have arms. Instead, their long bodies sported between eight and twelve legs.

Another one leaped at us from the front. Brag'mok swung his blade at it. The nightcrawler split in two, but the parts continued moving, reforming its missing half in less than a second. His strike had turned one creature into two.

Layla shot them both down as quickly as she had the first three.

Another loud shriek came from a distance.

"I think they might be regrouping," Layla said. "Now that they know that I can kill them, they're probably coming up with another strategy."

"Next time they attack, I don't think they'll be coming at us three or four at a time," Brag'mok said.

"I agree," Layla said. "If I were in their position, I'd try to overwhelm us. Come at us with so many at once that I couldn't possibly take them down."

"I can try and widen our area," I said. "Push a little more power into all the elements. You said they don't like earthen magic, right?"

"It doesn't hurt them," Brag'mok said. "They just find it...repulsive."

"You could swim through raw sewage," Layla said. "You'd survive just fine. But you'd be disgusted by it. Earthen magic is sort of like that to the nightcrawlers. They'll avoid it if they can, but it won't stop them if they really want us dead."

"It's a good idea," Brag'mok said. "If anything, it'll buy us a little more time. We're getting close. The village should be just over the next hill."

Layla nodded. "I can see the glow from their fires."

"I can barely believe it," Brag'mok said. "I think the Fury was right. They did survive out here."

"I need to rest after this," I said. "Wielding all this power, it's exhausting. But I can do it."

"We just need to make it to the village," Brag'mok said. "You'll be able to gather your energies once we're safe."

I inhaled deeply and focused my energies, drawing in some of the atmosphere I'd created around us. I churned the air, creating a giant whirlwind all around us, then I forced it outward.

I pressed more water into the wind, releasing the cool energy of that element. Then I drew on the heat of fire in my frame and turned the tongues of fire dancing around us into large infernos.

"It's working," Layla said as the nightcrawlers started shrieking again. This time, the tone of their shrieks was less definitive, less controlled. It was as if all of them were screaming at once.

"They're panicking," Brag'mok said. "This is unlike anything either the giants or the elves have thrown at them in a thousand years."

"I'm not sure how much longer I can keep this up," I said as my knees weakened.

Brag'mok stopped in his tracks and grabbed me, then threw me over his shoulder. "Just keep casting your magic, Caspar. We'll run you the rest of the way."

I'd never seen Brag'mok run so fast. Layla was just as fast.

I kept the magic going, unleashing a little more earth and aether to compliment the other elements.

As we crested the hill, I could see the village below.

It wasn't much—several huts, made mostly of mounds of mud and covered with dried-out leaves. But there were green grasses all around the village. A small group of maybe a dozen giants inside came forward as we approached.

"Brag'mok!" one of the giants roared as we charged onto their grounds.

"Hello, Gronk," Brag'mok said. "It's great to hear your voice. I didn't think any of you were still alive."

"We assumed you were dead, too," the giant Brag'mok had called Gronk said.

Brag'mok set me down on the ground. I knelt a second to catch my breath as I released the magic I'd been casting.

"Are you the only survivors?" Brag'mok asked.

"We are the last of our race," Gronk said. "But who are these? You dare bring an elf, and Brightborn no less, into our sanctuary?"

CHAPTER TWENTY-SEVEN

"The princess is with us," Brag'mok said.

Gronk grunted. "You trust her? Deceit runs in her blood!"

"It's true," I said. "She's trying to stop her father."

"Who are you, human?" Gronk asked, towering over me. He was about a foot shorter than Brag'mok but an imposing presence nonetheless.

"I am Caspar," I said.

"He is the chosen one of the ancient prophecy," Brag'mok said. "We've come to save you. To bring you with us to Earth."

"This is our home," Gronk said. "We have no intention of leaving."

"No intention?" Layla asked. "Isn't it your sacred purpose to protect the Earth? My father has already taken his legions there. We need you to help stop him."

Gronk shook his head. "We have already lost. We could not stop Brightborn here. Why do you think we'd be able to do so on Earth?"

"I bring the elementals," I said, "and the Furies will unite with us if you'll join us."

"The three races, born from the divine loins," Brag'mok said.

Gronk shook his head. "Just a story. A myth meant to give our ancient ancestors a sense of purpose. But it is nothing more."

"Not true," I said, my head still spinning from exhaustion. "The Furies sent us to find you."

"The legend says nothing of an elf joining us to protect the Earth," Gronk said.

"The prophecy says that the chosen one will unite the peoples," Layla said, clenching her fist around her bow, "and there are elves here who might also join us."

Gronk laughed. "You seriously expect us to join with elves to fight other elves on Earth?"

"That's what I expect," Brag'mok said. "The age of war on this world is over. The prophecies have been fulfilled, all except for the one that remains sealed."

"This is a matter to bring to the high priest," Gronk said.

"Vakgu is here?" Brag'mok asked. "Take us to him. He'll confirm that what we say is true."

Gronk grunted. "He is not. He did not make it. Targigoth has ascended to his place."

"Targigoth?" Brag'mok asked. "He's just a child."

Gronk nodded. "He is the only priest who remains, Brag'mok."

"Very well," Brag'mok said. "Does he have the scrolls?"

Gronk nodded. "Thankfully, they remain secure."

We followed Gronk through the onlooking giants. Looks of disdain directed at Layla, combined with curiosity—probably on account of me likely being the first human any of them had ever seen—followed us.

It wasn't unsurprising. Until now, Layla had been the daughter of their arch enemy. It had to be a surprise for a human to traverse through the shades of their broken world.

"Are all of these giants sorcerers?" I asked, stumbling beside Brag'mok.

"Some of them," Brag'mok said. "Gronk is probably the most accomplished of all our kind. We are fortunate he's survived."

I shook my head. "He doesn't exactly seem pleased to see us."

"Our people have lost much," Brag'mok said. "To subject what remains of our race to danger, to more war. It's a big ask."

"But can they really expect to live here, in this small oasis, forever?" I asked.

Brag'mok shook his head. "Of course not. But convincing them of that after all they've endured won't be easy."

"They hate me," Layla said, resting her hand on my back. "My presence here isn't making our case any stronger."

"Not necessarily true," Brag'mok said. "They know the prophecy. That the chosen one should appear with you cannot be a surprise. Still, centuries of disdain for the elves is not something easily shaken."

"I don't blame them," Layla said. "When I learned the truth about what my father planned, what the elves have always intended… I'm not exactly proud."

"You should never be ashamed of what you are," Brag'mok said. "You may be your father's daughter, but you are not your father."

"Still," Layla said, "the shame is real."

"Sometimes, the Bible speaks about generational sin," I said. "How the sins of the fathers become the sins of the children. I don't think that's about inherited sin. It's about learning to mimic the errors of your parents. In AA, you'd be surprised how many members are second or third-generation drunks. Several of them have children who struggle with the disease."

"That's different," Layla said. "There's an actual genetic component to alcoholism."

I nodded. "But our genes don't take us through the twelve steps. We don't blame our actions on an inherited disease. We take responsibility. We make amends, and we strive to do better today than we did yesterday."

"Exactly my point," Brag'mok said. "You could have done what your father desired. He sought to set you up as the chosen one. You could have stayed by his side and ruled. But you didn't. You took responsibility. You decided that your past, what your ancestors and family have done, didn't define you. You left behind everyone you ever knew and put your faith in a prophecy and a preacher."

Layla sighed. "I can't still help but feel shame over all my father has done."

"He feels no shame at all. That's what makes you and your father different, Princess," Brag'mok said. "The pain you feel over his actions proves it. It's because you aren't like him that it aches. You have chosen the harder path. The noble one. Because of you, elves will not forever be judged only by your father's actions. You've forged a new future, a better history for elven kind."

Layla wiped a tear from her eye. "Thank you. That might be one of the nicest things anyone has ever said to me."

"Do not thank me yet," Brag'mok said. "What I've said goes in both directions. Simply because the noble giants were dedicated to the protection of the Earth... Well... As we prepare to meet the high priest, remember that just as no one should be judged by his or her race, no one should be exonerated by it, either."

"What do you mean?" I asked.

"Targigoth... I'll simply say that of all the children born to the priestly caste, he's the last I'd have ever predicted would one day become high priest."

"He's just a child," I said. "Surely some immaturity is to be expected?"

Brag'mok grunted. "He may be a child. But this one, in particular, is insufferable."

"Come on," Layla said. "He's a kid. How bad can he be?"

"Hopefully, the burden of responsibility and authority has changed him," Brag'mok said. "That's all I'll say lest I skew your opinion of the high priest before you have a chance to meet him."

CHAPTER TWENTY-EIGHT

Gronk pulled back the large curtain that covered the entrance to one of the mud huts and held it open for us as we went inside.

Gronk closed the curtain and remained outside.

"Brag'mok!" the giant, who I presumed to be the high priest, exclaimed as he reclined on what resembled a large chaise, lined with a material similar to velvet.

"Hello Targigoth," Brag'mok said.

The high priest extended his hand. "Please, help me to my feet."

Brag'mok held out his hand, and the high priest grabbed it and stood up. As a child, he was still rather large. He was approximately my height. His hair was long, stringy, and tucked behind his ears. He glanced at me and then fixed his gaze on Layla.

"Well, hello, beautiful," Targogoth said.

Layla cocked her head. "It's a pleasure to meet you."

"The pleasure will indeed be yours by the end of the night," Targigoth said.

I cleared my throat. "I'm Caspar, by the way. Layla's husband."

Targigoth huffed. "You must be the one rumored to have fulfilled the prophecy."

"He is," Brag'mok said. "We've come to bring the remnant of the giants back to Earth that we might fulfill our sacred duty to defend the earth from the elven legion."

"And you'd like me to give my endorsement to this plan of yours, Brag'mok?" Targigoth asked.

"Please," Brag'mok said. "You know as well as I do that you cannot survive here in this small village forever. Our people are meant for more than that."

"What's in it for me?" Targigoth asked.

"The salvation of our people!" Brag'mok said. "You'll be remembered as the high priest who brought the giants to glory!"

"Maybe," Targigoth said. "But even if we were to succeed, I'd only be remembered in such a way long after my time has passed. I want to know what's in it for me now."

"What are you talking about?" Brag'mok asked. "The high priest is meant to be a servant to the people, to the scrolls of the prophecy."

"Tell me, Princess," Targigoth said. "Do you have any giant in you?"

"What are you talking about?" Layla asked. "You know I'm an elf."

"Would you like a little giant in you?" Targigoth asked, smirking.

"No!" Layla said. "I'm married, and you're just a child!"

"I'm no child!" Targigoth shouted. "I'm a virile young giant of twenty years. I have needs, fantasies you'd be well suited to fulfill."

"In our lifespan," Brag'mok said. "Twenty years makes you still a youth. What you ask is not befitting of your role, high priest."

Targigoth laughed out loud. "The look on the princess' face! So much disgust!"

"I'm not sleeping with you," Layla said, staring daggers at the high priest.

Targigoth waved his hand in the air. "I'm not serious, Princess. Can't you take a joke?"

"It's not funny," Layla snapped.

Targogoth laughed, clinging to his pooch of a belly. "But your reaction, it's certainly worth a good laugh."

"Like I said," Brag'mok said, looking at me. "Insufferable."

I shook my head. "I get it, funny ha-ha. See how desperate we are. See what we'd be willing to agree to for your support."

"See!" Targigoth said. "The human gets it! Just between you and me, human, elves don't have much of a sense of humor."

"I'm still standing here," Layla said. "It's not much of an inside joke between you and him."

The high priest reached beneath his chaise and pulled out a golden chest. "These are the prophecies, possessed by our high priests for centuries. Though, all the scrolls that have been revealed are well-known to all the giants. Unlike the elves, our priests have never held these scrolls secret."

"So you'll come with us?" I asked.

Targigoth raised his hand. "You come asking for me to interpret the prophecies, to tell our small tribe what they should do. The point is only that these prophecies are no secret. Each of our kin can determine for themselves if they believe the prophecy demands we should do what you ask or not."

"But you're the high priest," Brag'mok said. "Your recommendation would hold sway."

"Which is precisely why I am disinclined to make a recommendation or an interpretation," Targigoth said. "We've all lost much. The one thing that the giants still have is their freedom of choice. Who am I to tell them what they should do?"

"Strong leadership," I said, "does not rob people of their liberty."

"But what of these prophecies demands that we should follow your particular plan to bring us with you to Earth?"

"We'll unite with the elementals and the Furies," Brag'mok

THEOPHILUS MONROE & MICHAEL ANDERLE

said. "We'll finally become what our race was meant to be from the beginning."

"Again," Targigoth said, "the prophecies indicate that the chosen one would unite all the races. It does not say, specifically, that he'd lead us to join humans, elves, or even the Furies and elementals in this particular war."

"You have barely enough magic to sustain this village a month, much less indefinitely. If you make this decision now and use the magic that's left to help bring our people to Earth, you'll save not just their liberty but their lives!" Brag'mok had his hands on his hips as he stared at the high priest.

Targigoth took a deep breath. "What you say is true. I must admit, the fact that you've survived at all, Brag'mok, is something of a miracle."

"So you'll consider it?" I asked.

Torgigoth nodded. "I must consult with my ancestors."

"With your ancestors?" I asked.

Brag'mok nodded. "This is wise."

"What do you mean to consult with your ancestors?" I cocked my head.

"Care to explain, Brag'mok?" Torgigoth asked.

Brag'mok snorted. "The high priest inherits this ability, typically passed on by the laying on of hands from one high priest to the next. The high priest can release the gift when his life is nearing its end. There is a ritual that the priest can perform to commune with the high priests who've come before him."

"You received his gift when you became the high priest?" I asked.

Torgigoth nodded. "Vakgu, my predecessor, passed it along to me with his dying breath. But the ritual requires one who can wield earthen magic as fire."

"I can do that," I said. "I have all the elements."

"We'll also need water," Targigoth said. "Along with stones."

"What this ritual requires is the high priest to sit, in meditation, in extreme heat. It can take some time," Brag'mok said.

"Like a sweat lodge?" I asked.

Brag'mok nodded. "From what I understand of similar practices on Earth, yes, it is something like that."

"How long, exactly, will this take?" I asked.

"As long as it takes," Targigoth said. "I may choose one of our kind as a witness. Brag'mok, would you accompany me in the ritual?"

Brag'mok nodded. "It would be my honor."

"Then let us prepare the rite," Targigoth said. "I have the stones. Human, if you might simply provide some water and fire that we might heat the stones and create steam with the water."

"Of course," I said. "I can do that."

"Caspar," Brag'mok said. "Do this, then get whatever rest you need. I'd advise you and Layla to proceed to attempt to reach the elves while we undergo the rite."

I nodded. "Makes sense. You said you don't know how long this will take? Is there like a minimum amount of time?"

"At least a day," Targigoth said. "More likely closer to two days."

"You're going to sit in steam, like a sauna, for two whole days?" I asked.

"This is what it requires in order to activate the aspect of my ancestors that is within me," Targigot said. "I'll have an answer for you after the ritual is complete. Not a moment before."

CHAPTER TWENTY-NINE

At Targigoth's insistence, Gronk took Layla and me into one of the huts and offered us a place to rest. It wasn't much. There wasn't a proper bed, just a small, blanket-covered slab in the middle of the room. It probably wasn't a large room, by giant standards, but since it had to accommodate the full height of a giant, it was rather spacious for Layla and me.

We spooned together on the makeshift bed that the giants provided and fell immediately asleep.

I didn't know how long we slept. When I woke, it was daytime. Layla was already up and had left me there alone. I got up and stepped outside. Based on the position of the sun in the sky, which was bluer in hue than Earth's sun, it was midday. Since it had been dark when we arrived, I ascertained that I'd slept at least a half-day.

That meant we had another half-day at a minimum before the rite would be complete. It could be as much as a day and a half. Either way, we didn't have a lot of time to spare.

I wasn't sure how easy it would be to convince the elves to come with us. Probably no easier than it was proving to convince the giants. At least in this endeavor, we'd have the benefit of elf royalty on our side.

I was temporarily invigorated with energy. I'd probably spend all of it flying with Layla while also giving us enough air to breathe, to find the elves.

Layla hopped on my back, piggy-back style. I gathered the power of air and aether, the two elements I'd need to both fly and ensure that we had breathable air for the journey.

We took off into the skies, the warm air of New Albion striking me in the face as we soared over the giants' village and the barren but once luscious plains of Layla's home world.

I could see the old elven kingdom from miles away. Unlike the giants' village, which looked like something out of the stone age, the elven city was magnificent. Huge buildings with large twisted spires tickled the skyline. Even with the whole region devastated due to the absence of magic, the towers still glistened in New Albion's blue sun.

We soared over the city, looking for signs of life. Something other than a nightcrawler moving around, a patch of green grass, something...

Layla tapped my shoulder and pointed straight ahead at the base of one of the spires. "See the light?" she asked, shouting into my ear.

There was a light in a large picture window that covered one side of the ground level of one of the buildings.

I dove down toward it and did my best to land gracefully. Takeoffs were easy. I was still working on landings. Layla's extra weight didn't help. My legs buckled beneath me, and we tumbled to the ground.

"Sorry about that," I said, dusting myself off as I got back to my feet.

Layla giggled, shaking her head. "I guess I should have been expecting that."

"What's inside here?" I asked.

Layla shrugged. "There are a lot of buildings in the elven kingdom. This is a residential spire. The buildings were charged by magic before. It helped water the plant life inside. Each of these buildings was like its own ecosystem. I suppose, perhaps, a lingering spark of magic might have remained here, keeping the place lit. Or maybe…"

"Or some people might be living here?" I asked.

Layla nodded. "Even so, my father gave the impression that most of the elven kingdom was in safety. It's pretty clear that they aren't here."

"Think anyone's in there?" I asked.

Layla shrugged, stepped up to the glass, and tapped on the window. "I don't see anything. Let's go in and check it out."

I nodded. "Best have your bow ready. Just in case."

Layla nodded and retrieved an arrow from her quiver. She pressed her hand on a small plate beside the door. The plate illuminated at her touch, and the door rolled open, retracting into the left side wall of the entrance.

"Cool door," I said. "Does the thing read your palm or something?"

"As a royal, I have access to any building in the kingdom. So did my father and those who worked in what you'd call law enforcement. But mostly, only those who lived or worked in a spire would have access."

"Something's powering it still, anyway," I said.

Layla nodded. "I'm guessing there's some magic still coursing in the spire."

"The building is powered by magic?" I asked.

"Not exactly. Like I said, it's more that they were charged with magic that kept streams of water flowing within the buildings. We have the technology to extract the hydrogen from the water. It is our energy source."

"You use water like gasoline?" I asked. "That's freaking brilliant."

Layla nodded. "One of many technologies I'm sure my father has dangled in front of the President to gain his loyalty."

We looked around the inside of the building. Water poured through channels along the walls. The channels were connected to troughs where a variety of colorful plants I'd never seen and couldn't identify based on my limited experience with botanicals grew. "This is stunning. I can't imagine how beautiful this city must've been when it was full of magic."

Layla nodded. "It was marvelous, Caspar. Unlike anything you'd see anywhere on Earth. Imagine if Las Vegas was in the middle of a rainforest rather than the desert, and you'd have something of an idea."

"Puts St. Louis to shame. Not to mention our junkyard ranch."

Layla shrugged. "Perhaps. But I like the home we're building. It's quaint, sure, but it's ours."

"Any signs of anyone living here?" I asked.

"There's someone here. At least there was recently," Layla said.

"How can you be sure?"

Layla gestured at one of the plants. "The fruit on this vine was recently picked. Someone is eating from it."

"Are they like grapes?" I asked.

Layla shrugged. "A lot like grapes, actually. Very sweet."

"How long could someone survive in a spire like this?" I asked.

"As long as the magic remains, as long as water still flows. I'm not sure there's much magic here. But it just takes a spark to get one of these spires working. After that, the place produces its own energy."

"Where would someone be hiding?" I asked.

"It's a big spire," Layla said. "Hard to say."

"Maybe call out and ask?"

Layla shrugged. "Anyone home?"

The sound of footsteps from somewhere above us grabbed my attention. "You hear that? Where's it coming from?"

"Could be anywhere. The acoustics in these places can be deceptive. Hard to tell where a sound is really coming from."

"Hello?" I asked out loud, hoping for a response.

The footsteps stopped.

"Whoever is here knows we're here," Layla said.

I nodded to a spiral staircase.

Layla nodded. "We can go floor to floor. Whoever it is, we'll find them eventually."

We followed the staircase from floor to floor. I imagined that the place probably had twenty levels or more. The whole middle of the spire was open, and the staircase contoured alongside the troughs of water and plantlife.

The rooms, if you could call them that, were like an outer shell surrounding the perimeter of the spire.

"It must have been an experience living here," I said.

"Each floor would have housed a whole family," Layla said. "Not just parents and children, but extended family. As many as twenty people lived on each level."

"I believe it," I said as we went from room to room on the first floor. What I guessed were children's toys were scattered haphazardly across the floor of one room. As if whoever lived here left everything behind and there wasn't any time to tell the kids to clean their room.

There wasn't any furniture in the way we'd normally think of couches or dining tables. But there were hammocks, which I imagined were what the elves used in lieu of beds, hanging from beams attached to the walls.

"Anyone here?" Layla asked, her voice echoing through the rooms.

No response.

"Next floor?" I asked.

Layla nodded. She still had her bow ready. Whoever was here

wasn't likely a threat. Based on the fact that they hadn't shown themselves, I imagined they were probably as nervous about encountering us as we were them.

We climbed the stairs to the second floor. As we circled the floor, which was not as cluttered as the first one, we spotted a body lying in one of the hammocks. Whoever it was had long white hair hanging off the side.

We approached, and Layla put her hand on the man's chest.

"Echor?" Layla asked.

"I'm not leaving, Brightborn," the man said. "I'm sorry, Princess. I told your father before. I'm too old for a new adventure. This is my home, and this is where I plan to spend the rest of my days."

"Echor," Layla said. "I'm not with my father. He doesn't even know I'm here."

Echor grunted and rolled to the side, then lowered his feet off his hammock to the ground. "He doesn't know, you say?"

Layla shook her head. "How long have you been here, alone?"

Echor shrugged. "Several months. Who is this? He's not an elf."

"I'm a human," I said. "You can call me Caspar."

"Echor," the man said. "I must ask, why are you two here?"

"My father is trying to conquer Earth," Layla said.

Echor sighed. "Of *course* he is. The news of his plans came as a shock to most of us. But when he told them that the magic would be leaving us, nearly everyone left. A few, like me, stayed behind. They refused to leave."

"How long ago was this?" Layla asked.

"I can't say. I've lost track of time. Living alone, you stop counting days after a while. But he took most of the people to Earth. Then he and the legion returned for a time. But when the legion left, most of the magic went with them."

"How many more survivors are there?" Layla asked.

"I haven't seen a soul since magic left," Echor said. "I don't think many who stayed behind made it. I think I may be the only one who still lives."

"You said he took everyone to Earth?" Layla asked. "Any idea where they went?"

Echor shook his head. "Orders came to dress for a cold climate. Some place he referred to as the Arctic."

I snorted. "So there are elves at the North Pole after all. Priceless."

Layla backhanded me on my arm. "Excuse my husband. He has a knack for making jokes at the worst of moments."

"What?" I asked.

"I don't think I follow the joke," Echor said.

Layla rolled her eyes. "On Earth, they have a myth, a story about a man who lives on the north pole of Earth and has elves working for him to make toys for all the good boys and girls of the world."

"We call him Santa Claus," I said. "He delivers toys every Christmas Eve. I mean, that's the story. The parents really just buy them for their kids and tell them that Santa and the elves brought them."

Echor cocked his head. "So humans lie to their children about their own generosity and gifts?"

I nodded. "More or less."

"How strange," Echor said.

"You have no idea," Layla said. "Humans have a lot of weird customs. They actually think a fairy comes at night after their kids lose a tooth and leave them money instead."

"No one actually believes in the tooth fairy," I said. "Another story that kids are told."

"More lies?" Echor asked.

I shrugged. "I suppose it gives children something to look forward to. Makes the whole trauma of losing a tooth seem...exciting."

"But fairies have no interest in teeth," Echor said. "It doesn't even make sense. What would a fairy do with baby teeth?"

I shrugged. "Good question. I don't have an answer for that."

"Speaking of the fairies," Layla said. "I'm presuming that my father used fairies to take the people to Earth?"

Echor nodded. "I was curious why the fairies would suddenly be working together with the king. For as long as I knew, we'd hunted fairies for sport. Why would they want to help us?"

"The fairies who were helping him," I said, "came from Earth. They are narrowly focused on how humanity has threatened the planet. So much so that they don't realize that backing Brightborn is like using poison to cure a cold. It'll get rid of the cold, but the result will be far more devastating than ever intended."

Echor nodded. "It makes sense. If they'd spoken to the fairies, who've lived here in New Albion from the time of the ancients..."

"That's it," I said. "If we can bring back fairies who've been severed from the Furies, they can testify to Brightborn's misuse of magic! Even if we can't get him convicted in the human courts like Tisiphone proposed, we may be able to present a case that conflicts with Develin's testimony about Brightborn's actions."

"These fairies," Layla said. "They've been hunted for so long. There just aren't many of them. Those who remain, they're notoriously hard to find."

"They were," Echor said. "Before the elves left. But since, I've seen a few buzzing around the city."

"If we can capture one," Layla said.

I interrupted her. "No, not capture one. They can't be treated as prisoners. Let me speak to them. I'm human. They may be more willing to hear me out than they would an elf. No offense."

Layla shrugged. "None taken. That makes sense."

"After that," I said, "we'll head back to the giants. See if they've finished the ritual."

"Echor," Layla said. "Thank you. We'd love it if you came with us."

Echor shook his head. "I'll help you find a fairy. But my position has not changed. I've had a life consumed by chaos and war. For the first time, while it's certainly been lonely, I've known peace. I wish you well in your battle for Earth, but my story ends here. I'll enjoy whatever time I have in peace."

"I can respect that," I said.

Layla shook her head. "I can, too. I don't like it. I'd love to have your support back on Earth. But I totally get it."

"You don't need my support, Princess," Echor said. "I served in your grandfather's court and your father's."

"As high priest," Layla said, smiling. "I remember well. You used to be in charge of the prophecies."

"I retired from service," Echor said. "But technically, until a high priest dies, he retains his title. The current acting high priest is only acting as my proxy until I pass. Given the king's plans, I'm not particularly inclined to pass on my title officially."

"That's been a long time," Layla said. "I was just a young girl when you retired."

Echor laughed and turned to me. "You should have seen her when she was a child. Cute as can be, and a force of nature!"

"Some things never change!" I said, winking at Layla.

"I'll tell you," Echor said. "That little girl could have conquered the world herself. She had the whole legion wrapped around her little finger ever since she was just a toddler."

"I did not," Layla said, shaking her head. "No more than any kid might."

Echor shook his head. "Don't listen to her, Caspar. She was unique. Strong-willed and confident. When other kids were playing and singing songs, she was studying, learning to read, then studying strategies of war in the archives. I think she picked up her first bow at the age of six."

Layla nodded, laughing, "A good four years before most boys start training."

"Impressive," I said, raising my eyebrows. "Mind if I ask why you retired so young?"

"I was in my prime, as far as sorcerers go," Echor said. "Magic matures even as the body starts to decline. But when we had a chance to make peace with the orcs, the king decided instead to raid and pillage their villages. He took advantage of their goodwill to negotiate an end of the conflict, and I would no longer have a part in it. Just as I refuse to have a part in the king's conquests on Earth."

"We could use you," Layla said. "If what you say of the other elves is true. A leader like you at my side could help me rally them to break league with my father."

Echor pressed his lips together. "I appreciate the invitation, but like I said, my journey ends here. In peace, rather than at war."

CHAPTER THIRTY

"I think I should go after the fairies alone," I said.

"Caspar, if any nightcrawlers show up, you'll need my bow."

"Echor," I asked, "have you seen any nightcrawlers in the city?"

"I've only ventured out a few times," he said. "But so far, I don't think they've come here. There are still a few pockets of magic here in the royal quarter. I think it's keeping them away."

I nodded. "I'll be fine, Layla. If the fairies are reluctant to trust elves, perhaps they'll be more open to talking to me if I'm by myself."

"It's too risky, Caspar," Layla said, shaking her head.

"But he is right," Echor said. "You know how the fairies here are. They'll avoid contact at all costs if you're there. Besides, Princess, it would be nice to have a few moments of company before you depart. I've already been alone for so long."

Layla nodded. "Caspar, if you have to, just fly. Don't try to take on any nightcrawlers. You won't be able to stop them."

I smiled. "I know, Layla. I've got this."

Layla hugged me and kissed my cheek. "Just be careful, okay?"

"Always," I said. "When have you ever known me to act recklessly?"

Layla laughed. "Considering the first time we met, you charged an armed giant in an alley and got yourself stabbed."

I bit my cheek. "Okay, you have a point. But at the time, I didn't realize what I was facing."

"If you did, would you have still done it?" Layla asked.

I stroked my chin. "You know, if I knew everything then that I knew now, you bet I would."

"Even though it got you stabbed?" Layla asked.

I shrugged. "A knife to the gut is a small price to pay for meeting the love of my life."

Layla blushed a little. "I love you, Caspar."

I kissed Layla on the forehead. "I love you, too, Princess."

Echor suggested that I try the royal quarters first. That's where he'd seen the fairies before. There was still a little magic lingering there, so it was also the safest part of the elven city. Luckily for me, it was only a few blocks walk from Echor's spire to the royal quarter. Turn right when leaving the spire and pass two more towers, and I'd be right in the royal quarters. Easy peasy lemon squeezy.

The only problem was, without Layla's palm print to access any of the buildings, I'd have to limit my quest to the courtyards surrounding the royal spires. Worst case scenario, I figured, I'd come up empty-handed, and I could come back and get Layla to open up the buildings.

I was already a little tired from the flight. It took quite a bit of magic to get us here. But I wasn't half as exhausted as I was before when we first arrived at the giants' village.

Walking through the city was like exploring a ghost town. It was eerie and quiet. Every step I took sounded louder than it should. Only because I was the only living person there. I had air circling me, giving me enough oxygen to breathe, but I tried to keep it to a minimum to conserve my energy. I still needed to fly back to the giants' village, and after that, I was hopeful that I'd be leading a contingency of giants back to the portal to Earth. If I needed another nap first, I'd take it. But with events continuing to progress on Earth, both my legal situation and whatever Brightborn was scheming in his effort to establish a global government, the longer it took to get back, the more complicated both situations might be.

It was easy to see where the magic still lingered. One of the courts, outside where I guessed the elven royals must've previously lived, had a few trees in bloom—beautiful, multicolored blossoms representing all the colors of the rainbow. From a distance, it looked like a Skittle tree.

I had a sudden urge to taste the rainbow. I was hungry. The tree had fruit. Small, round fruit resembling young apples that were not yet ripe. I didn't know if they were edible, but they did look delicious. Tempting, but if they weren't edible, I wasn't prepared to handle diarrhea. Especially since I had no idea where the closest elven restroom might be.

I released my magic. The trees apparently provided enough oxygen to make the air breathable.

If fairies were the opposite of nightcrawlers, attracted to magic rather than repelled by it, this was where I'd find them.

I sat down at the base of the tree, leaning against its trunk.

I wasn't sure of the best way to attract a fairy. On Earth, they'd mess with you if you used magic in an irresponsible way. They'd probably do the same here, but I didn't want to give them any reason to see me as a foe. I was trying to attract their favor, not just their presence.

I thought about Ensley. Sure, he'd lived most of his life on Earth. He'd pulled his share of pranks on me, and for a time, he'd made my life a living hell. But he had been pure of heart. He'd sacrificed himself for what he knew was true—that Brightborn would be a scourge on the Earth and I offered the planet a better hope.

Somehow, if I could find a fairy here, I'd have to convince them of the same.

I released a few spurts of magic into the air—some of each element. Not enough to tire me out, but something that I hoped might at least get the fairies' attention.

As I released my magic, it settled into the ground around me. The patches of grass, already green, expanded quickly. Grass doesn't normally grow so fast, but like before when I'd charged New Albion's ley lines, the whole place sprouted into life in seconds. Even just a little magic seemed to have the same effect, albeit on a smaller scale.

Surely, the fairies would at least appreciate the fact that I was enlarging what was in short supply—inhabitable, magic-infused land.

I heard a giggle in my left ear.

I turned. A small orb of green light floated there, the frame of a small, female fairy in the middle of it.

She looked at me with wide eyes as her pointy ears wiggled back and forth.

"Hello," I said.

The fairy cocked her head. "Who are you?"

"A friend," I said. "I've come from Earth. My name's Caspar."

"Trixie," the fairy said. "You are a human?"

I nodded. "I am."

"Why are you here?" Trixie asked. "This world is failing."

"I know," I said. "I'm sorry that's happening. But I've come seeking your help. I was brought here by the Furies."

Trixie scratched her head. "I've never met a Fury. You mean, the Furies are real?"

I nodded. "They do not know the elves. The elves have come to Earth."

"The elves will destroy your world, Caspar," Trixie said. "Even as they did this one."

"That's why I need you," I said. "I need a fairy who can tell the Furies of the Earth the truth."

Trixie shook her head. "I'm just a girl. A young fairy. Why would they listen to me?"

I shrugged. "Because you've seen things that the fairies on Earth haven't. We need you, Trixie."

The fairy buzzed around me. I extended my hand, and she rested in my palm. Then, she gasped.

"You have magic, human," Trixie said. "More than you just cast here."

I nodded. "I do."

"Do all humans?" Trixie asked.

"As far as I know, I'm the only one."

"So you are the one?" Trixie asked. "The one meant to heal the divide between our kind?"

I shrugged. "I haven't heard that version of the prophecy. But I'm told that I've been chosen to unite all the races, all peoples."

Trixie climbed up my arm and put her hand on my cheek. "I sense something else. Your soul is bound to…"

"To Layla Brightborn. And also, to one of the drow on Earth."

Trixie yanked her hand away. "You've bound yourself to an elf? Why would you do that?"

"She's not like the others," I said. "Neither of these elves are. They are more like what elves used to be. A long time ago. When you all first came to this world."

Trixie bit her lip. "I don't know…"

"Have you ever met any of Earth's fairies?" I asked. "Some of them were here, for a while, working with the elves."

Trixie nodded. "They are… different than us. They would not listen to what we said. Why should these Furies be any different?"

"I don't know," I said, nodding. "But I know that we have a better chance of saving our world with your help, Trixie."

"My help? But if I went with you, I would be alone."

"How many of you are there here?" I asked.

"Not many," Trixie said. "Especially now that this world's magic has failed."

"You could all come with me," I said. "If not now, then after you come with me and see what I say is true. You could save them all, Trixie."

Trixie scratched the back of her head, glitter flying out of her green hair as she did. "No offense, but we've often been deceived by the elves. Trusting others, particularly since humans and elves are not all that dissimilar, is not easy."

"I get it," I said. "I had a fairy friend before. He connected to me, somehow. He burrowed into the back of my neck. It's how he knew my thoughts. He trusted me to the point that he tried to lead the fairies against the elves."

"You said tried."

I shook my head. "He failed. The other fairies, even though he was their king, killed him."

"And this is supposed to be an attractive proposition?" Trixie asked.

"He didn't have information he could use to appeal to the Furies. All he had was my mind, my intentions. But you are a witness to what the elves did to New Albion."

Trixie pressed her lips together. "If I were to do this, you would have more power, too. Even after I left you. How can I agree to this if I do not yet trust you? And how can I come to trust you if I do not do as you propose?"

"I suppose you'll have to decide for yourself if you can put enough faith in me to make it happen. The very fact that I'm here in New Albion suggests that what I told you is true. One of the Furies sent me here. Her portal remains open, awaiting our return."

"I'll do this, and if what you say is true, you'll return so that I can bring the rest of my people back with you to Earth?"

I smiled, extended my hand with my pinky finger extended. "Do fairies make pinkie promises?"

"Do we ever!" Trixie exclaimed, wrapping herself around my finger. "It means if you aren't telling the truth, I get to take your pinkie!"

"It what?" I asked. I would have yanked my pinkie away from her, but she was so wrapped around it there wasn't any way, minus grabbing her with my opposite hand and pulling her off to stop her.

Trixie giggled. "I'm messing with you, human. What would I ever do with a human pinkie?"

I took a deep breath and exhaled in relief. "Good, I'm rather attached to it myself."

Trixie cocked her head. "Was that supposed to be a joke?"

I nodded. "Yeah. Sorry. I know it's not the best…"

Trixie snorted and started laughing. "'I'm rather attached to it myself!' Oh boy! That's a good one!"

"I know," I said. "I'm something of a comedy genius."

"I'd believe it!" Trixie exclaimed.

She'd soon find out that my jokes were lame, and at least on Earth, elicited more groans than laughs. But for now, I'd take it. I once saw a statistic that more than sixty percent of men believed they'd be great at standup comedy if given a chance. Every man thinks he's hilarious. I'd had enough time preaching and hearing my jokes fall flat on the congregation to know better. If people laughed, it was at my expense when they saw how awkward I looked, starting to chuckle at my own jokes when no one else was laughing.

With the pinkie promise in the books—even if my fifth phalange wasn't on collateral—Trixie burrowed herself into the back of my neck.

I felt a sharp pain, which was quickly assuaged by the fairy's soothing, healing magic.

I didn't have anything to hide. Not from Trixie. Not from anyone. In AA, I'd done a thorough fourth step. I cataloged my character defects obsessively. Then, as the steps indicate, I shared them openly with another human being. Now, I was engaged in the manner of living that the Big Book demands—rigorous honesty. Perhaps that was why, ultimately, something about that lawyer we'd hired rubbed me the wrong way. I didn't want a pardon. I wanted an acquittal. I wanted the truth to be known, God's honest truth to be out and in the light. Sure, I felt guilty about Fred's death because I'm a human being. But I also knew, at the end of the day, it was Brightborn who was ultimately responsible.

My whole body tingled as Trixie's magic spread through my frame. She hadn't said anything yet. When Ensley had done this, I'd heard his voice in my mind. I'd presumed the same would happen with Trixie. But she was exploring my mind, my memories, and evaluating my trustworthiness.

"You stole the Bubblicious?" Trixie asked.

I cocked my head. "Are you serious?"

"When you were a kid. You stole a pack of Bubblicious from the place you called the supermarket."

I snorted. "Yeah. Is that really an issue?"

"I don't know..."

"Keep looking," I said. "I didn't keep it."

"Ah!" Trixie exclaimed. "Your mom made you bring it back and apologize to some woman called Manager!"

"It was a job title," I said. "I don't think that was the woman's actual name. Is that really the worst thing you found in my memories?"

"No," Trixie said. "The stuff when you were drinking...but you've made amends for that. It is honorable. I was just curious about this Bubblicious stuff. It looks, and from what your memories told me, it seems incredible."

I smiled. "It is. For the first couple minutes at least. It's like an explosion of sugar and imitation fruit flavors in your mouth."

Trixie started giggling again. "Oh my! I want to blow a bubble! Can I blow a bubble?"

I nodded. "You realize, one piece of Bubblicious is like the size of your whole head. A whole pack would last you a long time."

"Forget the price of your pinkie. Get me some Bubblicious. Oh, and some Fun Dip, and I'll do what you've asked with the Furies."

"It's a deal," I said, shaking my head. A pack of gum and some Fun Dip were a small price to pay for a move that could potentially save the world. "I'll even get you some Pixie Styx."

"That sounds disgusting!" Trixie protested.

"It's not that different than Fun Dip. Just comes in a straw rather than a packet with a sugar spoon."

"Pixies are like fairies, sort of. We're related. Would you want to eat something called ground-up human dust?"

I bit my lip. "Probably not. But it's just a name. I promise you if you eat Pixie Styx, you will not be committing any form of cannibalism."

"Still," Trixie said. "I think I'll pass. I just can't get past the name."

"It's okay," I said. "They aren't that great, anyway. Plenty of other candies you can try. I'll get you whatever you want."

I felt a sharp pain as Trixie extracted herself from the back of my neck. Again, her magic quickly healed the wound. I rubbed the spot where she exited.

"It's a deal," Trixie said. "I'll go back with you. I'll tell the Furies the truth about the elves, and I'll feast like a queen on your Earth delicacies of sugary-sweet goodness."

"First, we have to go back and get Layla."

"The elf?" Trixie asked. "I'm so nervous."

"She won't hurt you," I said. "I promise."

"I know, I know... I've seen your memories. I know she's good. But you must remember, to see an elf... Would you cuddle a viper, even if you had evidence that it was tame?"

I shook my head. "Probably not. But Layla isn't a viper. I promise."

"I know," Trixie said, taking a deep breath and releasing it. "But you'll have to excuse me if I keep my distance. From her, and from your cat."

I laughed. "I can't blame you on the latter part. He doesn't appreciate the smell of fairy."

"No cats do," Trixie said. "Not that I've met many. The elves only had a few felines, and from what I've seen in your memories, they aren't exactly like yours. But one thing they did have in common. Well, two things, actually. They don't like fairies, and like the elves, they are determined to dominate the world."

I smiled. "A fair assessment. Just so long as he thinks he already rules the world, we're good. I'm not one to ever tell him otherwise."

CHAPTER THIRTY-ONE

Having Trixie as an ally was helpful on several fronts. First, of course, she'd help make our case to the Furies. Second, I had the ability to make portals again. On a hostile New Albion, it was an enviable ability. With a fairy gate, I could not only get Layla and me back to the giants quickly, but we could create a portal in the giants' village that would take us all back to the gateway back to Earth. It also meant, ultimately, that the giants wouldn't have to use the rest of the magic they had remaining to make the trip. One less reason, I supposed, for them to refuse.

Not that I intended for the giants to ever come back. Nor did I think they'd ever want to. However, if they were at all reluctant to come with me, at least having the option to come back to New Albion on the table rather than presenting this as an irreversible decision might make their choice less anxiety stricken.

I was able to visualize the inside of Echor's spire. We created a portal, Trixie and I, and stepped through it together.

"Well, welcome back!" Layla exclaimed as we stepped through.

"It looks like it was a success!" Echor said with enthusiasm.

Trixie ducked behind my shoulder, peering over it to look at the two elves.

"She's a bit nervous being around elves," I said.

"Understandable," Echor said. "I must apologize on behalf of my race. We've not treated your kind with the honor you deserve."

Trixie huffed. "Thank you, sir."

"Just call me Echor," he said. "Sir is not necessary."

"As a Brightborn," Layla said. "I also apologize for our past indiscretions. It wasn't right to hunt your people like that."

"I appreciate it," Trixie said, her voice hushed more than before.

"She's reluctant," I said. "With good reason. But she's agreed to help us, provided once we've secured her position with the Furies, we come back to bring the rest of the New Albion fairies back with us to Earth."

Layla nodded, making eye contact with Trixie. "If we can't get the Earth fairies on our side, it will be of great value to have you as an ally."

Trixie nodded. "I will do what I can to help. Do not forget, Caspar. Our agreement also included Bubblicious."

I chuckled. "I won't forget. All the Earth candy and gum you could ever want."

"Are you sure you won't come with us?" I asked Echor. "We could really use your help, too."

"My decision has been made," Echor said. "It was a pleasure to meet you, Caspar, and a great gift to have a chance to enjoy a conversation with my princess."

"All right, Trixie. You ready to go meet the giants?" I asked.

Trixie nodded. "I like giants. They have always been kind to us."

I smiled. "All right, then. Let's go."

Layla hugged Echor and whispered something in his ear. He

nodded. I didn't bother asking. I was sure, more or less, that she was simply offering her gratitude for his assistance and well-wishes for his last days on New Albion.

I extended my hand, and he shook it awkwardly. I don't think handshakes were a part of elven custom, but he took the cue and picked up on the significance of the gesture.

"May the grace of the Furies be on your side," Echor said.

"Peace be with you," I said, nodding.

I visualized the giants' village, and drawing on fairy magic, formed a portal. Layla and I stepped through, with Trixie flying close behind.

We appeared right in front of the hut where Brag'mok and Targigoth were conducting their sweat lodge ritual.

Gronk approached us. "You were faster than anticipated."

I nodded and gestured toward Trixie, who perched herself on my shoulder. "We had the help of a fairy to travel back here."

"Impressive," Gronk said. "How are you, Trixie?"

"Wait," I said. "You two know each other?"

"Oh, we go way back!" Trixie exclaimed.

Gronk laughed. "We have a pretty strong relationship with the fairies. We've striven to preserve whatever magic used to vivify our planet, even as the elves wasted it in their effort to eliminate us."

"You didn't use magic to fight back against them?" I asked.

"We used what we had to in order to survive," Gronk said. "But we did not use magic as a weapon."

Layla shook her head. "It's incredible that you've been able to thwart the elves so effectively for centuries without using magic. If you had, think of the tragedies that your people had endured that could have been avoided."

"If we had, it would have expedited the crisis that has now befallen our world. We did what we could to sustain the planet, despite the likes of your father and those who came before him who squandered whatever magic they could find in an effort to squash our people."

"Then you'll be especially valuable allies on Earth," I said. "To face Brightborn again without resorting to his methods."

"Except for what you can do, of course," Layla piped up.

I nodded. "But even I am not prepared to weaponize the elemental powers."

"You can use them with or without our assistance," Gronk said, "to tame whatever the elven king attempts. If we'd had such mastery over the elements that it seems you have as the chosen one, we could have simply shut down the king when he tried to leverage the power of magic against us."

"So you're saying you agree that I'm the chosen one?" I asked.

"I'm saying," Gronk said. "That if the high priest confirms what you've told us, and *if* you are indeed the one the prophet foretold, then you should be able to quell any act of elemental or magical violence."

I pressed my lips together. "Well, let's hope that we get good news from the high priest. Any idea how much longer it will be?"

Gronk shook his head. "It could take another day. Or they could emerge at any moment. Either way, in my experience, the ancestors typically reveal something different to the high priest than whatever we thought was likely."

I huffed. "When dealing with priests and prophecies, interpretations are often vague and varied. I'm sure, based on what I know of your traditions, the answer will be just and honorable."

"Come with me," Gronk said. "I imagine all three of you could use something to eat."

I nodded. "That would be generous of you."

"Thank you," Layla said.

Gronk grunted and nodded. "You will be the first elf to dine with giants since our first ancestors arrived in New Albion, Princess."

A subtle smile formed at the corner of Layla's mouth. "Then I should say that I am quite honored. This is a rather momentous occasion."

"Indeed," Gronk said. "Momentous, or foreboding. I haven't decided which, yet."

CHAPTER THIRTY-TWO

Who would've thought that giants could be vegetarians? When I think about giants, I imagine massive beasts stomping around with their fee-fi-fo-fums and chomping on giant hunks of meat. Not a turkey leg. That would be too small. Maybe the hindquarter of a bull or something.

What they served us looked like quinoa, some kind of blubbery protein like tofu, and a collection of greens all mixed up in one bowl. By itself, it was rather bland. But then they passed their dressing. I don't know what was in it. I was a little bit afraid to ask. But it totally transformed the bowl into something scrumptious. A little bit like soy sauce, but with a richer, deeper, less salty flavor. It had a hint of sweetness to it.

"The giants have always been rumored to be good cooks," Layla said. "I had no idea."

"Do you know what all this stuff is?" I asked.

Layla shrugged. "Mostly. No clue what's in the dressing, though. That stuff is amazing. It's like sex in a bottle!"

"I seriously hope you're being metaphorical."

"My God, Caspar. Of course I am. Ew! What did you think I was suggesting?"

I chuckled to myself. "Sorry, I knew you weren't being literal. What can I say? Adolescent sense of humor."

Trixie didn't eat much. Just a couple grains of their quinoa-like substance was more than enough for her. So, she was buzzing around the room greeting the various giants who'd showed up to watch us eat.

Yes, us eating was almost like a show to these giants. Not entirely shocking. I knew, from my Biblical studies, that meals between notable persons were often public affairs. That's why Jesus was so heavily criticized about who he ate with. Sharing a meal with someone was more than an occasion for small talk in those days.

Gronk was the only giant who joined us. He was clearly their leader. We sat around a table together. It was an odd arrangement. Layla and I had to stand on our chairs to reach the top of the table. They offered us boosters, blocks of wood meant for giant children so they could reach the table. Based on the way the giants were joking about it, Layla declined, and I followed suit. Sure, the booster would have been practically beneficial. But since boosters were reserved for children, it would also be mildly humiliating.

Aside from such visual oddities, however, it struck me that this meal must've been something quite momentous for the giants. For the first time ever, both a human and an elf joining a giant for a meal. No wonder the whole village, albeit not at once, rotated in to watch us while we ate. For them, this was a meal on the scale of Jesus' Last Supper or the first Thanksgiving with the pilgrims. Sadly, what followed those meals wasn't pleasant. Jesus was betrayed, and well, we know how the colonists treated the natives.

Still, I was optimistic that this meal portended only good things.

If the giants came with us to Earth, we'd have to throw something together, adding Aerin and the drow. We'd serve McDonald's fries. Who doesn't like McDonald's fries? As far as the giants knew, they'd be luxurious. Maybe we'd throw together a vegetarian pizza.

Not St. Louis-style Provel cheese and cracker crust. We'd have to go deep dish, Chicago style. Much better, despite what the native St. Louisans might try to argue.

One step at a time. At the moment, I simply appreciated the gesture. Despite what Jack might tell you about his whole beanstalk debacle, the giants were good people.

I barely finished my last bite when one of the giants came bursting into the room.

"Gronk, sir! The ritual is done! The high priest would like to see our guests immediately."

Gronk nodded. We climbed down from our oversized chairs to the cheers of the giants who were still gathered in the room. It was awkward. Should I belch? In some cultures, burping after a meal is complimentary. I decided against it. They were already cheering. I didn't want to spoil the moment with a potential cross-cultural faux pas.

Layla and I followed Gronk outside, past a bonfire that the giants had built while we were eating. We approached Targigoth and Brag'mok, who stood side-by-side outside of the hut where they'd held their sweat lodge ritual.

Targigoth was holding a large scroll in his hands.

I approached them. Targigoth extended both hands, holding the scroll out to me.

"What is this?" I asked, taking it in both hands.

"It is the final prophecy," Targigoth said. "The ancestors tell us that the final seal can only be broken by the chosen one and that each of the races has their own final prophecy. If you open it and prove yourself the chosen one, and the contents of the prophecy do not tell us otherwise, the ancestors advised that we follow you to Earth."

I exchanged glances with Layla. "How do I open it?"

"Only the chosen one," Brag'mok explained, "can channel all five elements. Like the prisms that contained the celestial artifacts held by the drow, I believe a similar method will open the seal on the scroll."

"I concur," Targirath said. "It is fitting that all of the giants who remain have gathered to witness this event."

I cleared my throat. "All right, I'll see what I can do. Does it matter which element I use first?"

Targigoth shrugged. "We cannot say. I imagine it does not matter. Once all five elements are channeled into the seal, I believe, the prophecy will be revealed."

Trixie perched herself on my shoulder. "How exciting!"

"You have a fairy?" Brag'mok asked. "What of the elves?"

"The elves are already on Earth," I said. "But she's agreed to come with us and help with our appeal to the Furies."

"You are brave," Targigoth said, addressing Trixie. "We honor your decision, no matter the outcome of this revelation."

"Thanks!" Trixie said, giggling after she spoke.

I focused on the seal. It looked as though it was made of wax, but based on the fact that it had lasted for so many centuries, I figured there was a lot more to it than that. The seal itself was stamped with a symbol vaguely resembling an oak tree.

I remembered the trials. How I'd acquired water first and used it to subdue fire and then the subsequent elements in their proper order. It struck me that in this instance, it might be best to do them in the opposite order. Maybe it didn't matter. But it seemed appropriate.

I gathered aether, the human spirit, and focused it into the seal. The seal started to glow a golden hue. Then, I cast air, earth, fire, and water in that order. All the elements swirled around the seal in a luminescent display. Then, with a loud sound, vaguely similar to a trumpet's blast, the seal shattered, exploding into a shower of colors, almost like fireworks.

Targigoth unrolled the scroll. He examined it carefully, narrowing his eyes with a definite focus.

"What does it say?" I asked.

Targigoth cleared his throat. "It's unbelievable. Uncanny in its precision."

"And?" Layla asked.

Targigoth waived his hand. "Everyone gather around. This is something all should hear at once."

The giants surrounded us, their bodies casting a shadow over all of us.

"The noble giants shall fulfill their call," Targigoth said. "Under the leadership of the Chosen, they shall save the Earth from those who would harm it, human and elf alike. They shall serve the one who wields the power of the Divine, and together, they shall immerse Earth in blood."

"Immerse the Earth in blood?" I whispered to Layla. "What does that mean?"

Layla shook her head, "I don't know."

The whole crowd remained silent for a moment. Then, Gronk released a shout. His voice echoed back at us from a distance. Then, Brag'mok raised his fist into the air and shouted, too. Then all the giants did the same.

When their shouts subsided, Targigoth put his hand on my shoulder. "The giants are in your service, Naayak."

"Naayak?" I asked. "Only the drow have called me that."

"It is the name, known to all, for he who would lead us. For the chosen one."

CHAPTER THIRTY-THREE

Drawing on the magic Trixie left within me when she merged with me, I cast a portal leading to the one that Tisiphone had made. The one that would take us back to Earth.

I stepped through first, holding Layla's hand with Trixie on my shoulder. Brag'mok wasn't far behind. Gronk, Targigoth, and the rest of the giants followed. It was only a couple steps from the first portal that took us to Tisiphone's gateway and the gateway itself.

It's a bit jarring going from one portal directly into a transplanetary gateway. It's like your body is pulled apart on a molecular level, then put back together again just in time to be blown apart into a billion pieces all over again.

And I thought Humpty Dumpty had it rough.

I wobbled a bit on my feet as I reappeared in the stone circle. I moved out of the way, almost falling into Tisiphone's arms, who was waiting for my return.

It was a good thing I moved as fast as I did. Otherwise, I would have ended up on the bottom of a pile of giants who fell over one another as they set foot on Earth like a bunch of linemen trying to recover a fumble.

I looked around. On either side of Tisiphone stood the other two Furies, Alecto and Megara. Outside the perimeter of the stones, Aerin was standing there with Jag on one side and her father, Elrand, on the other. A whole crowd of drow, maybe half of all of them, were gathered behind them.

"What is going on?" I asked, running my fingers through my hair.

"You've brought the giants," Tisiphone said, not answering my question.

I nodded. "I did."

"And a fairy from the otherworld?" Alecto and Megara asked in unison.

I nodded. "Yes. This is Trixie."

"It's such an honor to meet you!" Trixie exclaimed.

"This is good," Tisiphone said. "Especially in light of all that has happened."

"But I've brought the giants. That means no Fury. No earthquake, right?"

"We will not unleash our wrath on your account," the three Furies said in unison.

"That's a relief." I nodded.

"But others have scorned our rule, and our fury cannot be appeased."

"Well, who the hell pissed you guys off now?" I asked.

The three Furies exchanged glances with one another. "Your other wife told us that your name has been cleared."

"What?" I asked, scratching my head, both relieved on that account but frustrated that they were still avoiding my questions.

"You were pardoned," Tisiphone said. "But Brighborn has evaded justice."

I snorted. "Of course. The President probably pardoned me to avoid dragging Brightborn's name through the mud."

"The Princess Nightshade may enter the circle," the three Furies said.

Aerin stepped inside and, wrapping her arms around me, had tears in her eyes. "I wish you had been here."

"Why?" I asked. "What happened?"

"After you left," Aerin said. "Human agents, the FBI, came and raided the ranch. My sisters rose up against them. It was a bloodbath."

I shook my head. "You attacked the FBI?"

"They fired the first shots," Aerin said. "It was in self-defense, but we lost nearly half of our number."

"What about the agents?" I asked.

"Dead. All of them." Aerin said. "We expected another assault. But instead, Collin called and informed us that a pardon was issued the moment your indictment was processed by the grand jury."

"If you just took out a whole team of agents, why would he pardon me?" I asked.

Aerin shook her head. "I cannot say. That is why we came here. It took several trips in the truck, but we made it. I came to seek the counsel of the Furies and see if they could bring you back, but they refused. They said your quest was of greater importance."

"It was," Tisiphone said. "After you left, we summoned Develin and the fairies. I anticipated your success and demanded they await a decision upon the testimony of the giants."

"The other fairies are here?" I asked.

Tisiphone shook her head. "They refused our summons."

I cocked my head. "They can do that?"

"They rejected our rule," Tisiphone said. "An unseelie abom-ination!"

"Unseelie! Unseelie! Unseelie!" the three Furies echoed in concert.

Trixie left my shoulder and buzzed around me before approaching the Furies. "Why would a fairy reject our mothers?"

"They've bound themselves to the elf king," Tisiphone said. "It is they who have unleashed our fury."

"Bound themselves?" I asked.

Trixie turned back to me. "It means they melded their minds together, the way I entered you before. Only to such a degree that now they are inseparable."

I shook my head. "There has to be a way to appease you. I've brought the giants. The three races, the protectors of the Earth, are now here, together."

"This is pleasing to us," the three Furies said before Tisiphone began speaking alone. "But it is they who scorned us. You cannot atone for their unseelie error."

"But that's exactly what Brightborn wants!" I protested. "He's trying to unleash a terror on this world, to force the world's governments to bend their collective knee to his rule!"

Tisiphone shook her head. "I am sorry for this, Naayak. But our wrath has already been set in motion. In three days' time, the earth will quake."

I grunted. "There has to be a way to undo it. I can't allow this."

"It is not only Brightborn whose murderous ways demand our justice," Tisiphone said. "But now your government has assaulted the drow. The humans, too, must be punished."

"So, what is it?" I asked. "Are you unleashing this earthquake to punish the unseelie fairies or the human government?"

"Both!" the three Furies said at once.

"We've come to defend the Earth!" Targigoth interjected, stepping in front of me. "We came to testify to the elves' treacheries."

"We are pleased that you have rejoined us," Tisiphone said. "But we no longer require your testimony. Brightborn has already shown us his true nature."

"How is this justice?" I asked. "The people who will suffer from this earthquake are innocent."

"I am the Fury of the unceasing," Alecto said. "My wrath is not uncalculated. Those who suffer are those who have merited it, I can guarantee."

"But this earthquake will destroy a whole city, and more!" I shouted. "Most of those people don't even know who Brightborn is, nor do they have any say in what the President has done!"

"Our ways are not your ways, human," Alecto said. "Once this is done, I trust you will return to us that you will uphold your agreement to unify the elementals with the giants and us. For this is one battle in a larger war for the Earth. Do not give us reason to question your loyalty."

I dropped my head, dejected. "I don't know what to say."

Layla and Aerin each put a hand on each of my shoulders. "Let's go," Layla said. "We've heard enough."

"There's nothing more we can do here," Aerin said.

I took a deep breath and exhaled. "All right. Well, thanks for whatever."

"The fairy must stay with us," Tisiphone said.

"Trixie? But she came with me."

"I will remain with the Furies," Trixie said, flying over to me and putting one hand on my cheek. "But my power remains within you. Do what you can, and I will do what I must."

CHAPTER THIRTY-FOUR

With a fairy portal, I brought us all back to the junkyard ranch except for Jag, who drove the truck back.

The city of St. Louis had seen several disasters in its history. Of course, it had been a while since the last. There was the great earthquake, the one that sent the Mississippi running in reverse. But after that, in the mid-1800s, there was a massive fire that destroyed much of the city. Cities tend to build or rebuild to prevent a repeat of the latest disaster. In the wake of the fire, most of the city was rebuilt with brick, hence the nickname of St. Louis being "Brick City." Of course, a lot of the city that had been built since was constructed differently. But the older parts of the city, much of it still in use, was made of brick. Wise if you're worried about another fire. Not so great to weather an earthquake.

"Where are all the bodies?" Aerin asked as we arrived.

"I imagine someone from the government came to gather them," I said. "Probably while you were gone."

"We have traditions for honoring our dead!" Aerin shouted, clenching her fist. "It would be one thing if they just gathered their own dead, but they can't take ours!"

I put my hand on Aerin's shoulder. She shrugged it off. "Not the sensation I want to feel right now."

I took a step back. I'd nearly forgotten that when she and I touched, she was consumed with desire. A consequence of the rings that bound us. "I'm sorry, Aerin."

"I can't believe the elf king has such an influence over your government. It's offensive."

"I agree," I said. "Perhaps we can honor them as if their bodies were still here?"

Aerin nodded. "We can conduct the death rite. But their spirits will not rest. Not with their bodies defiled."

I nodded. I didn't know the ins and outs of what the drow believed with respect to the afterlife, but I wasn't going to try and minimize her pain by offering a Christian explanation as an alternative. As far as I was concerned, it was not so important what happened to the bodies of the dead.

Some Christians abhor the notion of cremation on the grounds that the Bible says that Christ will raise the dead on the last day. But the way I saw it, if God formed humanity from the dust of the ground in the beginning, he could certainly re-form our bodies again from ashes. Considering the fact that these bodies would go unclaimed, I imagined that's what would happen. They'd be cremated and disposed of.

"Do whatever you need to do to honor them," I said. "I'm sorry this happened. If I'd been here, maybe things would have gone differently."

Aerin shook her head. "You might have saved their lives. But you could not have known."

"I should have," I said. "When I was broken out of custody, it was unthinkable that they wouldn't come after me."

"Still," Aerin said. "How could you have known they'd open fire on us?"

I shook my head. "I don't know. Still, I'm sorry I wasn't here."

Aerin nodded. "Do what you need to do. I will honor our

fallen, along with the surviving drow. But you have bigger issues to face."

I walked inside the farmhouse, Layla at my side. Agnus was curled up in a shivering ball in the corner of our bedroom.

I knelt and picked him up.

"You all right, buddy?" I asked.

"Humans suck," Agnus piped back.

I nodded. "I agree. A lot of them do. Did you see what happened?"

"I saw everything, Casp."

"You saw the government gather the bodies?" I asked.

Agnus snorted. "No. It was elves."

I looked at Layla, and her eyes met mine. "Elves, you say?"

"I hid here the whole time. Those elves suck, too, by the way."

"Again," I said, chuckling, "I can't disagree with you."

"That's interesting," Layla said. "Why would my father want the bodies?"

I shook my head. "Probably just to spite the drow. He's spent time with them before."

Layla sighed. "Makes sense. He's often done the same to the giants. Collected their dead before the giants could do it themselves."

"Why did he do that?" I asked.

"It's a head game," Layla said. "The giants, like the drow, believe that their death rites have importance. They're necessary to give their spirits rest."

I nodded. "I remember. That's what Brag'mok was originally here for. To collect B'iff's body."

"I wouldn't be at all surprised if it wasn't the FBI who attacked. It might have been the legion, dressed to look like agents."

"An interesting theory," I said. "Makes sense. It just doesn't seem like the FBI I know to shoot first. Not if the drow weren't fighting."

"I suppose we can't know for sure," Layla said. "But my father's people collected the bodies. Not just the agents, or the legionnaires as the case may be, but the drow, too. It's definitely a part of my father's MO."

"Doesn't defiling the dead run the risk of pissing off your enemy?" I asked.

Layla nodded. "An angry enemy is often impulsive. Less calculating. He's trying to bait us to attack before we're ready. When he has the upper hand."

"It works. I was inclined to do exactly that after Aerin finished her funeral rituals."

"I don't think his goal is to simply win another battle against us," Layla said. "He knows this would also distract you from the issue with the Furies."

I shook my head. "But why? You'd think that dealing with the Furies would be a distraction. Force me to have to deal with that, to try and save as many lives as possible when the earthquake happens."

"Then again," Layla said, pinching her chin. "My father knows that I know his strategies. If he somehow managed to convince the fairies to bind themselves to him, to stoke the Furies' wrath, he may be trying to drive a wedge between you and the Furies."

"Clearly," I said. "But in that case, why do something like this? Why assault the drow and steal their bodies?"

"To divide your attention, and to divide us. He knows that Aerin will want to fight first. The earthquake, this city, is of secondary concern to her. But it's your primary worry."

I continued petting Agnus as I thought about what Layla said. "If Aerin knows that Brightborn has the bodies, she'll want to recover them. Maybe he isn't trying to urge us to fight in vengeance so much as to send the drow on a wild goose chase to find the bodies. But he stoked the Furies' wrath because he knows if I'm occupied dealing with that, I won't be able to help the drow."

"Caspar put me down," Agnus piped up.

I set him down on the ground. "Everything okay, Agnus?"

"Have you been fraternizing with nasty fairies again?" Agnus asked.

"I have," I said. "Why do you ask?"

"Because you smell like butt!"

I pressed my lips together. "You know what, Agnus? You're brilliant!"

Agnus cocked his head. "Because I know the smell of fairies and butts?"

I chuckled. "No, because Brightborn doesn't know that I have fairy powers again."

"What are you thinking, Caspar?" Layla asked.

"Maybe we can do both," I said. "Your father doesn't know that I can portal myself, and even the bodies if we find them. We only have three days. But if I can do that, maybe I can find the bodies, bring them back to Aerin, and still have time to try and do something about the earthquake."

Layla shook her head. "We don't even know what we're going to do about the quake. You heard what the Furies said. It's already in motion. It can't be stopped."

"That's not necessarily true," I said. "I have power over the element of earth. I just don't know if I should use it."

"Wait," Layla said. "I can't believe I didn't think about that before."

"Agnus did," I said. "He suggested it back before I even turned myself in to the authorities."

"It's brilliant!" Layla exclaimed.

I nodded. "Except your father had that same idea. When he abducted me, he said, and I quote, 'it's a shame we don't know someone who has the power over earth.'"

Layla scratched her head. "He wouldn't say that if he wasn't trying to plant the idea in your head."

I bit my lip. "I was wrong. When I was talking to the Furies.

Unleashing the earthquake isn't what Brightborn wants. Not directly. He couldn't care less about the destruction it will cause, and it has nothing to do with his intention to force the government into submission. He wants me to try and stop it. His whole goal is to drive a wedge between the Furies and me. To divide the Furies from the elementals, and therefore the giants as well."

"Then what do we do?" Layla asked. "We can't stop the earthquake. But we can't let it happen, either."

A wave of anger came over me. I wanted to punch the wall, but I was worried if I did, I might take down the whole farmhouse. Not because I had such a forceful strike, sans infusing my punch with magic, but because the house was barely standing as it was.

Hungry. Angry. Lonely. Tired. An acronym, in AA HALT. Any of those conditions could put our sobriety in jeopardy. I wasn't going to drink. But I needed clarity.

"I need to go to a meeting," I said.

"What?" Layla asked. "You're seriously worried about drinking right now with so much at stake?"

"I'm always worried about drinking again," I said. "But that's not the point. I need to think. It won't take that long. I can portal myself there and back again. There's a meeting in about fifteen minutes I can catch."

Layla nodded. "Do what you need to do."

"Just keep an eye on Aerin," I said. "Make sure she doesn't do anything foolish. If we can find where the bodies are, maybe there'll be something we can do to help."

CHAPTER THIRTY-FIVE

I portaled myself to the spot behind the dumpster at the AA clubhouse. I'd used that spot before to portal in and out of meetings, back when I had Ensley's power. Trixie's power was the same.

It was a relatively safe spot to teleport myself. Of course, there was always a risk that some kind of object might be in the space I visualized. When Ensley was first teaching me how to use this power, I inadvertently portaled myself right into one of the pews at my former church. My butt cheeks were, literally, stuck in the wood of the pew.

Jokes about butts going "pew" were begging to be told. For once in my life, though, I had withheld my tongue. Ensley had a sense of humor, but it wasn't the sort of joke my late fairy friend would have appreciated. He was a connoisseur of practical jokes. Not dad jokes.

Thankfully, no mishaps happened on this occasion. Though, it was purely by dumb luck. Someone had tossed an old sofa that used to be in the entryway of the AA club behind the dumpster. I was about six inches away from having a leg stuck in one of the sofa's arm rests.

A leg stuck in an arm. Probably room for another joke there. Not as good as a butt stuck in a pew, though.

I made my way to the meeting room in the AA clubhouse. Rusty, my sponsor, was already there. He had a habit of arriving at most meetings about a half-hour in advance. He usually made the crappy coffee that was always flowing at our meetings. Our group had one of those massive Bunn coffee makers. The thing could make a pot in just a couple minutes, so I wasn't sure why it warranted him arriving a half-hour early. A bit ironic, actually, that the group spent so much on an industrial quality coffee maker while we never served anything above the grade of Maxwell House.

I once brought in a bag from Kaldi Coffee House, a St. Louis original and some of the best coffee ever roasted anywhere. People bitched about it. Pearls to swine, I suppose. Not that AA members were pigs. They were good people, but when it came to their taste in coffee, they were lowbrow.

Not that I was too good to refuse a cup. I grabbed the carafe and filled up one of the styrofoam cups that were stacked beside it.

"Been a while, Caspar," Rusty said as I took my seat. "I've been worried about your sobriety since you lost your church."

I nodded. "That's fair. I should have probably let you know what was going on. Surely you've seen some of it on the news."

Rusty shook his head. "I don't watch the news. It isn't good for my sobriety."

I chuckled. "Again, a fair point. I don't watch much of it myself anymore."

"So you were on the news? Usually, when people in these rooms make the news, there's more rather than less reason to be concerned."

I smiled. "You're right. And you wouldn't be wrong. I was in a bit of a legal mess for a minute. Blamed for something that was really someone else's fault. But I still had some responsibility for what happened."

"Did someone get hurt?" Rusty asked.

"Someone died," I said. "If I hadn't been there, it wouldn't have happened."

"You had that on your conscience, and you didn't find a way to get your ass to a meeting?"

I sighed. "I should have. I don't know. I was just so over-whelmed with everything I had to do."

"I can imagine," Rusty said. "But you're not drinking?"

"Nope," I said, shaking my head. "Don't even have the desire, really."

Rusty smiled. "You've come a long way."

"One day at a time," I quipped, reciting one of the many AA platitudes that we often quoted in meetings as if they were Bible verses.

"But are you still working your program?" Rusty asked.

I took a sip of my coffee. "I'm here, aren't I? What is it they say, meeting makers make it?"

"Meeting makers who are communicating with their sponsors and working the steps," Rusty said. "You've seen as I have a lot of people who just show up to meetings and don't do the work."

"Very few of those stay sober for long."

Rusty nodded and took a sip from his own cup of coffee. "When's the last time you did a fourth step?"

I shrugged. "When we did it. Like, five years ago."

"What's the tenth step, Caspar?"

I sighed. "Continued to take personal inventory and when we were wrong promptly admitted it."

"I'm not going to ask you about this legal situation since it seems you've found a way out of it. But have you taken a personal inventory over it?"

"Like I said, I wasn't primarily responsible."

"But you said it yourself, Caspar. If you weren't there… You're still blaming yourself."

"Which means I've taken inventory!"

Rusty shook his head. "Wallowing in guilt is not the same thing as taking inventory. We blamed ourselves for all kinds of shit when we were drinking. That wasn't the same thing as doing a fourth step, of taking inventory of our role in things that happened."

I took another sip of coffee. It wasn't just Fred's death that was weighing on me. It was the deaths of the drow warriors. I wasn't even there. Again, Brightborn was probably the one who owned the lion's share of guilt. But the drow had come to fight at my side, and when the battle came, I wasn't there.

Sure, I had my reasons. I did what had to be done, going to New Albion to find the giants. I'd probably saved them from the eventual devastation of their fallen world. Their magic wouldn't have sustained their village forever. But the prophecy had said that Earth would be immersed in blood. I was anxious that, given what I'd done, I'd simply brought the giants to Earth to die…as half the drow had died.

Rusty had a point. I already had more blood on my hands than I could ever wash off. Not to even mention the hundreds of thousands of giants on New Albion whom I'd never met, who didn't make it to the village. Then, there was B'iff and Ensley. Again, not my fault, but I still had a role in their deaths. I was there. I couldn't save them.

We started the meeting. Rusty was chairing. We said the Serenity Prayer. Another member recited "How it Works" from the Big Book.

"Does anyone have a topic they'd like to talk about today?" Rusty asked.

I raised my hand. "Yeah, I'm Caspar. I'm an alcoholic."

"Hi, Caspar," the rest of the room said in unison.

"Shit happens," I said.

"Shit happens?" Rusty asked.

"Yeah. How do we deal with shit that happens in sobriety? I mean, I've read the promises in the Big Book. Hell, sometimes we read them aloud at the end of meetings. It makes it sound like sobriety is all unicorns and rainbows. But it isn't. Shit still happens. Sometimes the shit is deeper than anything we ever dealt with while we were still drinking. How do we handle that and stay sober? How can we deal with shit happening without, at the very least, spiraling out of control in a cycle of shame and guilt?"

Rusty smiled. "A good topic. Who'd like to start?"

We went around the table clockwise, each person sharing their thoughts and experiences. No one had any magic answers that made my problems disappear. No one ever did at meetings. AA wasn't about solving our problems or making them disappear. It was about helping us through the piles of shit in our lives without drinking.

Holy hell, I didn't realize how true it was. Shit really does happen. Members talked about how they'd lost loved ones, spouses, and even their children, in sobriety. One member expressed his frustration that after he'd been sober for six months, he'd still had to go to jail for things he'd done in the past. Another member, an older woman named Cathy who had double-digit years of sobriety, revealed that when she was eight years sober, she was fired from a job that she'd somehow managed to maintain even when she was drinking.

Sometimes, in meetings, the topic leads into drunkalogues. People trying to one-up each other with stories about the awful things they have done or who'd been through the most crap. Those meetings aren't usually all that helpful. This wasn't like that. These were stories of people who'd had to deal with all kinds of suffering even while sober. It wasn't a matter of sizing up one's tribulations compared to others. It was about solidarity.

I wasn't unique. Sure, none of the members had so many

deaths weighing on their shoulders. But who was I to argue that the shit I was dealing with, that my experience of frustration, guilt, and pain, was worse when hearing the perspective of someone who'd lost a child, or gone to jail for more than a few hours, or lost a job that had defined them for years?

That last one, I could relate to. I'd experienced that, and the wounds were still fresh. It occurred to me that I hadn't even tried to deal with that. I'd lost my ministry. With so much going on, I hadn't had a moment to mourn that loss.

I knew I wasn't going through all I was facing alone. I had a wife. Okay, I had two wives. I had a cat and a bodybuilder friend who often surprised me with his insights.

But I was reminded, now, that I also had my group. Other alcoholics who actually understood the way my alcoholic mind worked.

After introducing the topic, I didn't share in the meeting. I'd gotten off my chest what I needed to when I talked to Rusty before the meeting started. Sure, I was vague on the details. But sometimes, we can get lost in the peculiarities of our situations and miss the forest for the trees. This was a meeting where I got more out of listening than talking.

I needed to be honest about how I was responsible for what happened. I couldn't undo the past, but I could learn from it. I could let go of the guilt, which wasn't helping me at all, and mourn what needed to be mourned. I needed to feel the pain of loss. Not drown it out with booze.

Only then would I find any clarity.

How, exactly, would I do that? Nearly everyone made the same suggestion. They had to turn it over to the God of their own understanding. The only way to cope with a guilt that is larger than oneself is to allow a power higher than oneself to assume the burden.

I couldn't remember the last time I'd said a prayer. Hard to believe that a former minister would *forget* to pray. Really, I always struggled with maintaining a constant prayer life. Seminary was more about gaining head-knowledge about my religion than developing helpful spiritual disciplines.

I had one more stop to make. I didn't know for sure if he'd be there. I knew I could portal myself there. I'd done it before. It was the first time where I learned to use a fairy portal.

Yes, the place where my butt got stuck in the pew.

CHAPTER THIRTY-SIX

From the back of the dumpster at the AA club to the Church of the Holy Cross, where I'd served as minister for the better part of the last decade. Where my former bishop, Philip, now served. I wasn't going there for nostalgia's sake. I wanted to see Philip. Sure, I might be persona non grata in my denomination, but he'd always supported me. He even seemed to believe, unlike the other powers that be, that there was something to this whole elven prophecy thing.

I only had a few days to figure out what to do about the earthquake.

I appeared in the chancel of the sanctuary at Holy Cross. It was the place where I'd often stood when I preached. Again, sort of like at AA, when I was a minister, if I made any mistake at all in my early years, it was that I thought being a good one was more about talking than listening.

Only when I used my ears, and bit my tongue, did I start to see real progress—at either AA or in the church.

Philip wasn't in the sanctuary. Not a surprise. It wasn't a place where I ever hung out. Some ministers, I supposed, would spend time there in the morning to pray. The atmosphere is more conducive to spiritual things than sitting behind a desk in the office. Even if, ultimately, God could show up wherever the hell he wanted.

The office that used to be mine was down a hallway behind the chancel. It was a handy arrangement. I could easily duck in and out of the service if I forgot something, or had to pee, or whatever.

Just so long as I remembered to turn my mic off before using the bathroom. I'd once, inadvertently, offered an embarrassing accompaniment to *How Great Thou Art* with the sound of pee hitting toilet water, followed by a flush.

To this day, I hadn't lived that one down. I half-expected that even if I ran into one of the congregation and we started reminiscing about old times, that would be one of the first stories that come up. "Hey, Pastor! Remember that time you peed over the P.A. system?"

I made my way back to the office door. Hearing the sound of classical music coming from the room, I was relieved to find that Philip was there. You never know. Minister's office hours are usually pretty uneventful. I often ducked out on mine to make hospital and nursing home calls.

The door was open, but I still reached across the opening in plain view and knocked on it for some reason. I don't know why. It was sort of dumb. But people did that to me all the time when my door was left open. I suppose appearing in an open doorway unannounced is a bit awkward. You can't just stand there randomly and be like, "Hey!" It feels like the appearance demands something more than that, an action, a gesture of some kind... If not a pointless knock, perhaps a song-and-dance number, or a walk-in song like professional wrestlers get when they walk on stage, or baseball players have when they walk up to the plate.

At the moment, mine would probably be Green Day's *Basket Case*—do you have the time to listen to me whine about nothing and everything all at once? With all the thoughts swirling around my cranium, it would be fitting. But instead, I settled for the knock accompanied by a "Hello, Philip."

"Caspar!" Philip said, standing from his desk. "What are you doing here?"

I sighed. "I know it's probably not appropriate for me to be here. I just don't have a pastor of my own, and I sort of need one."

Philip gestured to the empty chair on the opposite side of his desk. I pulled it out and sat down. Philip pulled his desk chair around to the front of his desk so that he was sitting beside me.

A real pro move. One they told us to try in our counseling class at seminary. Sitting behind a desk is too formal, almost business-like. People coming to talk to a pastor aren't usually there to talk business. Sitting on one side together communicates unity, the idea that we're on the same side with whoever we're counseling rather than an adversarial posture.

Until now, I figured I might have been the only one who used the two-desks-same-side strategy. Of course, now I wasn't the counselor; I wasn't the pastor. I was the one seeking counsel.

"I suppose you saw me on the news?" I asked.

Philip nodded. "Of course. Well, I didn't see it myself. But I heard about it almost right away. You know, people in the congregation talk."

I nodded. "Makes sense."

"What was that all about anyway?" Philip asked.

"You wouldn't believe it if I told you," I said.

"I believe that the son of a carpenter was the Son of God who rose from the dead. I'm used to believing in the unbelievable."

I chuckled. "Yeah, I suppose there's that. Believe it or not, we did it primarily as a public relations move. The President threatened me with charges related to someone's murder, and we sort of figured that if I did something big and great, it would make it less politically expedient for him to blackmail me."

"The President of the United States?" Philip asked, raising an eyebrow.

I chuckled. "Yeah. Told you it's pretty unbelievable."

Philip shook his head. "Not really."

"Because he's a politician?" I asked.

"Well, there's that," Philip said. "But because he's a human being. A fallen soul. A sinner, like the rest of us. From what I read about the depth of human depravity in the Bible, there's enough potential for evil inside each of us to destroy the world three times over. And with great power…"

"I know, comes great responsibility. A bit cliché, Philip, don't you think?"

"I was going to say comes great temptation, Caspar."

"Okay, not quite as cliché. I suppose that makes sense why the President might succumb."

"I wasn't talking just about the President. But there's that. I'm talking about you, too, Caspar. I'm not going to pretend to try and understand what this power is you have, but I know it's beyond the ordinary. Great power. Great temptation."

"But the whole great responsibility thing, even if it is cliché, is true, too," I said. "If you knew something bad was going to happen and you had a unique ability to stop it, but by doing that, you'd potentially cause more suffering in the long run, what would you do?"

"I think it depends on how strong that potential is," Philip said. "Here's the thing. Remember, when we took our theological ethics course, and they asked us to consider whether it would be just if we had the opportunity to go back in time with the knowledge we have about what would happen, to kill Hitler before he came to power?"

I snorted. "Yeah. The answer was that it's still wrong to kill, even if you're saving more lives. I think it's mostly bullshit, though."

"Why do you say that, Caspar?"

"I think I'd have a hard time justifying that decision if, after passing up the chance to travel through time and prevent the

Holocaust, I went to the future and talked to a Holocaust survivor."

"The issue isn't about whether you justify your actions," Philip said. "In theological ethics, we don't subscribe to the idea that the ends justify the means. But remember what Martin Luther once said about sinning?"

I chuckled. "Yeah, he said to sin boldly!"

"But to believe more boldly still," Philip said. "His statement is often misunderstood. But if you look at his words in context, it makes sense. Luther's point was that, for the Christian, because we are in a broken world, sometimes we are in situations where sinning is unavoidable. The point of the Christian life isn't to live without sin. It's to be honest about our sin. Even bold about it, not to hide it in our closets, so long as we're even bolder about our belief in God's grace."

"I get that," I said. "Sometimes even the right course of action is still stained with sin. In such instances, we have to trust in God's grace and mercy. But that still doesn't tell me which action I should pursue."

Philip pressed his lips together. He didn't know what I was talking about. But I did have a genuine dilemma. Use my power to stop the earthquake and save lives now. That was option number one. But it would possibly enrage the Furies even more. It might divide them from the elementals, and since the whole prophecy was about me uniting the peoples, even the original protector races, it would be the opposite of what I was meant to do. That was exactly what Brightborn wanted me to do. It was a *temptation* to save lives, but with the consequence of possibly breaking the prophecy. But in the end, if I didn't stay the course, it could cost an exponentially greater loss of life in the long run.

"Let's revise the whole Hitler time-travel dilemma a little," Philip said. "What if, rather than going back in time to kill him, you arrive in the past to find that some other time traveler hoping to prevent the Holocaust had strapped Hitler to train tracks, and you got there just in time to see a locomotive was barreling down on his position. But you look and there's a lever to pull, and you could divert the train down another track before it hit him. Are you, in this instance, ethically compelled to act to save Hitler? Does the fact you know that what he'll do if he survives change the equation at all? Is the whole dilemma different because you have more knowledge about what Hitler will eventually become than it would be if it was anyone else lying on those tracks?"

I shook my head. "I don't know."

"Or let's just take Hitler out of the equation. What if the train is heading down one path, and there are dozens of people in the cars who are going to die if it continues going that direction, but if you divert the train, it will hit one little old lady whose high heel is stuck in the tracks. In this case, the only way you could save the car with a young family inside would be to pull the lever, but by doing that, you'd kill the old lady. Do you act? Or do you leave it to the fates and mourn the loss of the young family?"

"Dude," I said, staring at Philip blankly. "You aren't making this any easier. In the first case, I don't think I'd save Hitler."

"But you aren't an executioner, Caspar. You'd still be guilty of killing him. Thou shalt not kill."

"I know... In the second situation, it would tear me up inside, but I'd have to save the young family."

"But in that situation, if you did nothing, you wouldn't have directly killed anyone. By acting, you actually commit the murder."

I grunted. "I don't know. My gut tells me that's the right thing to do. I shouldn't be in a position to choose who lives and dies."

"But in such a situation, the position has been thrust upon you. Whether you do nothing or do something, you have the power to change the outcome. It isn't a matter of what's right or wrong, Caspar. If you have been put into the situation, then it's

God's will that you be there. We could argue, from different ethical standpoints, that one action is preferable to the other."

I snorted. "Yeah, if we followed utilitarianism, saving the most people is always the ethical choice. The greatest good for the greatest number."

"But if you chose a different philosopher, by Kant's ethics, you'd have to act in terms of the universal application of the act. Is the act, itself, right or wrong in every situation?"

"Which one is right?" I asked. "Seems to me that in philosophical ethics, we just cling to whichever scheme justifies what we want to do, anyway. In the end, we act according to what our conscience, our gut, tells us is right."

"And for the Christian," Philip said. "We rest in grace. Because at the end of the day, we can't live perfect lives. We can't avoid sin totally. Even if we try to whenever we can. All have sinned, the Bible says, and all fall short of the glory of God. That's why, even in the Old Testament, there was a system for atoning for sin. Because God knew that after sin became a part of the world, we *would* sin. Assigning guilt isn't the issue, Caspar. It's what you do with that guilt that matters and what you'll decide to do next."

I shook my head. "But there are other people involved. Elves don't believe the same things we do."

Philip shrugged. "I'm sure they have a belief system, too. But I know what *you* believe, Caspar. What other people believe doesn't have any impact on how you bear the burden of your choices or how you choose to let go of that burden."

I shook my head. "You know, the Bible also says that we will not be tempted beyond what we can handle. That God will provide a way."

"Do you trust that?" Philip asked.

"Trust what? That God will provide a way? Sure, but what if I choose the wrong path and his way out was on the other one?"

"God isn't an ethics professor," Philip said. "He doesn't give you ethical conundrums just to confuse you."

I laughed. "Yeah, that's your role right now."

Philip nodded. "The point I'm making is that in any of the scenarios above, you can find a way to argue that either action is what's most ethical. But do you still have faith, in the end, that God is in the picture?"

I folded my hands together in my lap and nodded. "Yeah, I do. At the end of the day, the one thing I've never lost is my faith."

"Then whatever you do, act boldly. You might sin. But avoiding sin isn't the point. Do you believe that God is in charge? Believe it more boldly still. Because I don't know about you, but I have faith in a God who often accomplishes the impossible. A God who parted the Red Sea. Who turned water into wine. Who walked on water and rose from the dead."

"So you're saying I should just wait for God to come down from heaven and fix everything?"

Philip shook his head. "I'm saying you should follow your conscience. Do what you think is best and trust that in the end, God is in charge. I don't know what dilemma you're facing, Caspar, but I believe that even when we don't understand God's resolutions, at least in the Bible I read, when I get to the end of it, his plan is good and right and He loves us. Even the worst thing humans did to God in the Bible—crucifying His Son—was used by Him to give us something immeasurably loving: forgiveness. His love is greater than our sin."

CHAPTER THIRTY-SEVEN

I left Philip's office and returned to my old sanctuary. I didn't have a clear answer yet as to what I should do, but Philip's words helped. It was the first time since I was excommunicated from my church that I even thought about thinking about what my *faith* might have to say about what I was going through.

I knelt at the communion rail. There wasn't any service going on, and this was no Last Supper, but my mind was on how Jesus had prayed in the Garden of Gethsemane when he was facing the most daunting challenge of his life. He was so anxious about what he knew was coming that the New Testament tells us he sweated drops of blood.

What Jesus decided after saying his prayer was to submit to what evil men were planning to do to him. He allowed them to go through with their scheme to crucify him as if he was a common criminal. But he also kept the faith. He prayed that God would remove the cup of suffering from him, but in the end, he prayed, "Not *my* will, but *Thy* will be done."

I clasped my hands together and prayed the same thing. It became clear at that moment what I had to do. I *was* going to end up playing right into Brightborn's hands. However, I couldn't let the Furies unleash that earthquake on the city. The consequences of that would be too much to bear.

I might or might not be able to save lives later, but I *could* save people now.

I was going to help Aerin get the bodies back, and I was going to stop the earthquake. Even if it meant that the prophecy wouldn't unfold the way I expected it to. Even if it meant that it might set the elementals, and even the giants, against the Furies.

First, I had to go back and tell Aerin what we were going to do. I probably didn't have a lot of time to rescue the bodies of the drow from the elven legion before, well, the elves either desecrated the corpses, or they'd start to decay. Who was I kidding? Those bodies were probably already decomposing. But it was important to Aerin. The fallen drow deserved to be laid to rest in a way that fit with their own beliefs.

If I was going to cling to my faith in the midst of all this, I had to allow the drow who were helping me to do the same. I had to give them the best chance I could to honor their dead in accordance with *their* beliefs.

After that, I'd use every ounce of power I had to stop the earthquake. No matter the consequences.

I said one more prayer, the Serenity Prayer, and decided to muster up the courage to change the things I had the power to change. With that, I'd have to accept whatever things that might happen that I couldn't change. I couldn't let all those people suffer. I couldn't let the Furies destroy St. Louis. That was something I *did* have the ability to change. I had to admit that I couldn't control how the Furies might react.

I stood back from the communion rail and took a deep breath before I turned and, visualizing a spot on the grass in front of my farmhouse at the junkyard ranch, cast a fairy portal.

I jumped through it and found myself standing where I'd envisioned. No one else was standing there, thank God. It would be one kind of mess if I'd portaled myself into an inanimate object. It would be another thing, entirely, to portal myself into someone's body.

I walked around the back of the house where the drow campsite was set up. Aerin and several of the drow were gathered around a small fire. I placed my hand on her shoulder.

"Come with me," I said. "We're going to go retrieve your peoples' bodies."

"Caspar," Aerin said, shaking her head. "It's too risky. We can't do that."

I shook my head. "It's important to you. To all of you. You've risked a lot already, for my sake. I have to do this, Aerin, for yours."

A single tear fell down her cheek. "If we're going to do that, Caspar. There's something else you need to know."

"What's that?" I asked.

"They also took our prophecy. The final scroll."

"The elves stole the drows' version of the prophecy?" I asked.

Aerin nodded. I bit my lip. "When we were in New Albion, the giants showed me how to open up the final seal. They explained that every race's final prophecy is unique."

"The one they call Targigoth told me as much," Aerin said. "If we're going to go there and try and get the bodies, we need to retrieve the prophecy at the same time."

"I'll be coming with you," Layla said, stepping up behind me.

"As will I," Brag'mok added.

"This is a matter of concern for the drow," Aerin said. "I can't ask you all to risk your lives."

Brag'mok shook his head. "We are united behind our same chosen one. We may be different, come from different places, and have different beliefs, but we are still one people. We are now, at least."

"I don't think I'll be able to convince my sisters to stay behind either," Aerin said. "As you said, this is important to them. It's personal, now."

I nodded. "Let them come. We're going to have a lot of bodies to move, and we can use all the help we can get."

"Do we even know where to start looking?" Aerin asked.

I shook my head. "Not for certain. But we can start at Brightborn's mansion, where he took me before. I should be able to cast a portal to that room."

"We learned that the rest of the elves are hiding at the North Pole," Layla added. "Do you think they'd take them there?"

"I hope not. They could certainly travel there easily enough with the use of their unseelie fairies. I'm not sure I could do the same. I wouldn't be able to visualize anything there. Still, I suspect that they'll be here, somewhere in his mansion or at least nearby. Brightborn doesn't know that I have fairy abilities again. If I'm right, then this is exactly what he wants us to do. If he's trying to divide our attention between this issue and stopping the Furies, he knows there's no way we can get to the North Pole in the time we have left."

Layla shook her head. "Knowing my father, he'll have some trick up his sleeve to make this more complicated. I doubt he has bodies piled up in the living room of whatever house he's staying in."

"I agree," Brag'mok said. "If there's one thing we always expected when facing the elven legions on New Albion, it was the unexpected."

CHAPTER THIRTY-EIGHT

I went through the portal first. With as many people as we were taking with us to Brightborn's mansion, there was too much risk of portaling people into the middle of something or someone. At least if I went through first, and I found one of my limbs caught in something undesirable, I could portal myself out of it again.

The room hadn't changed. I didn't have to go back and let Aerin, Layla, Brag'mok, and the rest know. If I didn't come back in thirty seconds, they were supposed to assume that the coast was clear.

I looked around the room. No elven guards. No sign of Brightborn. No bodies piled up in the corner. I wasn't entirely sure that Brightborn hadn't abandoned the place. But I wasn't going to give up on it until we'd searched the whole mansion. It was the only place I could think to look.

Hell, even if we did figure out a way to travel to the North Pole, it wasn't like I had precise coordinates for the elves' whereabouts. Technically, Echor hadn't even said that they were *precisely* at the North Pole. Only that they were somewhere in the Arctic.

It wasn't a small room. I was pretty sure, though, that with fifty drow plus the rest of us, we were probably violating a fire code or something. With so many of us there, if Brightborn was near, he'd realize we were there in no time at all. He'd also figure out, almost immediately, that I had a fairy on my side.

Layla drew an arrow from her quiver and nocked it. Aerin unsheathed her sword. The rest of the drow did the same. Only Brag'mok left his broadsword at his side. This house wasn't meant for someone of his stature. Just making it through doorways or down the hall was going to be a squeeze.

We headed down the long hallway that led out of the only room in Brightborn's mansion that I'd yet to see. The hallway led to an open foyer. If we went to the right, it led to what looked like a small sitting area. There was another opening off of that room leading to a kitchen.

There was a giant staircase, large dark-stained wooden steps with an ornate, carved railing to match. I doubted the bodies were upstairs. Maybe there was a basement. Most of the old red brick mansions in St. Louis had thick foundations and damp basements. There was a small door under the staircase. I imagined it was either a closet or the basement.

I opened the door. The stench of death hit me like a ton of bricks. This was it.

"I think the bodies, or at least some of them, might be down there," I said.

Aerin nodded and pushed around me. She was eager to find out. I followed her from behind. Layla followed me. Brag'mok stayed upstairs with the other drow. The steps down to the basement were precarious. I doubted they'd hold Brag'mok's weight if he could even squeeze through the narrow door that led down there.

When we reached the bottom of the stairs, we saw three drow bodies, stretched out on the ground, completely naked.

"This isn't everyone," Aerin said. "There has to be more."

"What's that, lying next to the body on the right?" Layla asked.

"Looks like an envelope," I said.

Layla picked it up and opened it. "It's a message from my father."

"Of course it is," I said, shaking my head. "What does he have to say?"

"Consider this a gesture of goodwill," Layla said, reading the elven king's words out loud. "Good will?" Aerin asked. "If he had an ounce of good will, he wouldn't have attacked us, to begin with."

"No one else needs to die," Layla continued reading. "The rest of the bodies may be collected if my daughter and her two spouses come alone to the place where the princess was granted celestial power. If you wish to avoid more bloodshed, only these three can come, and all three must come together. Do not bother seeking the other bodies elsewhere. I can assure you, you will not find them. Come on Friday, one hour after sunset. Cordially, the Divine Emperor Brightborn."

"The Divine Emperor?" Aerin asked. "What hubris."

"I suppose that's what he intends to call himself as the ruler of his one-world government," I said.

Layla handed the letter to Aerin. "Friday? That's almost exactly three days from when we spoke to the Furies."

"When the earthquake is supposed to happen," I said, shaking my head. "I don't think his timing is accidental."

"I don't either," Layla said. "My father intends to present you with a conundrum. Either accept his invitation and claim the bodies or try to stop the earthquake."

I sighed. "We don't know exactly the minute that the earthquake will happen. I doubt he knows, either."

"He said nothing about the prophecy he stole, either," Aerin said.

"He can open the seal," I said. "The same way that he stole the artifacts, the rings, before. He'll just need to use five elves who can wield each of the elements."

"Maybe not," Aerin said. "The artifacts were sealed in a similar way, but not by Taliesin, the original Druid prophet. That may be why he wants all of us there, not just Layla."

"My father still intends to present me as the chosen one to his legions," Layla said. "If he can't open the prophecy himself, perhaps that's why he wants all three of us to come."

"We should search the rest of the mansion, just for good measure. Perhaps Targigoth will have more insight into how the seals work. He consulted with his giant ancestors before he learned how to open the giants' final prophecy."

"Good point, Caspar," Aerin said. "Send me back with the bodies, and I'll prepare the death rites for these three. When you're done searching the mansion, meet us back at the ranch with the rest. These three have waited long enough for their peace."

I nodded and formed a portal back to the ranch. "Stand in the middle of the bodies. I'll pull the portal over you so you don't have to carry them."

"Thank you, Caspar," Aerin said as she handed me Brightborn's letter and stepped into the middle of the room. I focused my mind and dropped the portal over Aerin and the three bodies. They disappeared from view, and I released the fairy power that sustained the portal.

Layla and I ran upstairs.

"Find the bodies?" Brag'mok asked.

I nodded. "Three of them. I sent Aerin back with them to the ranch."

"What about the rest?" Brag'mok asked.

I handed Brightborn's letter to Brag'mok. He unfolded it and read it.

"What a snake," Brag'mok said. "I wonder what he's up to."

"He didn't mention the stolen prophecy," Layla said. "We think he wants us three to go there to open the prophecy."

"When you and Targigoth were in the sweat lodge, did you see everything he saw?" I asked

Brag'mok shook his head. "Only he has the ability to speak to the ancestors."

"We'll have to talk to him about it," I said. "We're not sure if Brightborn can open the prophecy the same way he opened the boxes that contained the artifacts when he stole them before."

"It's possible," Brag'mok said. "But you're right. Targigoth could have more insight than I would on that matter."

Three of the drow warriors came down the stairs. Apparently, they'd already searched the rest of the house.

"Find anything upstairs?" I asked.

"Nothing of note," Rina, the drow warrior that Jag had taken an interest in, said. "It looks like hardly anyone has been here at all. The place is pristine. Not even any personal objects or clothes."

I nodded. "It seems that this place has served its purpose for Brightborn."

CHAPTER THIRTY-NINE

Since there wasn't much else to see at the mansion, Aerin hadn't gotten far in her funeral preparations by the time we arrived. Christian funerals are fairly predictable, and I'd officiated more than my fair share of them. We usually had a casket or, on occasion, an urn, set up front and center. I usually gave a homily. Sometimes we had a few eulogies, but as often as not, those were saved for the graveside service that followed the church service.

Whatever Aerin was setting up was, as Monty Python would put it, something *completely* different. Aerin had clothed the bodies. When the rest of us arrived, the drow warriors came to her aid and carried each of the three bodies around the smoldering campfire.

Jag was sitting at the fire, roasting what looked like a chicken breast on a stick over the flames. Rina came over and grabbed him by the arm. She whispered something in his ear—probably something to the effect that he might want to cook his food elsewhere given that they were about to conduct funeral rites for the dead.

Apparently, he felt he'd cooked it sufficiently. He ripped a giant chuck from the end of his skewer with his teeth as he walked away. Rina returned to the other drow as they started preparing the bodies.

Again, not in the ways that humans usually prepared their dead. Though, now that I think about it, it was probably less weird than what we do. Think about it. We take our dead, we drain all their blood, fill their bodies with disgusting chemicals, then put makeup on their faces to try and make them look alive, even though they never look anything remotely close to their own selves. Dead people usually have the exact expression you'd expect after getting chemicals shot up the pooper or into whatever other hole the mortician surgically created.

It was downright strange what we did. I mean, why were we putting formaldehyde in bodies, anyway? What exactly were we trying to preserve?

Given all of that, I was reluctant to judge what the drow were doing. The bodies weren't laid out in such a way to look like they were sleeping. They were on their backs, spread eagle as if they were making snow angels. They were dressed, not in black dresses, but in the colorful patterns the drow usually wore. They weren't adorned in makeup. There were no pretenses here, no attempt to make the dead look like themselves. Their eyes were opened rather than closed. Their jaws were agape. Since they'd been dead a while without any preservation, their eyes were sunk deep in their skulls. It was more than a little creepy.

But the goal of the rite wasn't, as I understood it, based on what Aerin had said about giving the mourning closure. It was about giving the souls of the deceased a peaceful exit from this world. The drow believed in reincarnation, so I presumed that they believed that the souls of the dead went to wherever souls went while waiting for reassignment to a new earthly existence.

Aerin came over and grabbed my arm. "Come here, Caspar. I'd like to show you what we're doing and explain it."

I nodded. "You don't have to. You can tell me about it afterward."

Aerin shook her head. "I'd like to show you now."

I shrugged. If I learned anything dealing with mourning, it was that people often wanted or expected odd things. Things that, frankly, didn't necessarily make sense. Sometimes people wanted photos with their deceased loved ones. Invariably, they'd say that they wished they hadn't done it later, that they couldn't bear to look at the photos. At the moment, though, the act of taking the picture was something that they thought would help. Some people laugh a lot at funerals. They share funny stories about the deceased, sometimes embarrassing things that the dead probably didn't want to be aired publicly. Interestingly, the ones who laughed the most were typically those who cried the most at certain parts of the service.

One thing I knew from experience was that people mourned differently. No two people go through the loss of someone they cared about in precisely the same way. If Aerin wanted me there, if explaining her traditions to me made her feel better, I was willing to comply.

"When does the service start?" I asked.

"It already has," Aerin said. "We don't have services the way you do. It's all a process of preparing the body, of offering the dead the clearest path from their bodies to the beyond."

"A path?" I asked. "What's that about?"

"You've heard of ghosts and vengeful spirits," Aerin said. "They are souls that did not have a clear path to the beyond. They were not properly prepared. Spirits of the dead, particularly those who die with something unresolved, can be easily distracted when they leave their bodies. If they do not have a clear focus, if their bodies are not positioned properly to direct them straight into the beyond, they may find themselves lost for a time. Wandering the world. Fulfilling an unfulfilled purpose. Exacting vengeance on someone who wronged them."

I cocked my head. "A spirit can do something like that? Become a ghost?"

"Ghosts require energy to manifest and engage with the world of the living," Aerin said. "Humans, for the most part having never touched Earth's magic, are rather helpless even when their spirits are lost. For the drow, although we do not wield magic, we're all attuned to it. Our dead, if not transitioned to the afterlife, can be quite powerful."

"Which is why it was so important to conduct this ritual," I said.

"I suspect Brightborn realizes this," Aerin said. "Typically, the spirit of a person will linger with the body for as long as a week, but not much longer than that. He knows that we'll be pressed on time to conclude our rites."

"Wouldn't he want you to do the rituals?" I asked. "You'd think an angry drow spirit released in the presence of the elven king wouldn't bode well for the king."

Aerin shook her head. "There are other methods, ways I'm sure he knows, to trap the spirits of the dead. To harness their power, like an enchantment, in something like a blade or another weapon. It's one reason, I believe, he's sure that we'd come no matter what threat there might be from the Furies at the same time."

"Why wouldn't he just harness their power for himself anyway?" I asked.

"Wielding a blade enchanted by the spirit of the deceased is risky," Aerin said. "Whoever wields it has great power, but whatever damage is done by the blade also wounds the soul of the living."

"Wounds the soul?" I asked.

"The spirit of one who wields such a blade will be melded with the spirit of the blade itself, until the two are indistinguishable. Eventually, it will be that the living is possessed by the spirit of the blade. They will become, in a way, possessed by the person who died and used to exact that person's vengeance."

"So the dead person takes over that person's body?" I asked.

"Not completely," Aerin said. "They will gain a greater influence over the host each time the blade is used. At most, the two spirits will share the body. It depends on the relationship between the two spirits. It can be adversarial or cooperative."

"If the elves did that to the fallen drow, it would certainly be adversarial."

"Yes," Aerin said. "But the destruction the legionnaires could unleash in the meantime using the power of such a blade would be profound. A single strike of such a blade, even indirectly, could separate spirits from the bodies they inhabit."

"So, how does this ritual prevent all of that from happening?" I asked.

Aerin reached into a small hip purse that she often wore and retrieved a mason jar full of glowing dust. "This can direct the spirit of the deceased."

"What is it?" I asked.

"A mixture of salt and ground limestone," Aerin said. "Enchanted with aether. I must sprinkle a circle around the body and then place some in the mouth of the deceased. The circle will prevent their spirits from leaving, and they'll go directly into the afterlife. The elves, if they wished to trap the spirits of the dead, would sprinkle their weapon with dust and use it to strike the body. The soul of the deceased would be transferred into the blade."

"And the elves know how to enchant like the drow do?" I asked.

Aerin shrugged. "I can't say for certain, but it is possible. I can't say that Brightborn doesn't know how to do it."

"Fascinating," I said, putting my hand on Aerin's back. "Thank you for sharing."

Aerin nodded. "Of course."

Aerin proceeded to sprinkle circles of the enchanted dust around each of the three bodies. The rest of the drow gathered around and, holding hands, started to sing. It was a beautiful but haunting song in another language. They all spoke English, but the drow also had an ancient language of their own.

As Aerin dropped some of the dust into each of the three fallen drows' mouths, their bodies started to glow with a golden hue that matched the magic of aether. The glow centered on their chests and then exploded into an impressive tornado of energy that swirled inside each of the circles before shooting into the sky and disappearing.

The drow raised their hands to the sky as their fallen ones migrated into the great beyond.

"May our sisters live on in our memories and in the care of the gods." Aerin, Rina, and the other drow exchanged tear-filled hugs.

It was over. It was a beautiful ritual. I was honored that Aerin made me a part of it.

CHAPTER FORTY

After the ritual was over, I wandered over to the giants, who were constructing shelters for themselves out of scrap metal as Brag'mok had done. Gronk was particularly impressive, tearing apart old cars with his bare hands.

Targigoth was the only one not participating. He wasn't just smaller than the other giants, but as high priest, I imagined he wasn't as accustomed to getting his hands dirty like the rest.

It was a good opportunity to talk to him about the prophecy.

I approached him as he was seated on the back bumper of Jag's fixed-up truck. "How's it going?" I asked, feeling the need to greet him somehow before diving into a barrage of questions about the prophecy.

"It is well," Targigoth said. "I was watching the ritual from afar. Intriguing."

I nodded. "I agree. I have a question. Since the elves stole the prophecy from the drow, I was wondering, could they open the seal with all five elements themselves?"

Targigoth shook his head. "I was holding the scroll when you opened it. I do not know who might serve as the high priestess amongst the drow, but whoever it is, she must have the scroll in her hands when the magic is cast into it."

I nodded. "I think, for the drow, Aerin is both the princess and their high priestess. She's the one in charge of the scrolls, anyway."

"Your magic loosened the seal, but it would only break when held by one who possesses the authority vested by the ancestors who cared for the scrolls in the past."

I nodded. "So Brightborn needs us to open it. That's probably why he wants only us three to meet up with him in two days."

"This is certainly a possibility," Targigoth said. "The elven king is likely intimidated by the final prophecy, particularly since each of the final prophecies is particular to each race."

"Do you think he's already opened his final scroll?" I asked.

"If, as you say, he could harness all five elements, it's certainly a possibility."

"He wants to know what the drow prophecy says," I said. "Probably so he can figure out how to manipulate its meaning to his purposes."

"This would be in line with our experience dealing with the elven king. He is, if nothing else, a master of deception."

"Do you think it's wise to do as he wants?" I asked.

Targigoth shrugged. "The elven king will do what he does. The prophecy is immutable. Its meaning might be open to interpretation. But what is foretold within it will come to pass, no matter how he might try to manipulate its meaning."

While we were talking, Gronk sauntered toward us, tossing what looked like the hood of one of the old cars to the side.

"Naayak," Gronk said. "We're making some progress here. But I must ask, how soon will you be ready to fight?"

"I don't know," I said. "We think we know where the elves are. But the elven king is pulling strings trying to consolidate his power, I think. The time will come."

Gronk nodded. "We'll be ready when the time is right. We stand prepared to fulfill our ancient purpose to defend the Earth."

"You should know," I said. "I'm going to try and stop the earthquake. It might cause some tension between our side and the Furies."

"You must do what is necessary," Gronk said. "The Furies will protect this world in their own way. We are united in purpose no less on that account. Even if our means toward the same end might differ."

I slapped Gronk on the shoulder. "If there's anything I can do. I know adjusting to this world can be difficult."

Gronk laughed. "It's actually surprisingly nice. As a sorcerer, I can feel the magic of this world all around. Could use something to eat, though."

"No meat, right?" I asked.

Gronk nodded. "Fruit. Brag'mok says that you haven't lived until you've tried an apple or an orange."

I smiled. "They can be delicious. I'll see what I can get for you. And some vegetables."

"I hear you have a vegetable that resembles little trees that I'd like to try."

"Broccoli?" I asked.

"That's not like e-coli, is it?"

I laughed. "No, totally different."

"Then yes!" Gronk exclaimed. "Get us some broccoli!"

"And some peas, maybe?"

"Pee? You consume that?"

I snorted. "No. Pea, with an A rather than two Es. Corn is also fantastic."

"Just don't get us any...what is it Brag'mok called it... Kale?"

I smiled. "I wouldn't do that to you. But there are some other leafy greens I'm sure you'd enjoy."

"Speaking of pee. Brag'mok said you have something called spareguts that makes your pee smell."

"Asparagus," I said, correcting Gronk's understandable mispronunciation of the word. "And yes, when you eat it, your urine will smell exactly like it about an hour later."

"Fascinating…"

"Indeed!" I said, chuckling. "I'll have Jag load up the truck and see what we can get you."

I sent Jag and Rina, along with Aerin since she had all the cash, to a farmers' market we'd seen signs for just a few miles down the road. I wasn't sure if they'd have enough there to feed the whole horde of giants, but I knew a farmers' market would have grade-A quality produce. They probably wouldn't know what to do when Jag pulled up the truck and told them to fill the bed.

We had two days to burn. There wasn't much sense in trying to find the bodies ourselves. Brightborn said we wouldn't find them, and as crafty as he was, we decided it wasn't worth wasting our energy to try. So, instead, I focused on trying to make the giants and drow feel at home.

I didn't know what was going to happen after we met with Brightborn. I didn't know how much havoc the earthquake would cause or what my chances were to stop it, but this wasn't our world anymore. It didn't just belong to humans. Sure, comparatively speaking, there weren't many giants. But what they'd given up, and after all they'd lost and endured, I felt responsible for making sure that they were welcome.

The rest of the world, humanity, might not ever accept giants in their midst. Elves could blend in. All they'd have to do is hide their ears. Even the drow, with their purplish skin and white hair, looked human enough that they could pass. They'd managed to do exactly that for centuries in India. But the giants, I knew, would have a hard time.

They didn't have many women amongst them—only three out of the whole bunch. A lot of male giants, without enough women for them to have families of their own, were bound to grow ill-content over time. At least, now, they'd have something to eat. A full stomach can go a long way.

CHAPTER FORTY-ONE

We decided to take the Eclipse. I could have portaled us into the middle of the Pruitt-Igoe forest, but as far as I knew, Brightborn still didn't have a clue that I had fairy powers. Best keep my cards held close to my chest.

So far, no tremors. No sign of the earthquake. Still, with every bump we hit on the road, my chest tightened, expecting the worst. We were almost three days on from the time the Furies told us the quake was coming. I was expecting it any minute.

The sun was setting on the horizon as we pulled up next to the forest. It was an odd place, several acres of forest in the middle of one of the most crime-ridden parts of the city—an old public housing project that failed back in the middle of the twentieth century. The project had been such a disaster that the forest had taken on an almost sacred significance to those who lived in the area. A few developers had proposed projects for the space over the years. Nothing had ever come to fruition.

· Hardly anyone who didn't have a death wish ever went into that forest. It was where Brightborn had forced me to kill Fred, but his blood wasn't the first to be spilled on those grounds. I had a keen sense, particularly now that I was in tune with aether, that the whole place was haunted.

I locked the car after Aerin, Layla, and I got out. Aerin had her sword at her side. Layla had her bow and a full set of celestially charged arrows in her quiver. Brightborn had said to come alone. He said nothing about coming unarmed.

A gust of wind struck me in the face. It smelled of death. "I think he has the bodies here."

Aerin nodded. "At least he stuck to his word."

"I wouldn't count on it," Layla said. "I'm sure he has something up his sleeve. He didn't demand this meeting out of the goodness of his heart."

"Your dad has a heart?" I asked. "Could have fooled me."

"It's in question," Layla said. "I've known the man my whole life. I certainly wouldn't ever refer to him as Daddy Dearest."

We entered the clearing where we'd met Brightborn in the forest before. He was waiting for us, holding the scroll of the drow prophecy in his hands. A pile of bodies was stacked, one on top of the other at the forest's edge. Of course, Brightborn had his legionnaires gathered around him, two of them with spears standing at his side. Probably his bodyguards.

"We're here," I said. "As you requested."

Brightborn nodded. "As I said, the bodies I left you before were meant to be a token of goodwill. I have no intention of any further bloodshed tonight."

"Then why do you have your whole legion here armed?" Layla asked.

"Why did you bring your weapons?" Brightborn asked. "Presumably for the same reason I came prepared. Let's hope that we can behave cordially and avoid any unnecessary violence."

"Cordially?" Aerin asked. "You've already slain half of my warriors. How can you expect this meeting to be cordial?"

Brightborn laughed. "Aerin, you're still the firecracker I almost married. I like that about you."

"Almost?" Aerin asked. "You never meant to marry me. It was a trick, like everything else you do."

"There are no tricks in my agenda," Brightborn said. "I imagine you already know my purpose here."

"You want us to open the drow prophecy?" I asked.

Brightborn nodded. "I would have myself if I could. But we cannot do it without both your power and the drow princess' blessing."

"You're hoping to use our dead, our warriors who never should have been killed to begin with, as some kind of even trade?"

"Aerin," Brightborn said. "I didn't say it was an even trade. The fact is that I have two things, here, you want. The bodies and the prophecy."

"Which you stole!" Aerin shouted.

"All is fair in matters of war," Brightborn said. "But there is no need for a war if we can set aside our differences."

"You mean our difference of opinion about whether you should rule the world?" I asked.

Brightborn smiled, flashing his white teeth. "Precisely."

"What about our prophecy?" Layla asked. "I presume you've seen it already."

Brightborn nodded. "It only confirms what I've been trying to tell you, daughter. *You*, not this human, are the chosen one. Think of how much good we could do in this world if you'd only accept this fact."

"Except it's not the truth!" Layla protested, her hands on her hips.

"Truth?" Brightborn asked. "What is truth?"

I snorted. I doubted that the elven king realized he was quoting Pontius Pilate. "The truth will reveal itself, Brightborn. You can't change what the prophet intended."

"Who says I'm the one changing the truth?" Brightborn asked. "You're the pretender, Mister Cruciger."

"We'll see about that," I said.

I was going to say more about the prophecy when I noticed a slight rumble beneath my feet. Just a tremor. This wasn't the one that would destroy the city. Something bigger was coming. Even the trees shook a little. I widened my stance, steadying myself on my feet.

"Don't you have somewhere else to be, human?" Brightborn asked. "We could stay here and debate our interpretations of my prophecy, or you could do what I've asked you to do and be on your way to save your precious city."

"Dammit, Brightborn!" I shouted.

The king laughed. "It's your choice, Cruciger. You could be out of here in minutes. I won't even try to stop you. All I need you and Aerin to do is open the prophecy and read it aloud."

"I don't think you were able to open our prophecy," Layla said. "If you could, you wouldn't need Caspar here. You have Aerin. You could just use your own sorcerers to cast the five elements onto the seal."

"Think what you will, daughter. Would I lie to you?"

"Do you really want me to answer that question?" Layla asked. "The reason you can't do it is because you don't have a proper high priest."

"Of course we do," Brightborn said.

"You don't!" Layla said. "Not a proper one. We've learned from the giants that a high priest must pass something along to the next on his deathbed. Your high priest, Echor, is still on New Albion."

Brightborn laughed. "As always, I'm a step ahead of you, daughter."

Brightborn gestured to his legions. One of the legionnaires stepped forward with another elf, with Echor, his hands tied and bound and a gag in his mouth.

"You're diabolical!" Layla shouted. "He wanted to die alone on New Albion!"

Brightborn shrugged. "Like you said, he had something he needed to pass along to the next high priest at his death. Sadly, he never did this for his successor when we were still on New Albion. I think it's high time we make it happen. Tell me, Layla, how would you like to be the chosen one *and* our next high priest?"

CHAPTER FORTY-TWO

Aerin stepped forward. "You already agreed if I opened this prophecy for you, you'd let me leave with the bodies."

"I will," Brightborn said. "You and your husband may leave. But my daughter will remain with me and assume the gifts at Echor's passing."

Layla shook her head. "You're going to kill him just so he can pass his office to me?"

Brightborn shook his head. "He need not be dead to do it. He only needs to be near his death, and based on his condition, he won't last long. Like I said, daughter, there is no need for bloodshed today."

"But what if I refuse?" Layla asked.

"I would like for you to open the prophecy," Brightborn said, "and only if I keep you here can I be sure that Mister Cruciger will return to help us open it. If he doesn't, well, I'd hate to put my own daughter on trial for her treasons."

I shook my head. "How many times are you going to threaten your daughter to force us to do what you want?"

Brightborn shrugged. "As many times as it takes to get what I want."

"But couldn't your sorcerers use the elements to do it without Caspar?" Layla asked.

"I'd like for the pretender to be here when the prophecy reveals that you are, in fact, the chosen one, daughter."

"And then what?" Layla asked.

"You're going to arrest me," I said. "Hold me as a prisoner."

"I promise we'll treat you well. Better than the human prisons would have. You're welcome, by the way, for my assistance in securing your pardon."

I shook my head. "Just another one of your manipulations."

"Let us hear the drow prophecy," Brightborn said. "Then, go and stop the earthquake. If you return, I can assure you, Layla will not be tried for her indiscretions. All will be forgiven."

"One thing at a time, Naayak," Aerin whispered to me before stepping forward. "Hand me the prophecy, Brightborn. We'll do what you asked."

"You realize, father," Layla said. "You can't keep me here. I have other powers I could use to escape."

"As you did before," Brightborn said. "But remember, I do still have Echor in custody. Do this willingly, and I'll gladly return him to New Albion so he can live out his last days as he wishes on that forsaken planet. Make any move to flee and evade this responsibility, and, well, I'll be forced to choose another high priest. When Echor dies, I'll make sure it's not as pleasant as he desires."

Echor grunted through his gag. He didn't need to speak. I was reasonably certain that he wanted to tell us to forget about it. To refuse to comply. But Layla wouldn't put him through that. If I knew anything about Layla, she was kind. She wouldn't allow anyone to suffer for her sake.

"Let's hear the drow prophecy," Brightborn said as the earth rumbled again beneath our feet. "How many more of these tremors will there be before the full quake is unleashed?"

Aerin nodded, and extending her hands, Brightborn set the scroll in them.

"I'm ready, Naayak," Aerin said.

I shook my head even as I focused my mind and channeled the elements into the seal, just as I had before with the giants. The colors swirled on the seal. A loud blare like the sound of a trumpet blasted before the seal shattered, and a fiery shower, like fireworks, blasted into the air and rained down over us.

Aerin opened the prophecy. She looked at it, her eyes narrowed. She took a deep breath.

"What does it say?" Brightborn asked.

"It has told me what I must do," Aerin said.

"Read it out loud, or give it to me that I might do it!" Brightborn demanded.

Aerin handed me the scroll. "Give it to him."

I cocked my head. "Are you sure?"

"I said, give it to him, Naayak."

I nodded and approached Brightborn and gave him the scroll.

As he unrolled it, I looked back at Aerin. She'd unsheathed her sword, and with her jar of enchanted dust that she'd used for the drow funeral, she doused her blade.

"Trust me," Aerin said.

Brightborn looked up from reading, his eyes wide in horror. "No, don't do it!"

Aerin plunged her own blade into her gut. I ran over to her and caught her as she fell to her knees.

"But the binding! If you die, Aerin…"

Aerin shook her head as she started coughing up blood. "We never consummated our marriage, Caspar. You need to take the blade once I die and swing it at them."

"Aerin, don't…*please*! I can heal you."

"Don't," Aerin said, coughing again. "This is what the prophecy demands."

I couldn't allow it. Maybe our marriage wasn't consummated. But we were bound in some sense. I needed her.

I tried to muster some magic. I know she said not to, but I couldn't lose her. I just couldn't.

But I was too late. Aerin's head fell as she took her last breath.

"Don't even think about it!" Brightborn screamed.

I grabbed the hilt of Aerin's blade and pulled it, soaked in her blood, from her body. "It's what the prophecy demands."

I swung the blade through the air. A blast of golden aether shot from the blade striking Brightborn and all the legion.

When it hit them, green orbs shot out of the back of their necks.

The unseelie fairies.

"Seize the pretender!" Brightborn commanded.

The legionnaires were all clutching at their necks. The fairies didn't leave them willingly, so they didn't heal them on their way out.

Develin, the king of the unseelie court of fairies, released a shriek—what I imagined was supposed to be a battle cry, and the fairies all gathered on his position and charged after me.

I gathered the power of air. Maybe I could blow them away. They weren't large.

Just as I was about to release it, more green orbs flew over my head. I recognized one of them.

It was Trixie.

They collided with the unseelie fairies, intercepting them before they could grab me. Or do whatever it was they were planning to do to hurt me.

"Get him!" Layla shouted. "Echor!"

I nodded. I ran over to Echor, who, while bound, had been released since the legionnaires were overwhelmed by pain, still clinging to their necks.

I quickly formed a portal over him and sent him back to the junkyard ranch.

"Now go!" Layla said. "Stop the earthquake!"

"Not yet!" I said. "The bodies! We can't leave them here!"

"Hurry!"

I ran over to the pile of drow bodies and quickly formed a large fairy portal, then sent them back to the ranch. Aerin wasn't in her body, but it didn't feel right leaving her corpse there, either. So, I transported her back, too.

"Now go, Caspar!"

"But you…"

"I'll get myself out of here," Layla said. "You need to go, now!"

I nodded and, forming another fairy portal, transported myself to the stone circle. I wasn't exactly sure where the epicenter of the quake was, but I knew that the faultline ran near there.

The three Furies were standing there as if waiting for me.

"Where's the earthquake centered?" I asked.

"You seek to stop it?" the Furies asked. "We cannot allow it. Not until our seelie court has exacted justice."

"Until what?" I asked.

"The fairies from the other world have pledged themselves to our service. We dispatched them to bind and arrest the unseelie."

"They're doing it now!" I said. "Come on. People are going to die!"

"We cannot permit it until we know they've succeeded," the Furies responded in unison.

The earth shook again beneath my feet. Stronger than before. One of the five stones surrounding us cracked. "If these stones are destroyed, what will happen to you?"

"We'll simply return to our realm," the Furies replied. "It is of no concern to us."

"Tisiphone," I said. "You stand to thwart murder, do you not? If your fury is still unleashed, if the earthquake still happens, people will die."

"It will remain the fault of the unseelie, who will soon be brought to justice."

"You can't secure justice for the dead," I said. "Punishing a murderer doesn't bring the dead back to life. You have to allow me to save them."

The three Furies exchanged glances. "We've consulted amongst ourselves. You may stop the earthquake. But if the seelie do not succeed, and the unseelie go unpunished, we will unleash another quake with many times greater magnitude than the first."

I nodded. "Thank you. Now, where do I have to go? Where's the epicenter of this thing?"

"To the east of here," Tisiphone said. "Approximately three of your miles."

I turned around. I always sucked with my cardinal directions. "Where the hell is east?"

The three Furies pointed, at the same time, in one direction.

I nodded and, mustering the power of air and aether, took off into the skies and flew in that direction. I didn't know how I'd figure out exactly how far three miles was, but I hoped I'd see some visual evidence of the quake.

I'd never experienced much in the way of earthquakes. We'd had a small one several years back, but nothing that caused any real destruction. I wasn't sure what I was looking for. I hoped I'd recognize it when I saw it.

It was hard to see in the dark, but the moon was up and gave me enough light that I could at least make out the tops of the trees.

I saw trees moving—two rows of them in opposite directions.

That had to be it.

I dove down to the spot, right in the middle of what I assumed was the New Madrid fault line.

I thrust my fists into the ground and unleashed every bit of earth magic I had into it. My body shook so much pressed against the earth that I thought my head was going to rattle right off of my shoulders.

The magic flowed out of me with a force that was almost as jarring as the earthquake itself.

It took everything I had. All my strength. All my focus. All my energy.

My vision blurred.

Then everything went black.

CHAPTER FORTY-THREE

Naayak...

Where in the world was I? Everything was dark—pitch black. I reached around my body and felt...sheets? How in the world did I get in bed? The last time I blacked out and didn't know how I'd gotten back in bed... Well, that was back when I was still drinking. Happened all the time.

I didn't... No. I hadn't been drinking. What was I doing before I got here?

I'm here, Naayak...

"Aerin?" I asked. Then it hit me. She'd killed herself. Fallen on her blade. If I was hearing her...

It's me, Naayak.

"Wait. If you're here...and you died...does that mean that I died?"

Aerin laughed. *No, you aren't dead. But you've been sleeping for almost twelve hours. You're still lying in the middle of the woods.*

That's right, I thought. The Furies. The earthquake. "Does that mean I stopped the earthquake?"

You did, Aerin said.

"Why can I hear you? If you died and..."

I bound myself to the blade, but my soul was still bound to you, too. So when you swung the blade, the only reason you didn't die when I did was that we hadn't consummated our marriage. Swinging that blade, I suppose, it was just as good as that. Like I told you before, when one wields such a blade, it mingles the two souls. Be careful about using the blade again in the future.

I snorted. "Well, if that's supposed to be as good as consummating a marriage, I hate to break it to you. It was sort of a letdown."

But it worked... I couldn't believe it when I read it in the prophecy. But I knew what I had to do.

"The prophecy told you to kill yourself?"

Not exactly. It said that the blood of the drow princess would water the Earth, and that the drow princess' sacrifice would shatter the union between the elves and the unseelie. Since I had the powder on me from the funeral, I knew at that moment what I had to do.

"It's hot in here."

The sun is up. It's a hot day.

I kicked the sheets off my body, or what felt like my body, and got out of what seemed to be a bed. I shuffled my feet, afraid of what I might step on, and made my way to the nearest wall. I groped around until I found a light switch and flipped it on.

"Why are we in my old apartment?" I asked.

We aren't. We're in your mind. This place must be a place of comfort for you.

The chorus of *The Old Apartment* by the Barenaked Ladies was suddenly running through my mind.

Aerin laughed. *I love that song!*

"Wait," I said. "First, where the hell are you because I don't see you. And second, how did you know I was thinking about a song?"

Because we're bound, Caspar. I am part of you. I explained to you how that worked when I was discussing the funeral rites.

I scratched my head. "If you're in my head, why is it I can hear you but can't see you?"

You can't get rid of me because I'm a part of you. But what you're seeing is what your subconscious wants to see.

"Where's Layla? And what about the fairies? They were battling. What happened there?"

You need to wake up and find out, Naayak.

"You realize it is just you and me in my head. You can just call me Caspar."

Aerin laughed. *After what you've done, I feel I should honor you.*

"I only did what anyone else in my position would do if they had the power I had. You're the one who deserves to be honored, Aerin. You paid the ultimate price."

Think of it this way. At least you and Layla can have a less confusing marriage situation together now.

I huffed. "That's one way to think of it. But if you're always going to be in my head, you'll always be there in the middle of it. If you can read my mind, even a song running through my head, then you'll be seeing what I see, feeling what I feel."

Only when you are touching my sword, Aerin said. *Which you are lying on top of right now. I was still pretty disoriented at being bound to you like this when you were talking to the Furies and stopped the quake. Since then, well, you've been unconscious.*

"Am I unconscious, like, injured? Or just asleep?"

You're alive, so that's good, but I don't know.

I sighed. "Layla must be looking all over for me if she got out of there. Lord, I hope she did. What about Brightborn? If the New Albion fairies didn't defeat the unseelie fairies, the Furies said they'd unleash a bigger earthquake."

You need to wake up, Caspar. You might be unconscious, but I can't sense anything wrong with your body. There's no reason why you shouldn't wake up unless your subconscious mind just doesn't want you to wake up.

"Why wouldn't I want to wake up?" I asked.

You tell me, Caspar. What were you thinking when you were trying to stop that earthquake?

"I thought I might not be strong enough. Maybe I was doing it wrong, the way I was wielding the magic."

Well, you did it right. You did stop the earthquake.

"I know. You told me that already. But you were asking me what I was thinking last before I passed out."

Perhaps you're afraid to wake up because you fear that all this, even my voice, is just a dream. You're afraid you'll wake up and find out either you failed or the seelie fairies failed to capture the unseelie. Rather than face the truth, perhaps, your mind finds it more comforting to just stay asleep.

"Avoiding the truth...that's something my alcoholic mind might certainly do. Especially if I'm afraid that the truth might hurt."

I know, Caspar. But you really need to face it. You need to wake up and find out. Because while my words are real, none of this is. This is not your old apartment.

I heard the front door open.

"Someone's here," I said, scrounging around in my closet, looking for my clothes. None of them were there.

You're already dressed, Caspar.

"I am?" I looked down. I was. "How the hell..."

Again, this is all being made in your mind.

I stepped out of the bedroom, and Layla was there, but she wasn't. So were Brag'mok and Jag. They were looking around the apartment but not really looking at anything in it.

"Hey, guys!" I shouted. "I'm right here..."

"Caspar!" Layla shouted. "Where are you?"

"I told you! I'm standing right here. Just turn around!"

You're only shouting in your mind. But what you're seeing, what you're hearing. That's real. They're looking for you.

I sighed. "Well, at least I know she made it out of Pruitt-Igoe."

Caspar... She won't be able to hear you unless you wake up.

I sighed. "I don't know how to do that. It's not like I want to be trapped in some prison of my mind."

Try walking out the front door?

I chuckled. Could it really be that simple? I walked over to the front door, literally walking through the apparition of Jag that was still wandering around the apartment of my mind.

I opened the door. I didn't see my old hallway. I saw the tops of trees. I stepped through it and felt my vision expand. I was lying in the woods.

"Layla!" I shouted.

"Caspar? Is that you?" Layla shouted back.

"Yes!"

I heard leaves crackling, dead leaves from last fall that hadn't decomposed. I heard sticks cracking under her feet, and I heard the thud of much heavier steps, too. It must've been Jag and Brag'mok.

Layla leaned over me. "Thank God we found you!"

I nodded. "Sorry, I think I was… Well, I blacked out."

"Can you stand up?" Layla asked.

I wiggled my toes. "I think so."

I slowly rolled over, made my way to my hands and knees. Brag'mok's giant hand grabbed my arm, and with his help I managed to get to my feet.

"Great to have you back, buddy!" Jag said, slapping me on the back and knocking me over again.

"Jag!" Layla said. "Seriously?"

"Dude, I'm so sorry!" Jag said, running over and grabbing me from behind and lifting me back to my feet.

I laughed as I picked up Aerin's sword. "Sorry, I'm still a little out of it. Would you believe it, when I was passed out, I could swear Aerin was talking to me?"

I was talking to you.

"Shit!" I said. "That was real?"

I told you it was.

"Yeah, but I didn't know if that was a real you, or a fake you, saying it was real."

"Caspar?" Layla asked. "What's going on?"

I sighed. "Somehow, when Aerin killed herself with this blade, with that enchanted dust on it, then I swung the blade, it mixed up our souls. Her spirit got stuck inside of the sword and now we're bound...still bound. Just differently, I guess."

"Aerin speaks inside your head?" Jag asked.

"When I'm holding the sword, yes," I said.

Jag laughed. "I mean, I knew the drow are into female supremacy, but that's a kind of role reversal I didn't think was possible."

"Dammit, Jag," I said. "That's not what I meant."

"Sorry, too soon?"

I sighed. "Yeah. Definitely too soon. I'm sure I'll find that joke funny later. In about twenty years."

"You should come back with us to the stone circle," Brag'mok said. "The Furies are waiting for you."

"The Furies?" I asked, shaking my head. "Please tell me that Trixie defeated Develin and the unseelie?"

"I don't know," Layla said. "When I left using my celestial magic, they were still fighting. But I couldn't stay there any longer. The legion healed themselves. They were going to come after me."

"Shit," I said. "I teleported Echor back to the junkyard ranch. The elves know about the ranch. They'll come for him."

"They're not there," Layla said. "The drow did their funeral rites, and then Jag called Dwight, and everyone piled into his eighteen-wheeler. I told them to go somewhere they couldn't be found until I texted and told them it was either safe to return or I found a new place."

I wiped a little sweat from my brow with my shirt sleeve. "Thank God you thought about that."

"Of course I did, Caspar," Layla said, kissing my cheek.

How sweet.

I snorted and planted the sword in the earth.

"What?" Layla asked.

"It's Aerin. She just made a comment when you kissed me. Said it was sweet."

"Wait," Layla said. "So Aerin can feel it when I kiss you?"

I nodded. "I think so."

Layla sighed. "I thought... I mean, not to be insensitive about her death, but I'd be lying if I said it didn't occur to me that our marriage might start to get a little more normal now."

"I'm just glad to know that she's still alive, in a way," I said. "I couldn't believe it when she sacrificed herself like that. She said the prophecy told her to do what she did."

Layla shook her head. "If we ever do open the last elven prophecy, the one my father has, I sure hope it portents something a little better for me."

"I agree," I said. I retrieved the sword and made a makeshift sheath from my belt as Layla and I followed Brag'mok and Jag through the woods.

"Any of you have any water?" I asked.

"One thing I wished we hadn't forgotten," Layla said. "I'm thirsty, too."

I nodded. "Well, I do have the power over the water elemental."

"What are you doing?"

I focused my power and, gathering water from the humid air, I formed a large, floating glob of water in front of us. I stepped up to it, pursed my lips, and pressed them into it, sucking the cool liquid into my mouth.

"Come on, Layla, get a drink."

"Caspar," Layla said. "We still don't know for sure which side of the fairies won. If they sense you using magic like that..."

I shook my head. "If the good fairies lost, we have more to worry about than that. The Furies said if the unseelie were not brought to justice, the next earthquake would be several times more powerful than the last."

"Do you think you could stop it again?" Layla asked.

I shook my head. "It took everything I had to stop that one. I really don't know."

We eventually made the three-mile hike back to the stone circle. The three Furies were standing there, waiting for me.

"Welcome back, Naayak," the Furies said in unison as I stepped inside the circle.

"So, did it work?" I asked. "Were the unseelie defeated?"

The three Furies waved their hands through the air and a whole army of fairies appeared. Trixie was in the middle, now wearing a small crystal crown on her head.

"You did it!" I shouted, smiling wider than I probably ever had.

"We sure did!" Trixie said, flexing her muscles as she buzzed around me like a hummingbird.

"What happened to the others? The unseelie?" I asked.

"We've bound them in the realm of the fae," the Furies all said in one voice. "They will not be returning to Earth until their sentence has been served."

"Their sentence?" I asked.

"A sentence appropriate for murder," Tisiphone said. "They've been sentenced to life without parole."

I raised my eyebrows. "You guys offer parole?"

Tisiphone smiled. "I was just translating our sentence into something that is comparable to the human legal system."

"So life for a fairy, how long is that, exactly?"

"A thousand years!" Trixie interjected. "Give or take a century."

I smiled. "Well, sucks to be them!"

"Indeed! It sucks to be them!" the Furies said in unison.

I cocked my head, then laughed. Apparently, the Furies were

gradually picking up on modern speak. "Well, we still have a war to fight."

"Now all three elements are truly united," the Furies continued, "we have a chance."

"I'd say we have better than a chance," I said. "Without the fairies, Brightborn is at a major disadvantage."

"It is not just Brightborn who you must now face," the Furies said. "The war you must wage is against more than his legion. The governments of this world are united behind him."

"Against all the governments of the world?" I asked. "I'm going to rescind my previous statement about him being at a disadvantage."

"For us, it is no change," the Furies said. "We have always been at odds with human powers."

"We'll need a place to go that's safe," I said. "A place where they can't find us. Until we figure out what to do."

"We can take care of that!" Trixie said.

"How so?" I asked.

"We can do more than teleport," Trixie said. "We're also masters of illusion. We will come with you and shroud your home village in a veil."

I shook my head. "They still know where the junkyard ranch is. Even if it's veiled, they'll find us there."

"They won't!" Trixie said. "What is within the veil is technically a part of the realm of the fae. If they go there and they are not welcome, they will simply pass through the place without realizing that you're there."

"Like a parallel dimension or something? In the same place, but not?" I asked.

"The realm of the fae," the Furies said. "Is all around us. It is here, but not here. Always there, but always imperceptible. What Queen Trixie proposes will suffice."

I nodded. "Thank you, all of you, for everything."

The Furies nodded, and in a flash of light, they disappeared.

I looked around. "All right, everyone. Who wants to take the portal?"

"And who wants to ride with me in the truck?" Jag asked.

"I'll take the portal," Brag'mok said. "No offense, Jag. But your protein and broccoli farts are the worst."

I laughed. "That, they are."

"Seriously?" Jag asked. "No one is going to ride with me?"

I looked around. "Let me just form the portal for them. Then, I'll ride with you, Jag."

"Thanks, buddy!" Jag said.

"You're going to regret it," Brag'mok said, shaking his head.

"Probably," I said. "But we'll leave the windows down."

CHAPTER FORTY-FOUR

We still had a war to fight. But we'd won a battle. We'd stopped the earthquake, saved St. Louis, and succeeded in separating the fairies from the elves.

At the very least, if Brightborn was going to travel anywhere, he'd have to do it the old-fashioned way. Meanwhile, with the seelie fairies on our side and the unseelie fairies in the hands of the Furies, we could portal anywhere I could visualize.

Jag called Dwight to let him know it was safe to bring the crew back to the ranch. Once they arrived, Trixie and the fairies cast their veil over the whole property. After I held up to my end of the deal, that is, and supplied them with all the Bubblicious and Fun Dip I could find at the local Walmart. One taste, and with a sugar high giving them a boost of energy, they had the ranch veiled in seconds.

Sure, it was a junkyard. We had a ton of crap I didn't know what to do with. But it was starting to feel like home even if it still needed a lot of work.

I wasn't sure what to do about St. Ensley's. Technically, Jag still held the title to the building. Was it really safe to go there? Could the fairies veil it, too? Usually, if you're running anything like a church, making it impossible to find was disadvantageous. I suppose if we told the members to go to platform nine and three-quarters, they might be able to find a way in. I'd have to discuss that later. There were other people, a whole crowd of folks, who supported us who had gone there looking for hope.

We'd figure something out. Eventually.

So, an army of drow, giants, a couple humans, an elf, and a cat...what in the world were we going to find to do to keep ourselves occupied while hiding behind a magical veil on an old ranch-turned-junkyard, turned base of operations?

In AA, we give coins out when someone hits thirty, sixty, ninety days sober. You get another one at six months and every year thereafter. We celebrate every small victory because each day sober is a day not drunk. In this war, I believed, we had to celebrate every win, especially as few and far between as they were.

The giants were building a fire so they could roast some asparagus. They were more excited to find out the whole pee smell thing worked than the phenomenon warranted, but like celebrating every win, it's worth experiencing even the most trivial joys that life has to offer.

This wasn't just a celebration of the victory. It was a celebration of Aerin's life. She was dead, technically speaking, but I could hear her voice in my head as long as my hand was on her sword. She was still with us, even if not in the flesh. She insisted that her sacrifice be celebrated, not mourned.

I pulled the Eclipse as close to the party, behind the farmhouse, as I could without it bottoming out on the ground. First, I tried my Alternative Rock station. Ace of Base again. Dammit. I switched the radio to classic rock.

Bon Jovi's *Livin' on a Prayer.*

Given how much prayer had played a role in everything, I figured it was appropriate. Besides, I was in the mood to rock out.

I wasn't the only one.

Agnus jumped onto the hood of the car and, banging his head, started singing along.

"We've got to hold on to what we've got," Agnus belted out, "it doesn't make a difference if we're naked or not!"

I chuckled. He might be botching the lyrics, but I wasn't going to correct him this time. I think I might have liked his version better, anyway. If you're naked, I'm not sure exactly what he thought Bon Jovi meant we were supposed to be holding on to...

Some questions are best left unanswered. Agnus could sing it however he liked.

Rina and Jag were dancing together to the music. I'd never seen him so happy. Not since the last time I saw him flex in the mirror. But this was a different kind of happiness, something he gleaned from someone else. I was happy for him.

Was Rina ready for the responsibility to take Aerin's place? Aerin had told me she was her choice to lead the drow. I'd tell Rina the next day. Tonight, I was intent on allowing everyone to enjoy themselves.

I felt a need to connect with Aerin. It was as simple as laying my hand on the hilt of her sword. My sword now, I guessed.

Have a minute to talk? Aerin asked inside my head.

"Sure," I said. "Let me get somewhere a little less loud."

I stepped into the farmhouse. Still plenty of noise, but at least in the farmhouse, I could hear myself think.

Do you think I could take over for a little? Just an hour or so.

"You can do that?" I asked.

I can if you allow it. You still hold the majority influence over your body, of course. But I think I'd enjoy one night to...you know...celebrate.

I scratched the back of my head. "Okay, but if you have to pee, try not to look."

Aerin laughed. *You caught me. I was going to spend the whole hour standing in front of the mirror totally naked.*

I shook my head. "You're welcome to if you'd like. But let me warn you, you might be a little underwhelmed."

I doubt that! Aerin exclaimed. *But seriously, this situation won't be easy for either of us.*

"Harder than navigating a polygamous marriage?" I asked.

It will be hard in different ways. Did you know that I can read your memories?

I scrunched my brow. "That has the potential to be embarrassing."

I didn't realize how often you used to stare at my butt when I wasn't looking.

I snorted. "I'm a man. Sorry. I didn't mean to."

It's fine! Aerin said. *I know you love Layla. But it's nice to know you appreciated the view.*

"Who wouldn't?" I asked. "But seriously. I don't know what to say. After what you did. You gave your life to save us."

I gave my body, Aerin said. *But life goes on, just in a different way.*

"Will you ever be able to move on?" I asked.

I can't say for sure. This isn't something I've ever done, and I haven't known anyone else who did it. I only knew it could be done. But someday, when all this is over, I hope I can.

"Give me another hour. I'd like to dance with Layla and let her know what's happening. No making out with my woman while you're at the helm, Aerin!"

I wouldn't think of it!

"You wouldn't?" I asked, raising my eyebrow.

Well, I might think of it. But I'd never do it. No worries, Caspar. No booze, either. I know the rules. Remember, I can read your mind. I won't do anything you don't want me to do. Really, I just want to talk to my dad. We'd barely been reacquainted before all this happened. I just need to say something to him, maybe give him some closure.

I glanced at Elrand. He'd come back here for the funeral rites the drow had conducted while I was still passed out in the woods. Now he was perched on the top of one of the junk heaps, staying mostly to himself. He'd just lost his daughter. I couldn't imagine what he was going through. The pain radiating off of his dejected posture was almost palpable.

"Take as much time as you need, Aerin."

Thank you, Caspar.

I glanced at Aerin's sword in my hand. "What should we do with it?"

You're the only one who can wield it. In anyone else's hands, it'll just be a normal sword. But you should be careful about how you use it. Every time you do, it will change our relationship. It may give me more power. It may have other effects I don't realize. Don't use it unless there's no other option.

I nodded and placed the sword against my bedroom wall. "Good to know."

Remember, Aerin said before I let go. *In an hour...*

I smiled. "I won't forget."

I went back outside and climbed into the Eclipse. I changed the music back to my go-to nineties alternative jam.

Iris, by the Goo Goo Dolls. I nodded, and for some reason, my eyes teared up as I looked at Layla through the car window.

So beautiful. So perfect.

I stepped out of the car and, extending my hand, I looked Layla in the eyes. "Would you dance with me?"

A small smile cracked at the corners of her lips. "It's about time you asked."

Layla took my hand and rested her other hand on my shoulder. I pulled her close to me as we swayed back and forth to the song.

Layla lowered her head, resting it on my chest. "I love you, Caspar."

"I love you, too."

Agnus circled us, nuzzling against my shin as we danced. He started singing.

This time, for once, he got the lyrics right.

AUTHOR NOTES - THEOPHILUS MONROE

JUNE 15, 2021

When I hear the phrase "Junkyard Dog" the first thing that comes to mind is a professional wrestler, back before the WWF had to change its name (after losing a trademark lawsuit to the World Wildlife Fund) to the WWE. He was a hulking man who wore a collar and chain. He dragged that chain with him when he went to stage and, not surprisingly, it was often used as a "prop/weapon" in his matches. I might be showing my age, here, but those were the "golden years" of pro wrestling, back when none of the wrestlers would admit that pro wrestling was "fake" (okay, "staged").

Caspar is still dragging the "chain" of his former life here, the old dogmas that bound him when he was in ministry, not to mention the double-ball-and-chain of having two wives. Add to that, he feels collared by the prospect of facing criminal charges and, of course, the fact that the furies intend to unleash their wrath on the mid-west. And, of course, he's living on a literal junkyard.

Now, I have a confession to make. I'd like to say I thought about all these deep, philosophical, implications of the title before I wrote the book. Nah. I was just trying to come up with more "Dog/Dogma" puns and this one jumped out. So, I ran with it. Sometimes, at least in my experience, it's just that simple. When the shoe fits, you wear it.

I toyed with the idea of sending Caspar to prison. He'd meet Cliff. Take up crochet as a hobby and get a few black eyes (how you get more than a couple is a challenge he'd certainly meet). But this would have been too much of a detour in the story to put him through the whole trial, conviction, introducing new "prison" characters only to leave them behind, etc. Still, it could have been fun. For the reader. And maybe Cliff. Not so much for Caspar. The way I saw it, he'd been through enough hell as it was —and I was eager to get some magic badassery involved.

Speaking of badassery, the stage is now set for the "Dogma Days of Summer." I'm really excited to see our former minister/chosen one start kicking ass and taking elf names that he can't pronounce. Not to mention, if his relationship status was "its complicated" before, well, what we saw happen at the end of *Junkyard Dogma* will undoubtedly add to the complexity of what might be the strangest love triangle in history.

I must also mention that I wrote about half of this book while recuperating from COVID. Thankfully, I have great editors. Things got a little loopy there, for a while, but I'm good. Salute to all my homies who've also endured the brunt of the pandemic. I just poured a little Mountain Dew on the floor, special for you. That'll get sticky. Thankfully, no more shortage of Clorox wipes.

Thanks again to Michael for his collaboration on this one and for all the good folks at LMBPN who've taken my zany story and taken it to the next level. And, of course, thank you to my wife and three sons who've endured more late-nights in front of the television while I busted my butt to get this one done. And, of course, thank YOU—yeah, you—the reader for sticking with this series! I'm humbled, every day, when I think about the fact that you've devoted a small portion of your life to reading my books.

Best!
Theo

AUTHOR NOTES - MICHAEL ANDERLE

JUNE 29, 2021

Thank you for both reading this story and these author notes in the back!

So, Theophilus had COVID…

I really don't have anything to beat that. I went through some trying legal contract stuff (while very much emotionally painful and a lot of work – it (usually) doesn't come with a chance of death.)

Theophilus is also right that we owe a lot to you, our readers, who picked up this book and continue this journey with us.

THANK YOU. (Again… It needs to be repeated. We do not get to enjoy our profession without you willing to pay for our stories.)

Anyone besides me want to watch a priest kick some ass?

Good, it's coming!

Have a great week or weekend, whatever works for your time of week!

Regards,

Michael Anderle

BOOKS BY MICHAEL ANDERLE

Sign up for the LMBPN email list to be notified of new releases and special deals!

https://lmbpn.com/email/

For a complete list of books by Michael Anderle, please visit:

www.lmbpn.com/ma-books/

CONNECT WITH THE AUTHORS

Connect with Theophilus Monroe

Website: www.theophilusmonroe.com

Social Media
https://www.facebook.com/pages/category/Author/
Theophilus-Monroe-Urban-Fantasy-Author-101469961530864/

Connect with Michael Anderle

Website: http://lmbpn.com

Email List: http://lmbpn.com/email/

Social Media:

https://www.facebook.com/LMBPNPublishing

https://twitter.com/MichaelAnderle

https://www.instagram.com/lmbpn_publishing/

https://www.bookbub.com/authors/michael-anderle